The Good Silver

OTHER BOOKS BY
MATTHEW DUNN

Day One

The Dummy Sign

Bingo Bango Bongo

Erased

Visit Matthew at:
www.matthewdunn.net

The Good Silver

By

Matthew Dunn

ONONDAGA HILL PUBLISHING

The Good Silver is a work of fiction. Many of the characters are inspired by historical figures; others are entirely imaginary creations of the author. Apart from the historical figures, any resemblance between these fictional characters and actual persons, living or dead, is purely coincidental.

Published by Onondaga Hill Publishing

ISBN-13: 978-0-9794908-2-8
ISBN-10: 0-9794908-2-0

Printed in the United States of America

Acknowledgements

To my lovely wife, Judy, for once again reading every word of the countless drafts I wrote to complete this novel. Many thanks to my family and friends for their support and encouragement, as well as special thanks to my sister-in-law, Debbie Barron, for her invaluable copyediting. To my friend, Matt Hotham, for all his hard work and candid advice. I could not have done it without any of you.

Finally, I would like to thank the city of Sherrill, my hometown, for giving me so many wonderful moments and memories over the years.

PROLOGUE

Syracuse University Campus
Syracuse, New York
February 14, 1879

At least it was not snowing, William thought as he walked briskly behind his best friend Charles, whose long legs and determined bearing set a pace difficult for William to match. However, it *was* very cold, well below freezing, and the wool sweater he'd thrown on hastily before stepping out into the twilight only twenty minutes ago had long since lost its will to shelter him. He had forgotten his hat and his gloves, exposing far more of his delicate skin to the elements than his mother could forgive, and his toes–his poor icicle toes, protected only by the thin cowhide of his Oxfords–now felt more attached to the frozen pathway than to his shivering body.

Had he exhibited the fortitude to refuse his friend's request, he would be sipping hot tea beside a glowing fire right now in the company of his sweetheart, Margaret–warm and bosomy Margaret. After all, it was Valentine's Day, and a young man like himself should be spending its ebb with a young lady–a warm and bosomy young lady. Was not that the order of the world? So why was he trailing along after his decidedly non-voluptuous friend braving the bitter cold, he asked himself. It was very simple. He could never say no to Charles.

Charles had arrived at William's tiny apartment just as he was finishing his supper, insisting that he come at once, saying that a lynch mob was gathering on campus and that they needed to hurry. "History could very well be made on this night," he said, "so grab your cloak and come with me, my friend."

Without hesitation, William snatched the incompetent pull-over off the back of a chair and followed Charles out into the cold, completely unaware of why he was doing so. They had walked almost a mile now and he still did not know. Over the course of their hike, he had not been able to move his frozen lips enough to ask.

Anticipating the opportunity to thaw, a thankful smile melted across William's red face as he finally saw their destination on the darkening horizon ahead–the Hall of Languages–the sole structure on the ten-year-old, 50-acre farmland campus of Syracuse University. He tucked his hands deep into his armpits, bowed his head, and trudged on knowing that relief was but a few minutes away.

Built of Onondaga limestone in the American Second Empire style borrowed from France, the Hall of Languages was the only building, of a planned seven, erected on the young college campus during the harsh economic recession of the 1870's. Elegantly styled in a double-pitched roof with a steep lower slope–the hallmark of the design,–it stood alone atop a quiet hill, tall and welcoming, a beacon to all in search of greater knowledge. Tonight, upon their teeth-chattering arrival, the two freshmen students found a large, gruff-looking man in a heavy overcoat, wool cap and boots blocking that normally unimpeded light.

As Charles attempted to move past what he would later describe as a dim-witted grizzly bear, the man extended his large, intimidating paw and said, "I'm sorry boys, but this convention can be attended by invitation only."

"A convention, you say?" Charles asked with a raised brow. "From what I've heard, I would liken it more to an assembly of hungry wolves; and a misguided rabble at that, if I dare be frank, sir."

If the mountainous sentinel took offense, he did not show it. He just stared at Charles, who defiantly stared back while icy white clouds spewed from their mouths, helplessly mixing in a fusion of brawn and brain before disappearing into the night air. As William expected, his best friend was not the first to blink.

"Shove off," the man growled.

"We're students here," Charles said unflinchingly. "We've paid our tuition and therefore we may go anywhere on campus we like. Chancellor Haven assured us of that during our orientation last fall."

"I don't know no Chancellor Haven," the man replied. "I was told to keep students, reporters and all other undesirable types out. So that's just what I intend to do," he continued as he pushed his barrel chest into Charles's opposing beaker, "I would advise you and your companion to go back to your books while you're still able to read."

Momentarily defeated, the regrouping Charles turned, seized William by the arm, and led him off without another word.

"Where are we going now?" William asked.

Charles snuck a peek back at the still grumbling obstacle and smiled. He then turned to William and said, "I know a side door that the dim-witted grizzly bear doesn't, and if luck is with us, its lock has not yet been repaired."

William wanted to ask Charles how he knew of the door and of its broken lock, but sensing that their conversation could still be overheard, he refrained. Further, he wondered how the door had fallen into its poor condition. As they made their way toward the eastern side of the building, William decided he didn't really want an answer to these questions. He simply wanted to get inside and get warm.

"I believe it was meant to be some sort of service entrance," Charles said, feeling the soothing rush of warm air dance across his face as he stepped through the broken-locked doorway. "We need only to follow this corridor to the stairs that ascend to the hallway that leads to the main vestibule. I believe that is where we will find the salivating wolves."

Searching for a radiator to huddle against, William ignored his friend's observations, choosing first to attend to his tingling fingers before asking Charles the question he had failed to ask back at his apartment. Relieved that he could find no signs of frostbite on his lethargically numb hands, William finally confronted his escort.

"Why are we here, Charles?" William asked.

"To witness an assault upon Utopia," Charles replied. "Come now, William, I know a place where we can hear everything they say."

As was his habit, William obligingly followed his friend.

"There is an impure emanation from it," a silver-haired gentleman said to the fifty or more men gathered around the room, all listening intently. Seated near the center, his dark attire alleging he was a clergyman, he had a newspaper folded in his lap. "Young people go there and return with these impure thoughts and associations in their minds."

Another similarly dressed man, who had yet to lower his chill-shielding coat lapel, reinforced the rising sentiment, saying, "Their institution is the outgrowth of vile passion!" The anger in his voice must have been too great to ignore as it triggered many to light their own torches and join the amassing intolerance.

"A nest of unclean birds."

"An immoral adulterous horde."

"A foul blot on the State of New York."

"A disgrace to civilization, I say."

"A *LASCIVIOUS LOT.*"

The condemnatory lava would have flowed for hours had not the silver-haired man diverted its path toward finding a way to "suppress the evil."

"Yes, I believe we all agree that they must be broken up."

"Extinguished!"

"Demolished!"

"Wiped out!"

"If we could get a moral sentiment aroused and public feeling turned against them...." one man offered.

"And sway the press into joining our cause instead of condemning our actions," another suggested, a stout man in an ill-fitting clerical collar speaking for the first time. "As teachers of the Gospel and defendants of public and domestic virtue in this part of the country, it is our duty to right the great wrong done to society by these immoral practices." Grabbing one of the many newspapers scattered about the room, he raised it over his head and shook it like a baby's rattle. "The truth must find its way onto these pages if we are to have any chance at all!"

"Perhaps we should have thought of that before we barred all reporters from attending tonight," someone said.

"Quite a valid point," the stout man replied, nodding his head in agreement. "We must leverage the power of the printed word to deracinate the evil rooting beneath our very feet. I propose that we provide the reporters that have collected outside our door with an abstract report of our proceeding here. Then, there can be no imprudent editorials."

Everyone agreed.

"But, the evil is too deep-seated to be easily eradicated," one man opined. "They have community empathy in their favor. By their thrift, their industry, their activity, they have vastly improved not only the large farm they occupy, but the neighborhood generally has risen in prosperity. Land is more valuable. The poor have employment. They do good work and have an excellent business reputation."

Undaunted, the silver-haired gentleman replied calmly, "then we must, as Hercules said, either find a way or make one."

Find a way or make one. The final words lingered in the cold vestibule like a thick midnight fog.

Hidden in an adjacent room, the completely puzzled William turned to Charles and asked who all these unfamiliar clergymen were so embattled with.

"The Oneida Community," Charles answered in a hushed tone. Keeping his better ear pressed hard against the conveniently thin wall, he then explained that the OC, as they were often referred, were a commune of several hundred people living about thirty-five miles east of Syracuse. "Professor Walls told me that they're Communists. He said they live in a huge mansion that they built themselves where the men can have relations with any woman they choose," he added excitedly.

Curious, but unconvinced, William asked, "But what if the woman is married or is unwilling?"

"All the members consider themselves married to the group rather than to one monogamous partner," Charles said. "They call it 'free love' and they practice it blissfully, so I am told."

"Free love?" William pondered aloud as he returned his now salaciously attentive ear to the wall, his thoughts conjuring scandalous images of his darling Margaret *and* her equally warm and bosomy older sister Annie.

Wide-eyed and grinning, Charles replied simply, "Utopia."

CHAPTER 1

Albany, New York
April 21, 2005

I knew she was dead the second I opened my eyes.

With the unnerving suddenness of an invisible assassin's gunshot, I snapped out of a black sleep and focused my stinging vision on the ceiling above. It looked like a blank canvas anxiously awaiting an artist's brush, except for the pale white grainy waves of plaster that I supposed imitated billowy clouds to assist an insomniac's quest for sleep. The small, silver-plated mechanism in the center reminded me where I was. Struggling to brush off the dust that clung stubbornly to my brain, I imagined the odd shaped thingamajig summoning rain, coaxed into unleashing a startling downpour by an unattended cigarette. It triggered an itch and with a shaky hand, I scratched my face. The television chained to the wall then came forward and testified, and as I dimly recalled stumbling into the cold, dull motel room in the early morning hours, I pulled the blankets up to my chin, feeling for the first time in my life that I was alone in the world.

"What kind of sick nonsense have you been telling your sister?" My father says in a black and white memory. I am eight years old and he towers over me. His face is tight with anger but I sense the jury is still out as my nervous eyes note his belt safely looped in the pants he has just come home from work in. *Thirty seconds to explain myself.*

"I...I just told her about a dream I had last night," I say.

"You told her she was going to get hit by a car and die," he replies sternly. "Now your mother tells me that she's been in her room crying all afternoon and won't come out; says she's never coming out."

I should say something–explain myself–but I do not. I don't know how to describe the nightmare I had the night before about my twin sister. I'm scared; scared for my sister and scared to fall asleep again; terrified that my father doesn't believe me and is about to teach me a lesson. I sit on my bed and look around my room, avoiding his stabbing eyes. Then, his right hand begins to move, reaching. *Is he going for the belt?* I feel the helpless tears coming. He scratches his head and then smoothes his thinning hair.

"Did you think you were being funny?" he asks. I recognize the tone–the jury is already in.

"No, sir," I reply, realizing that the only thing now is to escape with a lesser sentence.

"Well, it wasn't very funny and I don't want anything like this to happen again. Do you hear me?"

"Yes, sir."

He shakes his head. "Your mother is a wreck over this, and I, well I'm completely disgusted with you," he says. "Why you would make up something like that is beyond me."

But I didn't make it up, I want to tell him. But I don't. The storm is passing. I want it to go.

"As punishment for your little stunt, you're going to stack all the firewood delivered yesterday. And you're going to stack it right."

"But I thought everyone was going to pitch in," I say, forgetting about my escape plan. "It'll take weeks to do it all by myself. Maybe all summer!"

"I guess then you will have plenty of time to rethink what you did today, won't you."

Risking a stiffer jolt of my father's justice, I grimace. It does not slip by him.

"And I don't want any attitude while you're doing it. If I see anything less than a smile on your face, I'll tan your hide so brown you won't be able to sit down for a month. Do I make myself clear?"

Clear as day. Never again.

Dousing my father's invading image, I realized I was not alone.

From the corner of my eye, I squeezed off a snapshot of the rumpled mess of blond hair and boney flesh lying in bed next to me. I couldn't remember her name and became irritated as my selective ears locked onto the steady wheeze of stale air funneling in and out of her dry lips, the same ones that had lured me to this bed the night before; sensuously full lips that were now sputtering relentlessly.

"Thanks for waking me up," I said to the back of her head. She offered no reply and I could have continued to complain, gone into a rant about her deviated septum and how it was keeping the entire county awake, but I didn't. I knew, in all honesty, that it wasn't her puffing that had yanked me back to consciousness. It was my sister's distant scream.

It has always been her scream as long as I can remember—a wakeup alarm that accompanies me everywhere like an ugly facial scar, oddly shaped and discolored, but concealed by a well-placed tuft of hair. Only I know it is there. Not even my best friend, who once suspected something many years ago. But young minds are easily distracted…thank God.

"You look like shit," my friend Jeff says. Appearing in my still groggy mind in muted grays, I watch him flip open the tent flap. The sun is rising. "Another nightmare?" he asks.

"Yeah," I say, "started as soon as I shut my eyes."

"Didn't you bring some sleeping pills?" Jeff asks.

"I think my mom is hiding them somewhere," I reply. "But I'll find them."

"You've been awake for a while then. We're still going to the lake though, right?"

"You already know the answer to that," I say, trying to muster a smile.

Happily, Jeff retrieves a rusted old coffee can from just outside the tent and pokes at the mushy insides. His face beams. "It was cold last night, thought they might not make it," he says. The night before had been perfect for picking night crawlers and we had cashed in big time, filling our cache with what was now a bulging knot of slimly worm flesh. "They look better than you do," he says. "Good thing they don't know where they're headed."

"Probably slept more than I did," I say. I pull myself out of my sleeping bag and crawl over to the triangular entryway. The sun feels warm against my tired face, the chilly air sharp inside my lungs. I wipe my eyes, clearing away my sister's terrified face.

Always...her terrified face.

I rolled over, turning my back to the catch lying next to me, realizing that I hadn't gone fishing in years. It is then that I noticed that the cardboard motel room looked vaguely familiar.

The night before had been another one of my many grand escapes from what my parents had forever called "the responsible world," climaxing with a roaring ride down the Jack Daniels rapids, spilling over the falls and into this motel bed. Soaked in alcohol, my skin dripping with lust, I hurriedly shed my sensible shoes, eager for a wave of passion to pull me away from shore. Just another episode of my half-hour life, really, that had been in reruns ever since college, some ten years ago, and, as the song goes, kept me working for the weekend. Now, with the closing credits rolling up the screen once again, my head pounding and my tongue searching for moisture, I contemplated, perhaps for only the second time ever, the concept of being too old for this shit. My sister's lingering cry continued to echo in my head.

The muted snarl of a rasping guitar began to radiate from the wall behind my head. The rock-and-roll-loving neighbors were apparently awake and suddenly another jagged, steely edge of my memory slit a tender line of blood and I am back in college....

"Hey, dude," my roommate says. "Welcome back to the living."

The room is bright white and my eyes refuse to open. "What time is it?" I ask from my bed. My voice is gravel, my throat a patch of desert pavement.

"Past noon," he replies. "I told Jimmy to tell the professor you had a family emergency."

"Thanks," I say. "Why didn't you just wake me up instead?"

"Dude, I tried," he says, laughing. "But you were out cold. How many downers did you pop last night?"

"None," I say, prying my lids open a sliver. "I gave them up for Lent."

"It must have been the tequila shooters then," he says. "You were in the zone last night, dude. Incredible—a dorm legend in the making." He grabs a book off the desk, attempts a high-five against my wobbling hand and leaves. The night had been blackness and for that, I am grateful.

Blackness never screams for help.

Watching a nimble spider crawl up the wall, I wonder all these years later how I myself managed the climb to graduation.

I was younger and stronger then; the nightmares hadn't yet rendered me immobile.

Another fitful night and my body felt weak, as if the blood in my veins was slipping away through a small hissing pinhole, soaking into the sheets and staining the mattress forever. It felt beyond my control and I began to convulse. Not like an overloaded washing machine with one leg missing, but more like the spastic chills and gooseflesh brought on from a gusting winter wind that suddenly attacks on an otherwise peaceful, sunny day; unpredictable in a way that no matter of will or clothing can shelter.

"You're shaking," a whispery voice said. The wheezing had

stopped, replaced now by unseen fingers inching down my belly, fervently searching for acknowledgement. My thoughts shifted briefly toward the offer–an opportunity to consummate my get-away–but the spark quickly sputtered. This time the haunting nightmare had come true and it would take more than a probing lover to banish the fresh memory from my mind.

My only sister, the one who had followed me into this life while I lay crying upon our mother's breast inhaling my first breaths, was dead. The living being that had been the friendly ghost watching over me for all but those first few minutes of my thirty-two years, forever sensing my moods and forewarning mysteriously accurate premonitions that I had stubbornly learned to heed was gone, and I had no tears. As an adult, I had never cried, a trait my sister often teased me about ("A minor character flaw," she would chide in jest) and I was not about to change that now. But inside a voice was whispering; a low, clear voice, grinding repulsively against the cleverly decorated psyche I had spent years disguising. It was telling me there was no escape; convicting me of the crime; sentencing me to life behind the knowledge that I had done nothing to save her.

CHAPTER 2

I don't like funerals. I never have. I think it started when I was young–maybe eight or nine–and a newspaper boy delivering a backbreaking sack full of editorials and sports scores to almost everyone in town. It was the early edition, which meant I was the only one awake for miles at five in the morning–a time when the streets were empty and even the morning doves were still tucked beneath the blankets. I was Charlton Heston in the first scenes of The Omega Man, alone in a desolate place—the man I had thought was Moses—racing down the highway in a hot blue convertible and me on my gold banana bike roaring along the sidewalks, zombies around every corner. We only had one funeral home in town and the family that ran it lived on the second floor–a single flight of stairs above what I imagined at the time were dozens of corpses, all patiently waiting their turn in some macabre viewing room. They didn't like having their paper thrown onto the steps or in the bushes, so I had to enter a side porch to make the delivery and retrieve the weekly fee, which sat in a tea cup on a table a full six giant steps inside the door. At that time of day, the sun was just a sliver on the horizon—prime ghoul time my friend Jeff used to say—but I still had to go inside, into a place full of dead people. The morning a pissed-off bumblebee leaped out of that teacup and slapped my sleepy face was the same day I traded my route to fat Willy Williams for his collection of baseball cards. I have not been back since, but I know where I can find a dollar if I ever need one.

Our mother, Aislin Callaghan Gibson, sixty-six and, along with my father, recently retired, had organized a perfectly traditional Catholic funeral for my sister and was now presiding over the wake like a seasoned traffic cop, directing people to food and drink, and pulling unsuspecting pedestrians aside for "their fondest memories" of Melissa. The informal eulogy would have been tolerable, if not pleasant, if she hadn't dug out the karaoke system that Dad had bought her as a gag gift last Christmas and looped an endless symphonic version of "Wind Beneath My Wings" in the background. She wanted to know how people truly felt about her daughter, and standing off on the sidelines observing her from the dark alley that was the small hallway to the front door of my parents' modest split-level ranch, I got a sense she was asking everyone what they really thought of our whole family.

"Your mom sure knows how to cater a party," a soft voice said, emerging from the adjacent kitchen. I looked back over my shoulder and saw my sister's friend, Jessica Hartwell, juggling a china plate full of toothpick-impaled meatballs and mushrooms in one hand and two Coronas in the other. I relieved her of one of the beers, nodding in appreciation even though I knew I wasn't going to drink it, and smiled at the scent of my mother's cooking, a salivating blend of garlic, onion and cardamom. We both stood and watched as the family friend we all called Uncle Ralph lamented over how my sister Melissa had asked him to marry her. She had proposed to him when she was nine, strung out from a marathon of Oreo cookies and reruns of "The Brady Girls Get Married," and had wiggled into the first white dress she found in her closet. *He* was already in his seventies when she popped the question to which he gracefully, and somewhat reluctantly, declined. It appeared he now regretted turning her down.

"Mel certainly had a wide range of suitors," Jessica said before popping a meatball in her mouth and pulling the whittled dagger free.

Jessica was Melissa's best friend, her confidant, as Melissa called her. She had driven up from New York City earlier in the day to attend the wake, the funeral and whatever else my mother had up her sleeve. Like the rest of us, she was now riding out the melancholy festivities with a mix of sadness and trepidation. The schmaltzy little speeches of the toastmistress (my mother) and her unassuming guest stars were also giving Jessica the giggles, for which she quickly apologized.

"I'm sorry," she said, half choking and half laughing. "Your mother is just so sincere, Mel would be touched."

"And she would probably be laughing, too," I said, knowing how much Melissa enjoyed our mother's melodramatic style. "You could be the next Oprah!" Melissa would say to her, after receiving a laundry basket full of unsolicited opinions on everything from cancer-free diets to sex in the suburbs. "Who would want to sit for an hour listening to a graying old woman with failing eye sight and bad knees," my mother would always reply. I always agreed with my mother–who would listen? There were about seventy-five tonight, family and friends all gathered together, hanging on every word my mother said.

Having dismissed the forsaken bachelor–everyone's Uncle Ralph–my mother was back at the microphone coaxing her sister Mary to step forward and say a few words. A younger version of my mother, Mary Callaghan O'Shea didn't need to be asked twice, seizing the somber audience by the throat with a salvo of tear-inducing stories worthy of garnering my sister sainthood. "Never have I gazed upon more caring eyes than the twinkling brown stars of Melissa's," she said finally as her own eyes puddled and her lips began to quiver. "Her heart was as boundless as the heavens, her thoughtfulness as warm as the summer sun. She was my niece and she was sunshine," my Aunt Mary said as the flood of grief overwhelmed her, "always my sunshine."

My mother rescued her little sister, taking the microphone from her trembling hand before pulling her into a long, deep hug.

The room fell quiet, seventy-five thoughts stepping away momentarily from my mother's carefully laid buffet to reflect on the reason they were gathered in my parent's small home–the sudden death of my twin sister, Melissa.

Wiping away her sister's tears with a white laced handkerchief, my mother said, "She loved you terribly, Mary."

"Crazy Aunt Mary," Mary Callaghan O'Shea weakly chuckled, "crazy and stubborn because I was the only one who refused to call her Mel."

Mel was my sister's self-proclaimed nickname. She used it for all of her address, internet and telephone listings and, needless to say, it generated a fair amount of misguided fan mail, which was exactly the reason she did it—she was a pulse voyeur. You see, my sister, Melissa (Mel) Gibson, loved to get into your head and discover what, as she would say, "kept the fire stoked." What kept the heart pumping; what made it race; what made it skip a beat. I had always been her favorite subject (victim was the term I preferred) but even my "Paleolithic brain in a pin-striped suit" grew boring along with rest of our family and town, and when she was twenty-two she left us in Putney, Vermont for the bright lights of the big city. She wanted to be a journalist; a writer; an explorer of the great minds and cultures of the world! I can still see the excitement in her eyes the day she graduated college. She couldn't sit still; she couldn't wait to begin her journey.

It was over two hundred and fifty miles to New York City but Mel drove the old rusted-out, oil-choking Thunderbird our father bought her for graduation nonstop, securing freelance writing gigs from the New York Times, The New Yorker and others almost immediately upon her arrival in the Big Apple. She was smart and talented, *extremely* outgoing and not totally unpleasant to look at, as I would often tell her. "They'll love you there," I remember reassuring her, "you're spunky - New Yorkers love spunky." She hated that characterization, which of course was why I had continued to use it. *That's what brothers are for.*

Once again, my mother was at the microphone, only now looking my way with her commandeering eyes. She was extending her hand, clearly announcing it was my turn to speak, but instead of being a good little boy, I retreated down the hallway and escaped out the front door. Jessica consoled my mother with a sympathetic frown and followed me out into the unseasonably warm, mid-April night. She caught up to me in the driveway.

"Mel seemed to have a thing for Fords," I said, lacing my hand along the side of the red '64 Mustang Convertible my sister had bought just weeks ago. It had been a reward to herself when her one-hundredth story had been published, a weeklong series in the New York Times about poverty in the small towns of America. The exhaustive research had sent her around the country and "America's dirty little secret," as she called it, had chipped her audacious facade, a discovery I had made during one of the last conversations I had with her. Seeing so many hungry children just a few blocks off Main Street, USA had troubled my ever-upbeat sister, so much so, that I curtailed my usual sarcasm, passing up the opportunity to raze her over her latest hairstyle. I think now I should have, if only to have reminded her how much I loved her.

"How long did it take you to drive it back?" Jessica asked.

"About three hours or so," I replied, still gazing at the Detroit classic, its glossy smooth finish and silver accents glowing in the moonlight. "Just a blink of an eye in a sweet ride like this."

Jessica leaned against the front quarter panel of the Mustang and looked down at the beer she was holding with both hands, "I remember the first time I met Mel," she said in an affectionate tone. "It must have been eight or nine years ago. It was St. Patrick's Day and I was a rookie cop in Yonkers getting ready to march in the parade with a bunch of guys from the precinct when she pulled up in some god-awful rolling bucket of rust."

"The Thunderbird," I chuckled at the memory of it.

"The remnants of one," Jessica smiled. "Anyway, Mel was doing this story about what cops like about being in parades. You know Mel; she wanted to know the motivation. She wasn't looking to do a nasty expose or anything, just the less obvious truth hidden inside the blue uniform."

I couldn't help but grin. "I'm all too familiar with her routine."

"Yeah, I guess you would be. So, the parade master is yelling at us to step it up because we're falling behind the group we're supposed to follow, a dozen tubby Shriners in red fez hats riding those tiny motor scooters of theirs, while Mel is walking next to us peppering questions for the next two miles. She was *so* into it; you would have thought it was an interview with Elvis back from the grave." She paused and took a sip of her beer as the night fell quiet. Except for some crickets enjoying an early spring, the only sound I could hear was the faint giggle of delight my sister most certainly exhaled the first time she sat behind the wheel of her new "red sled."

"The story she did about us was great, though," Jessica said. "Made us look like heroes."

"She saw the good in everybody," I replied. "Buy hey, nobody's perfect."

Jessica laughed softly, "Mel told me about when you decided to become a tax auditor." She had a wry look now, but playful, like a kitten ready to pounce on a ball of yarn. "It was when you realized you didn't have the charisma to become an undertaker."

I laughed. I couldn't help it. It *was* something my sister would have said.

Just then, a voice echoed from the house. It was my father, Jonathan Gibson, the family patriarch, flexing his influential muscle at the request, I immediately assumed, of his wife, "Michael! Your mother needs you inside."

"Duty calls," Jessica said.

I briefly glanced toward the voice, watched the screen door close and then slid behind the wheel of the Mustang, latching the driver door quietly behind me. It was a tight fit for my six-two frame, the soft weathered leather pulling me into a tender embrace as the dashboard teased me with hints of thunderous accelerations and breakneck speeds. The rearview mirror complimented me on my reasonably good looks, a wave of not-yet-thinning black hair atop a wiry, well-organized frame. I looked at Jessica with optimistic brown eyes and began singing lyrics from a song I had heard a hundred times on the radio–something about having a fast car and the desire to escape. I sang it repeatedly. It was the only part of the song I knew.

"Tracy Chapman," she said, bobbing her head to my pathetic rhythm.

"Thank you for pointing that out, *Officer* Hartwell."

Jessica returned her gaze to her beer, blushing just enough to be noticeable in the moonlight. She had melted my butter the very first time I met her during one of my infrequent visits to Mel's place in New York City. She was tall, but not as tall as I was, with short, thick, wheat colored hair and a lean, athletic body that looked strong but sexy. The first time she looked at me with her striking green eyes, my neck muscles stiffened and I mumbled something clever about being frisked and handcuffed. Our wobbly relationship steadily grew from there; she routinely asks about my health and my career (How are you? How's work?), to which I answer with intricate detail (Ok. Not bad.) Now, with the binding link of my sister gone and our two-question repertoire on the verge of collapse, I found myself wondering who Jessica Hartwell really was.

With her soft eyes beaming at me now, she said, "I think it would mean a lot to your folks if you went in and said a few words."

"I'd rather you slide in next to me," I said, rattling the ignition keys. "Look, someone left the keys. It's an omen."

"Mel would be telling you the same thing."

"Mel wanted to be quietly cremated. My mother wants all of this," I said, waving my hand toward the house full of guests. "The wake; the Requiem Mass in the morning; and, of course, a repeat of tonight's *performance* after the burial tomorrow."

"I know she did, but...."

"I don't know which is harder; living as a traditional Catholic or dying as one."

"Cremation is against the rules. Mel knew your mother wouldn't allow it."

"Yeah, but I guess we both figured she'd be dead by the time our turn came so it wouldn't be a problem."

"That *is* the way it's supposed to happen."

"Maybe God is getting absent minded in his old age."

Jessica laughed at my sarcasm, and took a few timid steps toward the house before stopping. She was trying to lead me inside, like a mother luring a child out of the rain, but I just stared at the dashboard while my fingers caressed the soft leather steering wheel at ten and two o'clock.

"She was passionate," Jessica said, finally. "I think that's what I loved most about her."

"Spunky," I said as the tears filled my eyes. "She was spunky."

CHAPTER 3

The microphone felt heavy in my hand, my first stumbling words leaping from the speakers, startling my already thumping heart. I started over.

"As most of you know, Melissa and I are twins," I said. "Were twins," I added quietly. "Not identical. Mel was much better looking than me, right, Uncle Ralph?"

Earnestly, he nodded in agreement. A few people smiled, beams of light piercing the dark wall of somber faces. I paused, already instructed on what *not* to say....

"I don't want to hear another word," my father growls. He stares out at the road ahead, his unyielding fingers gripping the steering wheel as if he were wringing my neck. "We're going to bring back your sister's things and lay her to rest peacefully. Is that clear? Peacefully, the way God intended it. For Christ's sake, think about your mother. What this is doing to her."

"I'm sorry," I say, emptily gazing out the window at the passing farmland. It has been twenty-five years since I told my father–told anyone–about the nightmares I have about my sister. It may just as well have been five minutes ago. Nothing has changed.

"Sorry doesn't cut it, Michael," he says. "Your mother thinks Melissa died quietly in her sleep and that's where it ends. Ends! Do you hear me?"

"Yes sir," I say. *She was murdered*, I want to say. *The police are wrong. It wasn't an accident.* But I don't. I want it to end as much as he does–the nightmare of her death–the nightmares of my life. So, I swallow my need to empty my guilt and obediently ride shotgun for my father. *Maybe they will go away now*, I think, *now that one of them finally came true*. Driving west through New York toward a little place just east of Syracuse to collect the remains of my sister's existence, I count telephone poles.

My mother was staring at me now, anxiously mouthing something I couldn't make out, my father standing right behind her, his ever-present authoritative glare shrinking me by two feet. To him, I was eight years old again, and as my eyes glanced at his belt and then at the familiar surroundings of the house I grew up in, I *was* eight years old again. *Say what needs to be said, Michael*, he was telling me. *And say it right*.

The definition of Michael Gibson, at least in this household, was cut in stone long ago. So, I did as I was told, speaking the words my parents wanted to hear. Only this time, I meant them.

"Melissa was more than my sister," I said, "she was and remains a part of my very soul. She is the hope that keeps my own heart pumping, the thought that reminds me of what it is like to be truly loved. I loved my sister and, though she takes with her a piece of me that I know will never grow back, I still rejoice in her memory and invite you all to do the same."

My mother's tears told me I had done it right. My father's attention toward a late-arriving guest confirmed it. I had said what I had never been able to say to Mel when she was alive, and, at the same time, I had pleased my parents. Strangely, with my twin sister lying in a casket only a few feet from where I stood, I felt good.

CHAPTER 4

Three days without a drink was tough. Somehow, I had survived the gloomy jamboree of family friends and relatives I barely knew while fulfilling my promise to Mel *not* to get drunk at her funeral (or was it her wedding?). Now, I could settle into my favorite booth at the best, and only, dive in town with a clear conscience and absolute intentions of making the past week a muddled blur. The withdrawal tremors had arrived that morning like a rising tide, slow and deliberate, but I managed to ride them out long enough to cheerfully partake in my mother's "breakfast circus," an exhaustive carnival of fruits, starches and pan-fried animal flesh. I picked at my plate, nibbling on a single slice of bacon and a ladle of scrabbled eggs, leaving the rest of the pile to my father, who somehow had remained quite slim through the years of constant encouragement from my mother to "*EAT!*"

"How's the tape worm, Dad?" I said. He gave his standard reply while patting his near-washboard stomach, "Working as good as the day I bought it from the pet store." (His old story explained that as a newlywed he had purposely swallowed the parasite after experiencing the first month of his new bride's *expansive* cooking. To this day I'm really not sure if he's joking or not.)

Working now on my second beer, I sat stoically watching the static-filled Baseball Game of the Week on a dust-covered television along with a surprisingly thin Saturday afternoon crowd, anxious as any of them for the fermented barley and hops fog to roll over me. *You would think more people would need to escape once in a while,* I thought to myself. That's what drinking had become for me–an *occasional* escape. I wasn't ready to admit that the occasions were becoming more and more frequent, like the reasons for buying a Hallmark card.

The images from the wake were still too clear and had taken on a horrific life of their own. I could still see the photographs of Mel as a child, but they were spinning around her coffin now, her angelic face pitching and twirling in the invisible, weightless caldron churning at the base of my skull. The collection of her *favorite things*, as my mother called them, were dancing as if demonically possessed on the table next to her, and the flowers, the walls of flowers were enveloping me, suffocating me, pushing me down into a dark, bottomless hole.

"There should be a law against open coffins," I mumbled to the bartender as he handed me another beer. I went back to my booth and tried to breath steady in a futile attempt to fend off the lingering images of the nightmare I'd had again last night. But I couldn't stop it from flashing through my mind over and over– Mel surrounded by darkness, a blood red snake twisting and tightening around her neck as her trembling hand reached out to me. I took a big gulp of my drink and wiped my lips with my own quaking hand. My sister was six feet under and still the nightmares persisted. *Maybe I should join her.*

The first attack of the red menace had hit while I was working at my office. I can't even recall what I was doing when the vision came, but it had grabbed me and shook me like a kid with his piggy bank, and all my courage went jangling to the ground, a worthless pile of tarnished old coins. Evasively, I took the rest of the afternoon off to get an early jump on my weekend routine of boozing and skirt chasing. It worked, as it always had, and by sunset, the memory of my sister's terrifying plea was sitting on the bar with all the other empties waiting for the busboy to dispose of them in the recycling bin out back.

The police said that Mel had died that very night, only hours after my apparition. My recurring nightmares had always seemed so real, but they had never come true before. Not, that is, until now. I swallowed the cold pint in my hand and went to the bar for another. I didn't see Jessica walk in.

"A little early isn't it?" she said, noticing the train wreck of empty bottles in front of me.

"I like it when it's fresh and they take delivery in the morning," I replied.

"Mind if I join you?"

"No," I answered before raising my hand to her. "As long as we have an understanding of live and let live."

Jessica nodded indifferently and sat down across from me. I got the sense she didn't care if I sprouted roots in the place. Surprisingly, that bothered me.

"I need to ask you something," she said in a serious tone.

I gave her my best three-drinks-in-less-than-an-hour smile, "Yes, you can buy me a beer."

"I don't like to consciously contribute to an obvious problem," she replied. "I didn't vote for Bush and I'm not buying you a beer."

"Ok, then I'll buy you one. Sam! Two beers...and one for the lady."

"A Diet Coke for me Sam, thank you."

It was obvious that Sam had seen more interesting couples in his day and he got us our drinks without changing his flat facial expression. We drank for a few minutes, avoiding eye contact by taking in the ramshackle ambiance of the bar.

"Nice place," Jessica said, the sarcasm hidden behind her naturally beautiful, girl-next-door face.

"What's the question?"

She spoke frankly, "Did you, I mean, do you really love your sister?"

The question was a slap in the face but, before I could slap back, she put her warm hand onto mine and took me into her soothing green eyes. "I don't mean it the way you think," she said. "I don't believe Mel's death was an accident, as the police report claims. I think she was murdered. The question is: are you going to help me do something about it?"

CHAPTER 5

The answer to Jessica's first question was simple. I *did* love me sister, with every ounce of my being. The answer to her second question was murky at best, clouded by fear and carbonated indifference.

"So, you want me to help you play Columbo," I said, mockingly. "Don't you get enough cops-and-robbers-shit walking your beat down in Yonkers?" I put a fresh bottle to my lips but she stopped me before the comforting liquid could fall into my anxious mouth.

She squeezed my arm, her probing gaze penetrating my sarcasm, saying, "You *know* she was murdered."

My jaw tightened as I shook off her hand, angrily, and tilted the bottle up. *Yea, I know.*

Jessica pushed back in her seat and exhaled a sigh of frustration. At that moment, I hoped she would back off, forget the whole thing, and see that *it*, that *I* was a hopeless cause. She didn't see things the way I did. By ruling Mel's death accidental, the investigating authorities had indirectly absolved me from accessory and I was going to keep it that way. And, by order of my father, I had to think of my mother.

"Are you accusing your esteemed colleagues of lying?" I asked brashly.

Jessica didn't answer. Instead, she turned her eyes away, gazing out the neon-splashed bar window at the steady stream of cars carrying their indiscernible occupants off to adventures unknown. I wanted her to join them.

Taking a deep breath, her chest rising and falling from across the table, Jessica pulled several sheets of paper from her coat pocket and unfolded them in front her, saying, "Your father was nice enough to let me use his computer to check my email. I've gone weeks at a time without checking it. Mel used to scold me about it all the time and vowed to only communicate with me through email until I learned my lesson. Well, she sent me one the evening before she died, and I didn't read it until this morning." I could see the tears swelling in her eyes as she turned one of the sheets around and pushed it in front of me.

I struggled to focus and then read it aloud, "They are not very happy with the way I'm spinning this story. Call me on my cell as soon as you get this. I need some professional advice." I looked up at Jessica, "professional advice?"

"That was the term Mel used when she wanted my...a cop's take on a situation. She must have tripped onto something, accidentally or on purpose, I don't know, but something that made her wary. Mel never called me unless it was code red."

"Code red?"

"Serious. And something she couldn't figure out alone."

If I had had a few more drinks—a few more hours to distance my mind from my body—Jessica's words would have been spring snowflakes disappearing into the slush of my conscience, meaningless. I would have then waved her concerns off with a flick of my hand; scoffed at her suspicions with a loud laugh before ordering another round. But I hadn't turned that corner yet (not from the lack of trying) and I suddenly found myself swimming against my own inebriated current, curious about Mel's final adventure, Mel's final story. Curious, just like my sister.

"Was she doing something illegal?" I asked.

"Mel? Not a chance. More than likely it was someone or something to do with the story she was working on."

"Who is the *they* she refers to? *They* are not very happy? Her editor?"

"It could be, but that's not what my gut is telling me."

"It's easy enough to call him."

"I already have. He doesn't know a thing about how she was going to present the story. He said that was the way Mel always worked–not a word until she delivered the final product."

"That seems strange."

"Not really, a lot of writers work that way. I remember her saying that she didn't like other cooks stirring her pot while it was still on the fire. She said it spoiled the flavor."

"It sounds like somebody didn't care for the taste of it," I said, remembering a few powerful people in Washington were not exactly thrilled with Mel's last piece on rural poverty. It had made them look bad; made them look like they weren't tending to their own backyard while they preached about freedom overseas in the Middle East. This new story, at least what little I knew about it, didn't seem like the kind to have such a far-reaching ripple effect, but then you never know how deep a thread goes until it begins to unravel. I could see that Jessica was hell bent on giving this one a good solid tug.

"Without knowing her *spin*, it's going to be hard to decipher the motive," Jessica said.

"Well," I said pointing at the email, "this is not exactly a smoking gun. You got anything a little more...*incriminating*?"

Jessica was quickly learning that as more alcohol seeped into my veins my sarcasm grew. Her body language was now screaming in protest as she said, "Her laptop computer is missing and, consequently, so is her story."

"Probably swiped by the maid or a neighbor before the cops could tape off the room she was staying in," I concluded. "No reason to go all drama queen on me."

"I know what I know," she growled. "Haven't you ever felt something that didn't make logical sense but you still knew somehow it was true?"

That was a good question, but Jessica had no idea how hard she had hit the nail on the head, as the saying goes. No one did, not even Mel. Every time Mel and I had talked about "twin telepathy", as she called it, I had lied and said I had never experienced it. I told her she was the lucky one and there must have been a short circuit in my umbilical cord. She always felt bad for me, saying how wonderful it was to feel my presence wherever she was. To know what I was doing and feeling. I couldn't tell her that I felt her too. I had vowed never to tell her again about the nightmares, the ones in which she always had the lead role, and the one that always died at the end of the picture. I didn't want to have them; I wanted them to go away; I wanted them to leave me alone!

"No, I don't know what you mean," I answered. I looked away and stared at Sam as he wiped down the knotty pine bar he defended like the Black Knight.

Showing that she could be just as caustic as I could be, Jessica kept after me, saying, "That's funny, Mel could usually sense where *you* were, which seemed to be in the state of intoxication most of the time. You never had premonitions about her?"

I shrugged, keeping my eyes away from hers. *I don't drink that much*, I wanted to say. But I didn't. I didn't owe her or anyone else an explanation.

We sat in silence for a while, looking down at our drinks mostly, feeling each uneasy second pass. I was hoping she would leave but she looked too determined. She was playing the patient cop, hoping I would surrender and spill my guts. At least that was what I was thinking, but I knew I would have to give her something to be rid of her.

"So, what exactly was Mel working on anyway?" I asked.

Jessica's face relaxed a little and slowly she told me what she knew, how Melissa had gone to Central New York for a week, to a little place called Sherrill. It was a city actually, the smallest in the country, she thought, with an undersized population of around three thousand. She remembered her saying something about staying at an old mansion built one hundred and fifty years ago by some kind of Communist group.

I had already known where she had gone, I just hadn't pursued why, and consequently blurted out the most obvious puzzlement, "Communists?"

"Yeah, I know. I had the same reaction when Mel told me."

"Are we talking Russian Communism, as in Karl Marx, the Cold war and all that jazz?"

"No, Mel didn't think so. She thought it was some kind of communal living—socialism that existed back in the mid-to-late eighteen hundreds. I remember her saying something about group marriage and free love. Some kind of utopia, I think she said. But other than that, she didn't know a lot about it before she left."

"Was her story going to be about them? The free lovers?"

"That's what she said."

It sounded like a story that would attract Mel, examining a wedge of people who were going against the grain; radicals bucking the system; a dark knot in an otherwise beautifully smooth piece of oak that so many believed America to be. Mel loved the knots; she always said they were beautiful in their own way, and she lived to get into the middle to see what made them tick. Her approach (*naivety*, I believe was the term her editor once used in front of me) had gotten her in trouble more than once, but certainly nothing worth being killed over. Then I realized something didn't fit and I said, "You said this cult existed back in the eighteen hundreds?"

"Yes, but I didn't say it was a cult. I don't know what it was."

"Whatever it was, it's dead and buried now, and antiques were not Mel's thing. She liked the living and breathing models, the ones she could carefully dissect as they went about their daily routine. You can't do that in a graveyard or a history book."

Jessica smiled, knowingly. She knew my sister as well as I did, maybe better, and she also knew Mel wouldn't take on a story

about a relic. "Her editor told me they got a tip, an anonymous letter warning of a rebirth of the Communists and their alternative
sexual lifestyle. A rebirth of Utopia."

I couldn't help but laugh as I envisioned my sister going absolutely giddy with delight when her boss first mentioned the assignment. "So that's the story Mel was after," I said, knowing she
was probably streaking across the George Washington Bridge,
headed north to Central New York before her editor even finished
reading the unsigned letter to her. "Did she leave any notes?
Maybe a list of people she had been talking to?"

"I asked your father, but he didn't see anything like that in her
stuff. You went there with him to get her things, did *you* find anything?"

I didn't answer her, instead rising from my chair to retrieve a
refill of my pain reliever from Sam. I tried once again to entice Jessica into joining me, but she declined. With beer in hand, I sat back
down, nearly landing on the floor in the process, content knowing
my medication was doing its job.

"Well?" Jessica asked, impatiently.

"Well, what?"

"Did you find any of her notes in the room she was staying in?
She was a fiend about taking notes."

I stared at the ballgame on the television, the bend in my
bender once again in sight, hoping she would take the hint.

She coolly pulled a menu from behind the array of condiments
on the side of the table and began scanning the choices, a look of
stubborn resolve painted across her face. "I don't have to be back
to work until a week from Monday, so take your time."

I was beginning to see why my sister liked her; she was just
like Mel, headstrong like a mother grizzly, but cute as a bear cub–a
lethal combination for most men, including me. It may have been
my developing attraction to her, but as the minutes passed, I
found myself wanting to tell her more, wanting to peel off my armor just a little.

"I didn't go into her room, or even the mansion for that matter. I waited in the parking lot in back until Dad brought me the keys to the Mustang."

Jessica didn't respond, looking at me for a moment before returning her disapproving eyes to the menu.

"I know what you're thinking, *what a chicken-shit*. And you know what, you're right."

"That's not what I was thinking."

"Well, you should be. More than you know."

Jessica put her menu down and I knew right then I had said too much. I instinctively pulled my invisible shield back up and began the damage control, "Not many clues, eh, Sherlock? Or maybe I should call you Dr. Watson, the bumbling sidekick to the now dearly-departed Ms. Holmes."

Jessica shook her head in disgust, "What happened to you, or have you always been this way?"

I didn't answer. Looking away, my father's dogmatic voice began to jackhammer at the back of my brain, "This is where it ends, Michael. Ends! Ends! Ends! Is that clear?" *Clear as the need for another beer.*

"Do you even care that Mel is dead!?" Jess asked, pleading.

I glanced over at Sam, looking perhaps for some sympathy, thinking for some reason that he would know what it was like to be on the receiving end of an infuriated woman. But his face was expressionless as always, and he stood at the bar watching the game, looking like the professional he was at pretending to ignore the tongue fight erupting just a few yards away.

Suddenly, Jessica's plastic-coated cardboard menu smacked me in the face. She had thrown it at me as she sprang up from the table. I could feel a tiny trickle of blood crawling down the bridge of my nose. I looked for a napkin but didn't see one. Embarrassed, I wiped at my bleeding nose with my shirtsleeve, which only served to smear half my face red.

She was standing now, leaning toward me with both hands on

the table; her eyes burning a green fire that made me pull back in a flash of fear.

"God only knows why Mel spent so much time worrying about you," she said with a quiet rage, "chasing every premonition she ever had about you until she knew you were safe and YOU, in the meantime, are crawling into every bottle you can find, oblivious to her existence."

She was going too far and even the drunken fog couldn't keep it out, "I loved Mel!" I screamed. I repeated it three times, my voice lowering with each chorus until it was nothing more that a trembling whisper, "I still love Mel."

"Then do something about it!"

"Jessica, she's dead! Nothing I do now can change that; nothing!"

I was staring into her eyes now and, as I searched them for compassion, I saw them change. The fury was leaving, slipping away like clouds yielding to the sun. She sat back down and handed me a pink and purple polka-dot handkerchief she pulled from her handbag. I wiped my face with it as my throbbing pulse began to slow.

"If you tell anyone about that," she said, pointing at the handkerchief, "I'll have to kill you. And call me Jess, I hate Jessica. It sounds too MTV'ish, at least for a cop anyway."

I nodded in agreement, trying to smile but failing.

"With or without you, I'm going to find out what really happened to Mel," Jessica said. "I'm going to Sherrill on Monday and I'm not leaving there until I have the answer."

CHAPTER 6

My mother had insisted that Jessica stay with us through the weekend, making it difficult for me to avoid her or the idea of investigating my sister's death. By Sunday night, I was mentally exhausted. As I sat alone at the kitchen table knowing I should go to bed, I began looking forward to returning to Albany, New York, where I lived in a spacious townhouse with a roommate I tolerated, a cockatoo I despised, and a dog I truly loved. The cockatoo talked too much for his future to remain rosy and the roommate too little to remind me he was human. He was a technonerd who built websites by day and played online video games all night. But we managed to get along, mainly because he paid his share of the bills on time and stayed out of my way. My dog, a German Shepard named Saxy, short for the German name Saxonia, was as close to my lover as an animal could get without getting me locked up. She never fussed or argued, had no in-laws to visit and would bring me a beer whenever I asked. *What more could a man ask for.* I couldn't wait to get back and rub her belly, back into the steady routine of work and weekend wipeouts. *The nightmares will fade,* I told myself, *if God has any mercy at all.*

I had to get through tonight first. I really wanted a beer, a sixpack at least, but I knew I had a shit-load of work waiting for me, and a Monday morning hangover was the last thing I needed following the emotional decathlon I had just endured. It had been a long stretch: my sister's funeral; a judgmental, avenging friend to deflect; staying with my parents for an entire weekend! Unbelievably, I was ready to go back to work. It was tax season, just after the April 15th deadline, a time when an auditor like me gets to have some fun auditing the rest of the country (or in my case, the rest of New York State). I had already missed a good part of last week and needed to get back. As I was contemplating just how many files had accumulated on the desk, Jess walked in and sat right down next to me.

"Does this mean anything to you?" she asked as she placed a printed email in front of me.

I looked at the paper. It was from Mel, but she had sent it to herself.

"Where did you get this?" I asked.

"It's from the hotmail account she had, you know, one of those free email accounts you can get from Microsoft. I found it in her archive folder." A shy grin appeared, "We shared passwords."

"Why did she have...," I started to inquire but stopped realizing that *I* had several anonymous email accounts and, knowing what I used mine for, I really didn't what to know what my sister did with hers.

"She sent herself reminders every now and then, kind of like electronic sticky notes. Based on the date, I'm sure it has something to do with the story she was writing."

I studied the email, which contained a list of five condensed questions. "Putney Origin?" I asked, reading aloud the first item.

Jessica shrugged, "You're from Putney, born and raised, as I understand it. Do the other four mean anything to you?"

I continued down the list, "Perfectionism? Complex Marriage? Male Continence? Utopia?" I had no idea what these things meant and I'm sure my face looked as puzzled as I felt. "I think my original comment was correct; this definitely sounds like a religious cult to me."

"You've never heard these terms before?"

For one of the few times that weekend I was honest with her, saying, "Nothing comes to mind." I handed the sheet back to her, eager to let it go.

"Well, hopefully, I'll find some clues tomorrow."

"You're going through with it?" I asked, with a hint of surprise and amusement in my voice.

"I'm leaving at six."

"AM?"

"Yeah, you remember, when the sun comes up."

It had taken her a few days, but I could see now she was comfortable and quite adept at giving me some of my own medicine, as they say. "Well then, I guess I should say goodbye now," I said.

"Are you sure you won't go with me?" she asked.

I shook my head, concentrating on the hairline crack in the rectangular pine table where I had eaten cornflakes my entire life. I had never noticed it before but it now provided me a suitable distraction. I also noticed it was annoying the hell out of Jess.

"So, you're just going to let it die, let *Mel* die without as much as a whimper of protest."

I kept shaking my head. I didn't want to hear it. "Give it up, Jess," I barked. I then lowered my voice to spare my sleeping, or possibly preoccupied, parents and said, "Everyone says it was an accident; the police; the coroner–everyone but you."

She pushed back in her chair and threw up her arms, "Have you read that police report? *Accidental death by autoerotic asphyxiation*," she said, mockingly. "Accidental, my ass!"

"Shhh, quiet down," I said, waving my arms as if that would cleanse the air of her uproar. Whispering, I then said, "My mother doesn't know all the wicked details and my father will kill us both is she finds out. For all she knows, Mel died in her sleep from a defective heart."

"How could your father tell her that?"

"It's better than what the report said."

"Well...."

"Well, nothing. You don't know my mother. Something like

that might destroy her. Mel was her little angel and masturbation doesn't go with the image."

She leaned into the table toward me and said very directly, "Mel wasn't into autoerotic anything, let alone strangling herself to get off."

"How do you know that? She was as open-minded as anyone I've ever met. I'm sure she liked to doodle as much as the next person. Don't you?"

Jess' anger grew as she said, "That's none of your business, and don't change the subject."

"I was just curious," I said, hoping that I *could* change the subject.

"I just know; that's all. She could talk the talk, but she didn't walk the walk. Hell, she would blush when we went shopping for bras at Victoria's Secret in the mall."

"Everyone has secrets," I said, thinking about one of my own.

Jessica's face quieted and tiny tears began to trickle down her cheeks. I could only imagine she was remembering some of the more intimate feelings she and my sister had shared, and I began to wonder if perhaps they had been lovers. Now that would have been a well-camouflaged secret, especially since I could recall the constant stream of boyfriends (semi-serious, Mel would faithfully label them) I had met during visits to Mel's place or at family gatherings in Putney. No, I concluded, that that would be a stretch even for cosmopolitan Mel, and I decided that Jess was probably the sister she never had, perhaps even seeing Jess as the *sibling* she never fully had.

"I knew her," Jess finally said. "She shared herself like no one I've ever known and that's why I know the reports are wrong. The police are wrong, damn it, and I will never be able to think of her again if I don't at least try to find out why."

"What about going to the District Attorney and asking for an independent investigation? I'm sure they could do a better job than you or I could."

"I already checked into that; it could take weeks, maybe months before the D.A. would even look at the case to determine if an investigation is warranted. By that time Mel's killer could be long gone."

"If it is as suspicious as you say it is, I would think they would jump all over it?"

"Everything I can lay in front of them, the *official* evidence, is stamped with big black letters–ACCIDENTAL DEATH! The police report detailing the scene when the first officers arrived; the C.I.D. detective's supplemental report, which was a piss-poor effort if you ask me. It looks like the guy spent a half day on the case, filled out his report, and stuffed the file in a drawer with a hundred other forgotten cases."

"C.I.D.?"

"Criminal Investigation Division; almost every city police department has one. Even a little place like Sherrill has crime that requires investigation."

"And his report indicates no foul play?" I asked.

"Nothing. And the medical examiner's report lines up perfectly with the others and *he* signed the death certificate. It looks to me like they all sat down and did their homework together and came up with the same answers."

"Now I see; you've developed your own little conspiracy theory."

"I know it sounds that way, but trust me, I'm not *that* paranoid."

"Paranoia will destroy ya," I sang, off key, in a lame attempt to lighten the mood. It was from a song I couldn't name, by a group I didn't know, but I had the hook in my head, making me grossly susceptible to any consumer product the tune promoted.

"I just know that investigations take time and diligence, and I don't see the evidence of either one in these reports."

"Maybe the Sherrill Police Department is swamped with cases...wait a minute, how do you know all this, all the details in their reports?"

Jess sat back in her chair and folded her arms. She was taking a defensive stance, one I had seen many times during tax audits when I would ask someone to produce the birth certificates for the fourteen children they had listed as dependents on their tax return (believe it or not, producing live bodies is easier than producing authentic-looking documents). It told me something was amiss. To put it more bluntly, a lie was being covered or some other type of deception. I didn't think Jess was lying about the reports. Why would she make up something that didn't support her belief? No, there was something else brewing here and I knew if I let her talk, eventually she would tell me what it was. She did not keep me waiting.

"I've got a friend that works in the Yonkers C.I.D.," she said. "He made a courtesy call to the Sherrill P.D. and got copies of the reports."

"A friend?"

"Yeah, a friend," she said as her eyes tailed away.

The guy was more than a friend, that was obvious, and I felt a pinch of jealously that made me laugh inside. I had never been the jealous type, mainly because I didn't let women in. I kept them at arms length so I could ogle instead of cuddle. Developing attachments wasn't in my bylaws and it struck me funny that for some unknown reason I was flirting with breaking one of my own rules.

"Why didn't you just call yourself?"

"It's a procedural thing–chain of command protocol. Feathers ruffle easily when grunts like me go wading into somebody else's pool."

I nodded as if I understood. "So, what else did your *friend* have to say about it all?" I then asked.

Jess told me that her connection in the Yonkers C.I.D. had gotten everything but a copy of the toxicology report, which would be available in several weeks. She quickly added that she didn't think it would provide anything new. Jess said her friend agreed with the Sherrill P.D., that strangulation was indeed the cause of death, and concluded that the likelihood of anything abnormal showing up inside her body was remote. He did express concern, she said, that there were only a few photos taken at the scene and no sketches or diagrams were prepared, at least none had been faxed down to him. That, he said, raised a flag in his mind and was something he would pursue further when he could break away from the three homicide cases he was currently working on in the Big Apple. Jess said he had suggested getting a private investigator but it would be expensive and good ones were hard to find. She reminded him that Mel was her best friend and therefore she would be the best P.I. to have on the case. He didn't argue, she claimed.

"What about an autopsy?" I asked. "Were we stupid not to have that done?"

"That was your parents' decision and, like most grieving families, they chose not to. It's hard to make difficult decisions when the emotions are running so high. People don't really sit down and examine the situation calmly until months later. That's when the questions start flying about what really happened and people sometimes regret the less stressful road they traveled at the time. In the heat of the moment, it's tough to be completely rational."

"Isn't that what you're doing? Being irrational in the heat of the moment?"

Her face tightened. "I'm trained to keep a level head under stress and, even though I loved Mel like a sister, I know there's more to what I'm feeling than just inconsolable loss and a reckless desire for justice."

I believed her, but I didn't say it. She sensed something that went beyond the police reports, crime scene photos and blood analysis; something only a deep bond could spawn. Right at that moment, I realized that Jess and my sister Mel had truly been like sisters. Another pang of jealously bounced up and hit me square in the nose. I squirmed in my chair a little and said, "I think the police know what they're doing, they're the experts. We should let them do their job."

"They've done all they're going to do," she said, her voice more urgent now, almost pleading. "It's up to us now."

"Us? Why exactly do you need me to help, anyway? I'm just an accountant with no personality, remember? You're the cop, so go do your cop thing."

"I'm used to working with a partner; someone to bounce my ideas off. And since I can't show up there in any official capacity that rules out my normal partner."

"So, I would be Starsky to your Hutch?"

"You know what I mean. Two set of eyes and ears; two lines of questioning. You do ask good questions, I have to admit that. I wouldn't want you auditing *my* tax returns."

She was scratching my belly now and even though it felt good, I was not about to budge. "Two heads are better than one, is that the idea?"

"More like one and a half," she grinned. "But yeah, that's the idea."

Jess was trying her damnedest to find a hole in my armor and pull me over to her side, to crumble my walls with the anguish-laced sentiment in her eyes. It might have work, but thanks to my own desire to cancel my nightmare reruns and the dictatorial sentiment from my father, my mind was already made up. "Well, good luck tomorrow," I said abruptly, tracing my finger along the crack in the table. "Let me know how it goes."

Jess had no reply, looking sickened and disappointed as she left me as she had found me, alone in my parent's kitchen secretly wondering what I would do all night while the rest of them slept. She didn't know about my little demon, the nightmares that visited each night when I dared to shut sober eyes. I wasn't about to tell her. I wasn't ready to tell anyone, and I wasn't about to go to sleep, either.

CHAPTER 7

My sister, Mel, is lying in a bed. She is sound asleep on her back with a patchwork quilt draped over her. It stops just below the delicate mound of her breasts, which are hidden beneath a pale cotton t-shirt. Her breaths are slow and steady. Her fingers twitch as if she is typing a story in her dreams and I can almost hear her mumble as her mouth gestures in rhythm with her hands. She is alone, yet I sense she is not truly alone.

The room that encases her is unfamiliar to me. A friend's spare bedroom, one of Jessica's perhaps? Or one of the many hotels that she has stayed in during her travels around the country chasing *life stories*, as she used to call them. As I stare into the half-light, I believe that this is an old room—a leftover from another time. The weathered patina of the unpretentious rocker sitting in the corner is definitely not Holiday Inn, the simple lines of the surrounding woodwork warm and inviting, suggesting a quaint bed and breakfast. Scanning across the walls, ghostly black and white pictures of stout bearded men and placid women begin to speak to me with their eyes; they are telling me that this was once *their* home; that this was a very large home to many people; that this was their *mansion*.

A shadow looms across the bed and begins to inch its way toward my sister's unsuspecting face. It is a human shadow for sure, but not clearly a man or a woman. I watch with peculiar curiosity at first, unable to move as its murky form swallows the entire bed until finally its owner appears; a black faceless figure moving slowly into the frame.

Everything is muted shades of gray, the bed, the walls, the furniture, and even my sister, except the squirming, glowing red snake that dangles precariously from the hand of the unwelcome visitor. My curiosity has vanished, replaced now with sheer terror, and I try desperately to yell to her, to warn my sister, but the room remains silent even though I can feel my lungs exploding. The spook is moving closer to her now, lifting the snake up into both hands, when suddenly Mel awakens. She stares unbelievingly at the figure and at the serpent before turning her eyes toward me, screaming in silent words, "Michael!" Her face is a tapestry of pain and horror as the defiling beast wraps itself around her neck. She pulls at it with both hands frantically, helplessly. But it is no use, she cannot wrestle free and she reaches out to me, her staggering eyes pleading with me to help her. I try to reach back, to take her hand and pull her from the monster, her fingertips just inches from mine, but I can get no closer. I awake with a start. Sweat drips off my cold neck and I am back in my parent's home.

They always start out good, the nightmares, that is. At first, they are *pleasant dreams*, just like my mother promised when she would tuck me in at night when I was a boy. Safe and sound, my sister would be driving in her car or walking down the street with me observing from above, like an angel assigned to watch over her. A simple scene, boring really, something any father babysitting his kids at the playground would smile at and confidently return to the confines of his newspaper. The beginning has always the good part, the only good part.

I had tried to avoid sleep so often now that even an overdose of caffeine doesn't keep me awake anymore. I looked at the clock on the bedside table and saw that it was just after two in the morning. I rolled onto my back and gazed up at the ceiling. Mel was dead and still the nightmares came. I shook my head. Then, I got up, and went into the bathroom. At the sink, I splashed my face with cold water. I stared at my reflection in the medicine cabinet mirror, noticing a hint of darkness under each of my eyes. "You're getting too old for this shit," I said to the person looking back at me. There was no reply.

I went down to the kitchen, opened a bottle of heavily caffeinated soda, and busied myself with as many quiet and mindless activities as I could think of. I found six quarters and a dime digging into the cushions of the living room sofa before rearranging all the books by author on the shelves I remembered my father building when I first started high school. He had done a masterful job except for one shelf that my mother insisted looked "cockeyed." Somehow, I managed to burn off an hour before reluctantly returning to the kitchen table. The chairs had straight backs and flat seats with no cushions, and were so rigid that it was impossible to get completely comfortable, let alone fall asleep in one. I stayed there waiting for morning, or another idea, whichever would come to me first.

CHAPTER 8

I heard my mother yelling at Jess and then the distinctive whack of the metal screen door I had helped install over twenty years ago. My father had "tweaked" the attached hydraulic closer at least a hundred times but it still didn't work "worth a damn." It continued to proclaim our comings and goings like a square dance caller, keeping everyone in step with everyone else. I heard Jess yell back that she was fine and didn't need another piece of toast. My mother countered with an offer of eggs and sausage. There was another, "I'm fine Mrs. Gibson, really," followed by a, "Say goodbye to Michael for me." Then I noticed the sun stirring over the distant horizon and I heard a flock of geese honking overhead. I peered up just in time to catch a glimpse of them; their powerful wings pumping to a steady, unheard beat; their harmonious formation looking like an Indian arrowhead slicing through the sky. I had been awake for over four hours, waiting patiently, but was now cold, cranky, and anxious to hear the sound of Jess's car door slamming. Her car keys jingled as she inserted them into the ignition and started the engine, a mild rustling-of-autumn-leaves sound that only a 4-cylinder foreign compact would make. *Detroit would never put a wimp like this on the road,* I thought to myself, even though I knew they probably did. I waited until she looked in her rearview mirror before I spoke.

"I thought you said *six* o'clock," I grumbled as I sat up in the backseat where I had been lounging since three that morning. "It's already pushing seven and its cold out here."

Her smile was modest, subdued almost, but I could tell she was happy I had reconsidered her offer. "What made you change your mind?" she asked as she backed out of my parent's driveway.

"I know if I didn't go, I'd never hear the end of it," I said. There is a lot of time to think when the rest of the world is sleeping and I did my share sitting in the cramped quarters of Jess's car. I owed my sister something, of that much I was sure. Exactly what, I didn't know. I hoped I would find it where we were going. The nightmares would only get worse if I didn't go, I had concluded, and as I fought my way into the front seat next to my sister's best friend, I realized that my father would require me to explain myself. I had already decided that this time I would, whether he liked it or not.

CHAPTER 9

Although my vision was fuzzy when I opened my eyes, there was no mistaking the familiar chestnut brown siding and sunflower yellow door of my Albany townhouse. I had slept peacefully for the hour it took Jess to drive from Vermont and I awoke now with an optimism I didn't recognize. I went inside to swap clean clothes for the dirty clothes in my suitcase, then called my boss, leaving a message in his voicemail box that I would need the week off and would call him again later in the day. Leaving the message was the easy way out. As I locked the front door and headed back to Jess and her murmuring vehicle, I could already envision the spit shooting from my screaming boss's mouth as he stood shaking the walls of my luxurious 8 x 8 cubical.

"You're not even going to take the dog out for a quickie?" Jess asked.

"She's at the kennel," I said. "Probably scoping out some poodle as we speak. But I could go back inside and ask my roommate if he's interested."

Blushing, Jess assured me that was *not* what she meant.

Soon we were on the New York State Thruway, heading west at a seventy-mile-an-hour clip. I decided to ask an obvious question, "So, what's our plan of attack?"

Jess looked at me, broke out in a sheepish grin and returned her eyes to the road.

"You don't have a plan?"

She shook her head. "I figured I would think of something along the way."

"Something like...flashing your *Yonkers Finest* badge and telling everyone to freeze?" I asked.

"Well," she answered hesitantly as her cheeks blushed.

I laughed. I was surprised that she might actually be considering it. "Do you honestly think that the good folks of Sherrill will just belly up to the witness stand and start blabbing the minute they hear your siren wailing?"

"No...."

"Of course they won't. Whatever happened that night has already been neatly tied up, carefully locked down and secretly sealed away like the bones of Jimmy Hoffa. Its going to take some calculated persuasion to dig it all up again."

Jess gave me a quizzical look, "Do all tax auditors talk like that?"

"The better ones," I replied.

We sat in silence for the next ten miles, both of us trying to think of a plan that would impress the other *and* actually have a chance of working, until Jess said, "Have you got a better idea?"

"I'm working on it," I replied just as we were passing the sign for an approaching rest area. "Pull in here, I need some caffeine."

"Ay-ay captain," she answered with a smirk.

We went inside and sat down, she with her coffee and I with a heavily caffeinated soda. Having heard a thousand and one tall tales from the country's fine citizenry during tax season, I found it very easy to formulate a ruse that would cloak our true intentions. I suggested that we arrive in Sherrill under some false pretense and use different names. At least, I should anyway. I said we could be a rich couple on their honeymoon exploring the northeast who just happened to be passing through when we stumbled upon the quaint little city and completely fell in love with it. We want to consider investing by establishing a kick-ass spa and resort, which, we would explain, is our passion and the source of our *considerable* wealth. "When you have 237 properties all across the United States and another 121 abroad, the money does tend to accumulate," I reminded Jess.

"It *would* give us an excuse to start nosing around," Jess said. "Ask questions about local history that should help us reconstruct what Mel was writing about."

"Exactly; and once the smell of money gets out, they'll be lining up at our door; the mayor; the shop owners; hell, probably even the women's auxiliary!"

"But we'll have to be subtle with our questions about this communist group Mel was investigating."

"That's easy; we'll just throw a few lures in the water and wait to see who takes the bait. People love to talk; they just keep things to themselves until they find a willing listener."

"And that's us!"

I was impressed with Jess. She had caught on quickly to the bait-hook-and-reel tactics that had taken me several years to learn as a tax auditor. It was looking like we would make a good team. Spying on her now with only a small table between us, her always fresh-as-a-daisy face focused for the fight ahead, her lithe, curving body seemingly coiled to strike, I began to contemplate some of the potential side benefits of our little charade.

"Of course, we'll have to share one room," I said, looking out a window and trying to act casual about it. "To make it all look authentic—our marriage and ravenous passion for each other, that is." I checked for her reaction out of the corner of my eye. She was staring back at me, her head was slightly tilted; frowning just as my mother had the first time I told her that the dog ate my algebra homework. I wasn't discouraged, adding, "And one bed, king size of course, would really help seal the deal."

Jess let the crease of a smile play across her face, "We're not sleeping together," she said firmly. She scooped up her coffee and headed back to the car.

I watched her walk away, enjoying the subtle carnal shuffle of her firm behind (although at that moment, *tight* might have been the better adjective), and felt an encouraging tickle of lust. I was being sexist and I knew it, but then, many of life's simple pleasures are. I grabbed my soda and chased after her.

"We have to make it look believable," I said. "But don't worry; I'll be a perfect gentleman."

We were back outside now and were standing in front of her car when she said, "And you are assuming that I will be a perfect lady?"

It wasn't exactly what I thought she would say. I was expecting more rebuttals, a carefully presented case for the defense that would free her from my proposed marital bondage. Maybe even a cold hard slap in the face. But I wasn't prepared for the fresh tickle she had just delivered to my loins. I stood there speechless, thinking, *is she being serious or just yanking my chain?*

Jess watched amused as I struggled for a reply. I couldn't get anything out of my mouth, nothing understandable at least, and I stood looking as awkward as a ten year old at his first dance. Her bravado had me flustered and I could see she was enjoying it.

Finally, she said, "I like your plan, most of it anyway. I think I'll stick with my own name though, I don't see how anyone could connect it to Mel."

"You don't think she would have mentioned you to someone?"

"No; but if she did, it would have just been my first name and I doubt anyone would remember."

"Yeah, I agree. Not much risk there."

"And that means that you get to be Mr. Jessica Hartwell."

I was beginning to see why she was a cop. She liked to be in charge and didn't appear hesitant to lead one either. I wondered if she had brought her handcuffs and decided to save that flirtatious question for the right moment. Instead I said, "You'd like that, wouldn't you; me as your little henpecked husband."

"I wouldn't ask you to do that," Jess said, laughing. "Now get in the car, bitch!"

Once again, we were zipping along the highway, a rather bland stretch of road currently shrouded in the pubescent days of a Northeast spring; an endless blemish of barren trees and dirt frosted thickets. This time of year, before the tulips have risen from the earth like rainbow zombies and the apple orchards twinkle in pink and white, there was only the pale reminder that another winter has just passed through and left us "a frightful mess," as my mother called it. But still, the steadily warming air brought hope to those of us who lived here all our lives, serving as an annual reminder that life will still blossom as soon as it gets its chance. Sitting there, as Jess searched for a good radio station, I reminded myself that this was my chance to start anew, to fix some old mistakes. I thought of Mel and struggled with the tears, wishing with all my heart that I had made this journey a week ago, when she was still alive.

"You got quiet all of a sudden," Jess said. "Are you thinking about Mel?"

"Yeah," I replied, wiping my eyes. "And I was thinking that maybe I would be Mick. What do you think?"

"Hmmm, Mick Hartwell; it's got a rich and rude ring to it."

"It does, doesn't it," I said, smiling. "We can live in the Hamptons, but only during the summer months, of course."

"And in Palm Springs in the winter," Jess added, excitedly.

"Maybe Rome, or Paris during the holidays?"

"Why not both, after all, we *are* disgustingly rich."

"I like the way you think," I said, and I really meant it. There was more to this woman than the sum of her body parts and it put me in unfamiliar territory. There's an old joke that God gave man a brain and a penis, but only enough blood to run one at a time. As Jess and I rolled west on the still hibernating New York State Thruway, I could almost feel the pulsating rush of my own blood migrating north.

Putney, Vermont
November 16, 1847

"I think you should leave the state, John," Larkin said.

"That doesn't sound very legal, coming from my lawyer," John replied.

"I'm not being your lawyer right now. It's the advice of your brother-in-law."

"I will not abandon my followers and run away just to save my own skin," John said firmly.

The formal announcement of his sexual experimentation had not produced the reaction John had expected. Some of the followers in his association–a handful of families that regarded themselves as one family–were outraged. The town that surrounded them almost immediately began holding public indignation meetings, which only served to fuel the fire that was now burning out of control. Momentarily sheltered on the group's farm in his home town of Putney, John had looked to his friend for guidance.

"The sheriff has a new warrant for your arrest," Larkin said. "Adultery is a very serious charge."

John knew the allegation, arrested several weeks earlier and indicted under bond of $2,000 for trial in the following spring. It had come after he publicly proclaimed that he and his wife had entered into an enlargement of their marital relations with another couple. The union was based, he said, on his study of the New Testament. "In the Kingdom of Heaven, the institution of marriage, which assigns the exclusive possession of one woman to one man, does not exist. The new commandment," he declared, "is that we love one another."

As the flames of intolerance scorched the walls around him, he still believed what he had read in the scriptures and was prepared to face his accusers. He stayed in Putney after the first arrest, intending to surrender to the authorities without bail, on the condition that his flock be left in peace. But that was before other members of his tiny group had been similarly charged. *And* before the threats of mob violence and rumors of being tarred and feathered had grown in force and fury. His theories on marriage and birth control, which he and many of his followers openly practiced, were proving more than his orthodox neighbors in the small Vermont village could overlook. The air of acceptance the commune had breathed contently for years now reeked of prejudice and its stench was leading John to concede that his brother-in-law was right. He had to leave.

"I will go," John said. "But know that I only do so to prevent an outbreak of lynch law among the barbarians of Putney."

Relieved to hear John agree, Larkin assured him he was doing the right thing.

With no one giving chase, John left, wondering if the Putney Association, as it was called, had been a failure, a condition he was already quite familiar with. A graduate of Yale Theological School fifteen years earlier, John had earned his license to preach only to then have it revoked after a stormy hearing before the school's faculty association. Labeled a heretic for his unconventional views on what constituted perfect holiness in the Free Church, the then twenty-two year-old was subsequently cut off from his college, his church and his family to then wander New England virtually penniless, preaching his beliefs to all who would listen. A passionate student of the Bible, it was that very faith in God and the unyielding desire to preach Christ that had delivered him from that sorry fate and would quickly squelch any feeling of defeat that intended to follow him out of Vermont.

The following spring, the undaunted thirty-six-year-old son of a well-to-do congressman and Dartmouth graduate, reunited with his flock of nearly one hundred men, women and children.

"We shall move the entire group to a secluded valley in Up-state New York where I have purchased 160 acres of land," John said to an elated Larkin. "Until recently, it had been territory reserved to the Oneida Indians, but now it belongs to us. There is already a handful of Putney converts settled there. The property has a farmhouse, a few outbuildings, and a sawmill powered by a flowing creek that meanders through the valley. The soil is good and the water privilege excellent, an ideal location to begin anew," he said proudly, "the perfect setting to increase our communion with God's invisible kingdom."

John had no idea at the time that their new home would be the place branded into the minds of witnesses and historians alike, as Utopia.

CHAPTER 10

The cordial green and white sign read "Welcome to Sherrill–The Silver City–Smallest City in New York State." The place didn't look silver, nor did it appear big enough to even be a city. In fact, if Jess and I had blinked, we might have missed it. It was rural America to a tee; four stoplights, one grocery store, and sleepy little parks wedged into every available open lot. In less than five minutes, we turned a full lap around the place, continually veering left at the major intersections as if running under caution in a NASCAR race, before looking at each other with puzzled grins that said, "Is that all there is?" It did have a warm and cozy feel, like a visit to grandma's house–over the river and through the woods. As we pulled up to a mailman to ask directions, I had a strange feeling there was more here than met the just-visiting eye.

"You're looking for the Mansion House," the middle-aged mail carrier said after deciphering our purposely-incoherent questions about an old place on a hill built before the constitution had been signed. "And it's not quite that old; built mostly in the 1860's actually; a few additions after that; not really on a hill either; I would call it a little mound myself, of course it would depend on where you were standing at the time; beautiful architecture; they don't build'em like that anymore; you folks aren't from around here, are you? Just passing through? If you're looking for a nice lunch the best place is a few blocks over called the...." Twenty minutes later, we continued on our way.

As we wandered down the main street, gazing out our half opened windows, I wondered what my sister had found in the Norman Rockwell houses that were now curiously peeking back at Jess and me from behind their sentinel walls of pine, oak, and maple trees. Inside, was there nothing but homemakers? Baking cookies and folding laundry as their toddlers sat hypnotized by cartoon characters running amok on glowing television screens? What secrets might they be protecting? A scandalous affair with a discontented neighbor? Probably, that kind of thing happens everywhere. Maybe an illegal high-stakes poker game on Saturday night, one the Chief of Police hosts when it is his turn. Could there be a murderer hiding somewhere behind this provincial façade? That *was* the question.

"That must be it," Jess said, pointing straight ahead over the dashboard.

It was a mansion all right, one hundred thousand square feet, my statistically inclined mind guessed, three stories high and clad almost completely in amber and red brick, with tall, skinny, white-trimmed windows that watched possessively over the rolling acreage of quiescent lawns and gardens. My first impression was that it looked a bit out a place, like what Abraham Lincoln might look like standing in the middle of Time Square. But, as we pulled up the drive, our gawking eyes caressed by the gentle breeze invading our car, a sense of place and purpose swept over me. Suddenly, and strangely, I couldn't imagine this old place being anywhere else in the world. We stopped in front of the strapping, white-pillar terraced entry, wandered to the front door in touristy fashion, and went inside.

"Good morning," an attentive elderly woman said as we walked in. "Is this your first visit with us?" She looked to be about my mother's age, which was the yardstick I used to measure all senior citizens by, but much thinner and her face was pale like baking flour. She wore small wire-rim glasses and a faint blue, uninteresting waist-cinched dress that buttoned tightly at the neck and fell prudently past her knees. Her completely gray hair provided the only noticeable statement of color in flesh or attire, leaving her warm smile as the next thing to catch my eye.

"Why, yes it is," Jess said, cheerfully. "We were just driving by when we spotted it from the road and just *had* to come in for a closer look." Jess was already into her role and I decided to follow her, whether she was ready or not.

I grabbed Jess at the waist and pulled her to me, "We're on our honeymoon," I said, before kissing the top of her head. I could feel her muscles tighten in my arms, but I held her tightly, enjoying the curve of her hip against my fingers and the smell of her hair as it brushed against my chin.

"How wonderful!" the woman said. "Where are you from?"

"Albany," I said at the very instant Jess said, "New York City."

The woman looked at us both, mildly amused, but seemingly unconcerned with our conflicting answers. "Well, you have certainly come a long way," she said as she turned and walked toward a leaflet-adorned table.

Jess and I looked at each other and winced.

"Actually, I'm from Albany originally and my wife is from New York, the Big Apple." I squeezed Jess affectionately, and said, "She was just a pretty young thing working in a paper mill down in Yonkers when I found her and realized I couldn't live without her. I marched into that old factory, told her I loved her, and carried her out in my arms," I said, feeling Jess wiggle nervously the whole time. "Smartest thing I ever did in my life, right, Lollipop?"

"Uh-uh," was all Jess said. She wrestled free from my grip just before the woman turned back around toward us.

"We don't do a formal tour on Mondays," the woman said as she handed Jess a handful of literature, appearing uninterested in my courtship story, "only Wednesday through Saturday, but you are free to wander around today if you like. If you have any questions, just ask for Harry, that's me, its short for Harriet, Harriet Kinney. I'll be right here in the lobby most of the day." She offered a modest smile and then disappeared down the hall toward the sound of a ringing telephone.

I reached out to take one of the brochures from Jess's hand, but she abruptly pulled it away, saying, "You call me Lollipop again and you'll find yourself eating your lunch through a straw."

"I'm just playing my part," I said, grinning.

"Really?" She retorted, "What movie did you steal it from?"

"*An Officer and a Gentleman*; people say I remind them of Richard Gere."

She pulled back, examining me thoroughly in a way that made me feel self-conscious. She shook her head saying, "I don't see it."

I turned 90 degrees and said, "It's my profile; do you see it now?"

"Nope."

"You didn't even look!"

"I've seen enough of you to know I've seen too much," she chuckled as she opened one of the brochures. "And what's with the busy fingers? I'm not a piano. Next time, I break them."

I raised an eyebrow at her, "Next time?"

"Don't even think about it. Remember what we're here for."

Just as Jess said that, I caught my reflection in a large wall mirror and saw Mel staring back at me. We weren't identical twins, but we shared our mother's eyes and our father's nose, and could fool no one into believing we were *not* related when standing next to each other. Seeing her deep brown eyes staring back at me accomplished what Jess had prompted–we were here to dig up Mel. I felt a shiver as I began to comprehend how difficult this was actually going to be.

"Let's go outside and walk around the place," Jess said. "We need to get our bearings."

I followed Jess out the same way we had come in, settling in next to her as we strolled around the perimeter of the noble structure. It glittered like an antique ruby in the late morning sun, its white dovetail cornerstones looking like giant zippers lacing its fiery walls together, a labyrinth of ivy stretching like fingers up and onto the roof.

"Whoever the masons were, they certainly knew their craft," I said, looking up at the intricate brickwork.

"It *is* beautiful," Jess added. "Knowing Mel, I'm sure she was smitten the moment she arrived."

"Yeah, I'll bet she was," I sighed.

Strolling on, we found ourselves entering a courtyard where a giant barrel trunk tree stood in the middle looming majestically over the smaller inhabitants that decorated a meandering pathway. There was a line of grey dormer windows along each mansard roof, suggesting to me a platoon of army soldiers standing at attention atop protecting castle walls. Aside from the plantings, though, the quad was empty. I began to wonder if anyone lived here.

"It sure is quiet," I observed. "You would think people would be outside enjoying this beautiful spring day."

Just as I spoke, a crow cawed from overhead in the trees somewhere. Then, a second one answered and then a third as if they were playing a game of Marco Polo.

Jess didn't respond to my comment about the empty courtyard, and, looking at her, I could see her eyes bouncing from empty window to empty window as if searching for something or someone. I studied them along with her, feeling their dark gaze looking past us, indifferent to our presence. "What are you looking for?" I finally asked.

"Nothing, really; I was just curious about which room Mel had stayed in."

I was looking directly at a second floor window, the only one I had noticed with the shades half drawn and instantly Mel's terrified face flashed before my eyes. She was inside that very window and I felt a sudden rush of fear. I closed my eyes tightly, trying to clear my head. After summoning the courage to open them again, I looked at the window a second time. Mel was gone.

"There are some real nice rooms up there," a low, raspy voice said.

Startled, Jess and I turned to see a rather large man, very tanned and sturdy, wearing a god-awful (I was picking up Jess's slang already) green and yellow hat that reeked of mud and grease and who knows what else. It reminded me of the pine-tar encrusted batting helmets that the Boston Red Sox players favor, but after looking at the man in his entirety, I concluded it was one of his better choices when he had dressed himself that morning. His dungarees and collared button down shirt were something from the fifties, I guessed, a mix of earth tones–actual dirt and crud. His thin, deliberate eyes were a steel gray, a color that matched his rebellious hair almost perfectly. What truly stood out, as the three of us stood there assessing the moment, was the clean-as-a-whistle chain saw dangling from his left hand and...the distinct odor of cow manure.

He noticed my gaze and said, "Dirty tools mean dirty work; can't tolerate dirty work."

That seemed to be a contradiction, at least upon first glance at the man, but I wasn't about to argue the point. My mind was blank, my illusory script lost in the transitory panic, and I looked at Jess hoping she was staying cooler than I was. She wasn't; she was disoriented and mumbling something about how nice the weather was. *Aren't we a pair of whiz-bang detectives?*

The man pointed toward the window where I had seen Mel's image, saying, "Them rooms up there are the best for a long stay. The plumbin' is good, hot water almost every mornin'. It's quieter too, facin' the courtyard instead of the road."

Sensing our uneasiness, or perhaps having said all he wanted to say, the man turned and disappeared around a corner of one of the buildings. Rattled, Jess looked over at me just as I released a nervous chuckle.

"Who the hell was that?" she asked.

"The groundskeeper, I would imagine," I replied, "and, perhaps, our first suspect?"

CHAPTER 11

Homer Tubb scratched a jagged battle line in the dirt floor of the shed he had come to think of as his home with the tip of his pristine chainsaw. The scent of spring had stirred the fire in his belly weeks ago and now with the arrival of fresh visitors, the embers began to glow a deeper orange, as if crying out in hunger. "We are the most vulnerable when we are coming out of the deep winter sleep," his grandfather had told him in this very same shed when he was only seven years old. The two of them had just come from the graveyard where Homer's parents had been lowered to rest. He could still remember pulling at the scratchy collar of the fancy white shirt he had worn under the black suit his aunt had shown up with that morning as he listened to his somber grandfather explain to him about life and death.

"Be watchful, lad," his grandfather said. "The Reaper is a sly fox who always wears a different mask."

Homer hadn't known what he meant at the time, divine theory didn't mean much to a boy who had just watched two strangers throw shovel loads of dirt into a deep square hole, a hole that already contained two pine boxes filled with the only life he ever knew. The sound of the dry earth and stone slapping down against the bare wood was a haunting sound, a sound a man never forgets, but thirty-five years does provide a man time to develop his own theory about such things as life and death and how the Reaper might disguise himself. Nearly half a century of watching and learning the unyielding nature of life had cemented Homer's mind with the image of the dark harvester. As he gazed upon the courtyard through the lone cracked and tarnished window of the Mansion House maintenance shed, where so many years ago he decided to leave his parents behind and follow in his grandfather's footsteps, he recognized his enemy, and understood what he needed to do.

"We know why you're here," Homer Tubb said in a needled whisper to the friends that surrounded him, ancient-looking implements of wood and steel that hung from the rafters and the walls like soldier marionettes. "Every spring you come to frolic in all that our blood has built but, just as before, you will find no playground here, no solace from *your* long sleep." He said nothing more. His face fell placid as he turned from the window and went to his workbench, a spectacular slab of prehistoric oak that carried the aged scars of a medieval warrior, and began to sharpen his tools.

CHAPTER 12

Harriet, Harry to her friends, escorted Jess and me to a small but comfortable room, one of eight in the section our courtyard acquaintance had recommended. It was a sparsely decorated room with a wide chest of drawers, a humble nightstand with a lamp, and a wingback chair clothed in a crisp green leaf and red rose pattern that jumped out at us the moment we entered. The king size bed dominated the space, strategically placed in the center for easy access to neighboring amenities (the bigger rooms had two double beds, Harriet had told us, to which I had replied with a wink, "That is not how we plan to spend our honeymoon."). A slender doorway opened to a bright white bathroom suited with a cast iron tub and sink bound to the building by exposed piping that weaved and curled in odd directions before vanishing into the floor. There was no television or radio; leaving only the touchtone phone on the nightstand to remind us that we were living in the 21st century. The blinds of the lone window were open, leading me to conclude this had not been Mel's room.

"Lunch is served between twelve and one, if you're hungry; dinner at six o'clock sharp," Harriet said sweetly. "You need anything else, you know where to find me." She left us with a smile once again, and closed the door behind her. Jess stood quietly, anxiously assessing the bed.

"I'll hang a sheet down the middle if it'll make you happy," I said. "But I'm not sleeping in that chair." I then looked at the floor, thinking that might be her next suggestion, but it looked as uninviting as the chair, a speckled mocha Berber that reminded me a little of the gardener's dungarees.

"No, it'll be fine," she replied unconvincingly, "as long as you stay on your side."

"If *I* stay on *my* side?" I chuckled, recalling her quip that she would remain a lady during our visit.

Lazily, we unpacked our things, Jess insisting on the right side of the closet, the right side of the dresser, *and* the right side of the bed, before sitting down at the foot of the bed to survey our simple surroundings. So far, we had stumbled out of the gate (answering Harriet with two different places of origin), froze under inquiring eyes (the gardener's, who nearly scared us both back to Putney), and argued over wardrobe space. If Mel was watching from above, she was certainly laughing by now.

"We need to regroup," I said, feeling an overpowering urge to find a bar and pitch a tent. The ache was beginning to cloud my mind and the details of our original plan were growing distant and faint.

"I agree," Jess replied.

"You're a cop, where do you think we should start?"

"I don't know. I ride in a patrol car all day. We get a call on the radio, we go where they tell us, and we straighten out whatever mess we find when we get there. Not much detective work in that."

"Don't you ask questions? Try and figure out who done it?"

"It's fairly obvious who *did* what to whom on the calls we get. It's all minor stuff—domestic disputes, petty larceny, drunk and disorderly. Homicide takes care of the murders."

I shook my head discouragingly and said, "Now you tell me." My mouth was dry and a dull pain began to throb in my forehead.

Jess stood up and went to the window as I sat trying to control and hide my quivering hands. I could usually fend off the withdrawal tremors for several days, provided my stress levels were normal, but the current situation was anything *but* normal. I could feel the beginnings of a strong quake mounting. Jess hadn't noticed yet, the physical symptoms well hidden under my seasoned mask.

"Let's just stick with your plan, I think it will work," she said, her attention still focused outside the window. "We'll poke around like innocent tourists, ask questions, and see where it leads us." She looked back at me, and, noticing my edgy expression, asked, "Are you all right?"

I snapped up and stretched my limbs, a move I had perfected many years ago, telling her I was just tired from the drive and hungry. "My blood sugar is low, I need something to eat. Are you hungry?"

"Yeah, now that you mention it, I am."

I looked at my watch. It was nearly quarter to one meaning lunch would soon be over, according to Harriet, and I didn't want to miss our first chance to mingle with the tenants, one of whom might be my sister's murderer. "Well then, let's go, Lollipa...ah, before the kitchen closes." I opened our door and followed Jess out into the hallway, praying they might serve a spot of wine with lunch.

CHAPTER 13

By the time we found our way to the main dining room, it was almost empty, except for an elderly couple who looked to be a bit older than my parents enjoying a small cup of ice cream dessert. The woman noticed us standing awkwardly in the doorway and motioned us forward with her hand while saying in a distinctively aged voice, "Come on in, kids, you can still get a sandwich or a bowl of soup if you're hungry." We accepted her friendly invitation and walked in cautiously, Jess a half step behind me. The man didn't look up at us, he was clearly consumed with his ice cream. As we approached, I noticed he was wearing a tiny earphone that bled a thin white wire down his neck, off his shoulder and into the bulging breast pocket of his plaid flannel shirt. He looked quite spry for his age, his snowy head nodding like a bobble head doll. I thought it quite a contrast, this old gentleman with what looked like an iPod in his pocket, and I smiled at the thought of him listening to rap music.

"Sit down," the woman said. "We'd love some company, wouldn't we, dear?" She had to nudge her companion in the elbow before he looked up. Once he did, he just smiled at us and dove back into his ice cream. "Don't mind him, sit down," she insisted.

I pulled out a chair for Jess like the good husband I was pretending to be and then sat down next to her, directly across from our host. "Hi, I'm Michael–Mick, and this is Jess, my beautiful wife of two days. We were married just this past Saturday."

"Oh, isn't that exciting," the woman said, "so then you must be on your honeymoon."

"Yes, we are," Jess said, although without the enthusiasm one would expect from a new bride.

I quickly seized the conversation by repeating the elaborate tale of my proposal to Jess, embellishing the poor-working-girl rescue with a white limousine and a drive into the sunset. I was enjoying telling the story, as much for my own creativity as for Jess's nearly imperceptible look of agitation.

After enduring the ever-lengthening version of our romance and several failed attempts to derail me, Jess finally got a word in, asking, "Who built this place? I've never seen anything quite like it."

The woman sat back in her chair, a broad smile cresting over her face as she said, "Dearie, if only I had a nickel for every time someone asked me that." She was literally beaming now–a proud grandmother preparing to introduce her well-accomplished grandchildren–as she began her story. "Well, this grand old home was built by the Oneida Community back in 1861, the main section, that is, with several wings being added over the next twenty years or so. It has always been called the Mansion House, although no one can say why and I've never been able to find any reference to it. They had considered calling it the Communistery, they were Communists, you see, but that certainly does not have an air of elegance to it, at least I don't think so, do you? Did you know there was an "Old Mansion House"? It was built in 1849 out of logs cut from their wooded farms and clay bricks they fashioned by hand. It's gone now, replaced by this Community home. That was back when they called themselves Perfectionists, just after John had brought the family from Putney. That's in Vermont, have you ever heard of it?"

Just as I was about to lie by saying I'd never heard of Putney, a clock chime erupted in another room telling us it was one o'clock, prompting the elderly gentleman to slowly rise to his feet and the woman to abruptly stop the story we were now very anxious to hear more of. "Oh, how the time does fly," the woman said. She looked disappointed as she stood and I wondered if it was because she had to leave or because she had to curtail her story. "I do regret having to run off but we've used up our morning. Perhaps we can visit some other time. Are you planning to stay for a few days?"

Jess and I nodded in unison.

"Yes," I said. "We expect to be here a while."

"Wonderful! That will give me a chance to tell you all about us. Now you best peek your head in the kitchen and tell Grace what you would like for lunch. She slips out back about this time for a snort and a smoke, and then you won't see her again until suppertime." With that, she slipped her hand under the old man's arm, who then proceeded to escort her proudly out of the dining room, the two of them looking as if they owned the place.

"Interesting couple," I said, after they had disappeared out the entranceway.

"Did you hear her say they were Communists?" Jess said, excitedly, "and Perfectionists before that?"

"Yes, I was sitting right next to you when she said it."

"And Putney; she mentioned someone named John came from there. We should check him out."

"First of all, I'm sure he has been dead for some time and, second, John is a pretty common name," I said. "Let's get a last name before we add him to the suspect list."

Jess laughed at herself. "You know what I mean. We need to talk to them some more and find out about this John guy and the Oneida Community she mentioned."

"The old woman's story did touch upon several points from Mel's email reminder to herself, so I think it would be a good place to start."

Jess nodded and said, "I wonder what she meant when she

said 'we've used up our morning?'

"I don't know, maybe they take naps. Old people do that."

"Maybe, but they didn't look tired to me. Did they look tired to you?"

Jess was looking across the room to where the couple had just exited. I waited until she looked at me again before I frowned and asked, "Suspicious behavior, Dr. Watson?"

"Don't be sarcastic; they just seem…I don't know."

"They're just a sweet old couple living out their golden years in a grand old mansion."

"They didn't say they lived here."

"Well, no, but I assumed…."

"We don't even know their names."

Jess was right, they didn't mention their names. But there is nothing unusual about that, strangers chat all the time on trains and buses without exchanging names. Were we thinking it peculiar because of our own hidden agenda? Would everyone who crossed our path over the next few days become a suspect? I could hear the paranoia whistling outside my door, begging to be let in.

"Ok, let's get a grip here," I said. "I don't think Mel was murdered by Ethel and Norman Thayer."

"Who?"

"Don't you watch *any* movies? They were the old folks in *On Golden Pond*–Katherine Hepburn and Henry Fonda? It was about…never mind. You can do what you want but I'm not adding them to *my* list."

"Well, I'm not ruling out anyone just yet."

"Suit yourself, I'm getting something to eat," I said, and I got up and walked into the kitchen. It was completely empty and as clean as a Catholic's conscience after a Saturday afternoon confession. "Damn!" I said under my breath. I turned around and went back to the dining room. To my surprise, a middle-aged woman dressed in restaurant whites was cleaning up the table where we had been sitting. Jess was standing off to the side so as not to be in the way.

"Where did she come from?" I whispered to Jess as I joined her.

"I don't know, all of sudden she was just there."

"You really shouldn't be using these," the woman said in an irritated tone. "This is the good silver and we don't use the good silver anymore, not since the master of the house passed on. How did you get it?"

Puzzled, Jess and I just looked at each other. "It was here when we arrived. The elderly couple was using it."

The woman stopped and looked at us suspiciously, "What couple? I saw you two walk in just after I cleaned the whole place up. There was no one else in here then."

Neither one of us knew what to say. Since we didn't have any names to recite, we both stood there with our mouths hanging open. I would have described the old folks to her, just to prove we weren't making it up, but for some reason I couldn't picture them clearly. We had sat there with them just moments ago for a good fifteen minutes and now their faces were a blur. Jess was right, there was something about them…something…I don't know.

The woman showed little patience for the situation. After zestfully scowling at us, she proceeded to scoop up the small pile of forks, spoons and knives (the *good silver*, as she called it) and some soiled china she had swept together with her arm, and stormed back into the kitchen muttering to herself the whole time, "I can't even sneak a cigarette without…."

Before Jess could ask, I just shook my head and said, "I have no idea."

Driven by hunger, we went into town and found the restaurant the postman had suggested. It was a good lunch, just as he had promised, with hot, flavorsome food served by a prompt and talkative waitress. Even the other patrons were friendly, a host of local businessmen and women, and a few retired folks all curious as to the journey that had brought us to their "neck of the woods," as the postman had put it earlier that morning. It was relaxing, very informative and tainted only by an unspoken thought that Jess and I may have just seen a pair of ghosts.

The Mansion House
Summer 1862

After many long months of construction, the Great Hall was finally finished. Frescoed by German artists from floor to ceiling, the room had a large stage at the head with a proscenium arch of wood, a u-shaped balcony and a gallery to accommodate the entire community of over two hundred–men, women, and all the many children. Warming light poured in from a row of statuesque windows standing serenely behind the stage, the soft beams casting a heavenly glow upon the oil paintings that adorned the walls, symbolic figures representing Justice, Music, Astronomy and History. This would be the heart of the new Mansion. The place where the members would gather each evening to discuss religion and community business, listen to lectures on self-improvement, sing hymns and enjoy theatrical presentations by other members. Today the builders gathered within its welcoming arms to celebrate its completion.

A balding man with a trim beard and mustache took the stage first, his closely fitted coat, silky collared vest, and stiff, horizontally bound necktie projecting a ceremonial air. He welcomed the congregation and then proceeded to read the 33rd Psalm: *Sing joyfully to the LORD, you righteous; it is fitting for the upright to praise him....*

The final speaker, the man who had opened his doors and his heart to the small group from Putney nearly fifteen years ago, then reminisced over their journey in relation to the accommodations where they now found themselves.

"That first summer after our Community started," he said with a heartfelt smile, "is now a warm, fading memory. The old barn where we would meet as we do today, gone." He paused, relishing the acknowledgement in the eyes of his large family and on the face of his good friend, John, who sat directly in front of the stage in his favorite oak Windsor arm chair, a collie minding his flock. "We have come a long, long way in fifteen years," he said. "but we still have so very much ahead us. We have found a home in this valley, a foundation we can build upon." He then scanned the festive surroundings as he said. "And today we celebrate a symbol of our good fortune–this great hall. It is here–we are here–because of our faith in the Lord. We have peace in our minds because of our faith in the Lord. We feel each other in our hearts because of our faith in the Lord. We have honest work to be done because of our faith in the Lord. He asks nothing more of us, nor we of him."

Then, with a nod to the leader of the group's small band that stood poised at the back of the stage, the proud man led the gathering in the singing of the Community hymn: "Let Us Go, Brothers, Go."

Let us go, brothers, go
To the Eden of heart-love,
Where the fruits of life grow,
And no death e'er can part love;
Where the pure currents flow
Form all gushing hearts together,
And the wedding of the Lamb
Is the feast of joy forever. Let us go, brother, go!
We will build us a dome
On our beautiful plantation,
And we'll all have one home,
And one family relation;

We'll battle with the wiles
Of the dark world of Mammon,
And return with its spoils
To the home of our dear ones. Let us go, brother, go!
When the rude winds of wrath
Idly rave round our dwelling,
And the slanderer's breath
Like a simoon is swelling,
Then so merrily we'll sing
As the storm blusters o'er us,
Til the very heavens ring
With our hearts joyful chorus. Let us go, brother, go!
Now love's sunshine's begun,
And the spirit-flowers are blooming;
And the feeling that we're one
All our hearts is perfuming;
Towards one home let us all
Se our faces together
Where true love shall dwell
In peace and joy forever. Let us go, brother, go!

CHAPTER 14

Having successfully refueled our tanks during our afternoon meal stop where we discovered that the city's epithet ("The Silver City") was a reference to its chief employer, Oneida Ltd., the world's largest manufacturer of stainless steel and silver plated flatware, Jess and I set out to explore the checkerboard streets of Sherrill. Revitalized by the warm sun and the taste of spring in the air, we were searching, I suppose, for a sign that read, "Mel was here." But it all appeared very ordinary; everything in its place. From the unbroken rows of agreeable houses painted in optimistic colors to the perky shopping plaza that boasted the finest silverware at discount prices, it hummed contentedly to itself as we rolled past, smiling and waving as if we, too, were just another neighbor on our way to the market. That was the odd thing about this place; it didn't make me feel like a stranger. I felt at home. As I struggled to get comfortable with that feeling, I wondered if Mel had felt it, too. She loved people. It was her strength and her weakness at the same time, and I could only answer the question with a resounding *yes*! But I knew in my gut that her unwavering heart could have also unknowingly opened itself to a killer.

"Oh, look! There's a library," Jess said as she pulled around a corner. "Let's go in and see what local history books they have."

"That's a good idea," I replied. "It will keep me from falling asleep in your car after that big lunch we ate."

As I stepped through the doorway and into the Sherrill-Kenwood Free Library, my nostrils filled with the distinctive smell of ancient books and old newspapers. It had opened only an hour ago, apparently choosing to make itself available in the evening rather than the morning, but it looked deserted as Jess and I scanned the interior for the librarian and the card catalog. I spotted the latter first and poked Jess before we both headed toward it.

"Where do you think we should start?" I asked.

"Well, Communism is going to be way too broad," Jess answered as she studied the countless tiny drawers that filled the brawny oak cabinet that was as tall as she was. "Our *friend* said the Oneida Community had built the Mansion House so...." She pulled out the drawer labeled "Om-Oz" and began leafing through the cards. She quickly found there were many cards that began with Oneida-something.

"Are you looking for books about the Oneida Community?" a seemingly invisible voice spoke.

We both looked up and found a dapperly dressed, balding man about the age of my father looking me squarely in the eye. "Yes, we are," I answered, noticing that his red paisley-print suspenders matched his jovial bow tie perfectly. I watched him push his bifocal glasses back up his nose and blink nervously before he turned and headed away, limping slightly as he walked.

"We have a special section right over here," he said. We followed him over to it. "This table here has some of the more popular and newer titles, and the shelf right behind it has a whole bunch more."

"There are *new* books?" Jess asked. I was thinking the same thing, that this was an old topic–a one hundred and fifty-year-old topic—so why would people still be writing about it? Maybe for the same reason my sister was?

"Oh yes," he said. "Someone is always writing a new book about the Community; putting a fresh spin on it, as you young people say. People love reading about their social experiment with free love and communal living. Utopia, some people call it. Sexy stuff, as you young people say."

"Free love?" I asked, recalling it as one of the phrases that Jess had remembered Mel mentioning.

"A lot of folks believe that is what they practiced, though some others would tell you otherwise," the bow-tied man said. "A lascivious lot if you ask me, that Community."

"Not a fan, I take it?" I asked.

"Not my place to judge," he replied tersely. His posture stiffened and I noticed his eyes were twitching double time. "My job is to keep the records; keep the history, that's all." He then limped off without another word, leaving us to peruse the dozens of volumes about Utopia, socialism, free love and a number of other provocative topics. I only hoped there were plenty of pictures.

"There are lots more over at the Mansion House," his voice echoed from somewhere in the library. "They have their own library. It puts our little section on the Community to shame, I'm sad to say."

"Maybe we should just look there?" I said. "That's where Mel would have started."

"You're probably right, but let's browse through some of these first, just in case," Jess said.

"In case of what?"

"I don't know, but since we're here, we might as well look."

"Irrefutable logic," I chuckled, "a talent of no use to a cop in Yonkers."

Jess scowled and then began looking through the pile of books. She had almost forgotten about my sarcastic humor, which had been surprisingly quiet most of the day. I could be ruthless at times, usually assisted by ludicrous amounts of alcohol. I never knew where to draw the line and, once on a roll, I just kept rolling. I found it hilarious, but then most things are when the beer goggles are so firmly strapped to your head it would take a sado-masochistic surgeon with a crowbar to pry them off. The next day the recollection of my lampooning would always be long gone, floating away down the selective memory river, leaving me guilt free and poised to strike again. Mel hated my "antics," as she referred to my less-endearing habits. I think she got that word from our mother who was a vast dictionary of geriatric slang, always warning me when I was a teenager not to get my *keister* in a *pickle*, but always giving me some *bread* on my way out of the *joint* to do just that. Mel knew me better than anyone; knew all about most of my pickles, except for the one about the nightmares–the real reason I had started drinking to begin with.

"Look, here's one that Mel checked out," Jess said, as she pulled a pale white index card from the back cover of the book she was skimming through and held it out in front of me. "See, she signed it out last week."

There was no mistaking Mel's signature. It was an elegant script, tilted slightly to the right with the "l" of Melissa and the "b" of Gibson rising above the other letters like bridge towers. It was actually readable, too, unlike my own, and the only time she used her given first name instead of her preferred nickname. It was dated a week ago today. I stared at my sister's handwriting, feeling a sudden stab of regret, followed by an irrepressible need for a drink.

I took a deep breath and read the book title aloud, *Free Love in Utopia*. I looked at Jess. She wore the same curious expression that was now spreading across my face. "Sounds a like a real page turner."

"We definitely have to read *this* book."

"No argument here. Did you find any others that Mel signed out?"

"No. You?"

"Not a one, but I didn't look through them all. There's so many."

"Yeah, this Community is quite a hot topic around here."

"It's surprising, considering it existed over one hundred years ago."

"And possibly *still* exists," Jess reminded me.

That *is* what the anonymous letter had said. A rebirth, it had warned. *Free Love in Utopia* in the 21st century, right here, right now, in Anytown, USA. *Unbelievable.*

Jess was apparently done browsing titles and checking sign-out cards when she said, "Let's take this one out, go back to the Mansion House, and see what they have in their library. The librarian said they had a lot more than they have here."

"Ok," I replied, lost in a daydream about *Free Love in Utopia.* What would that be? What would it look like, feel like? My thoughts wandered down their own deviant path, conjuring visions of naked Playboy centerfolds lying seductively on laced covered brass beds scattered about a lavish garden filled with rose bushes and wild flowers. Of course, I was the only man present, except for an old hunch-backed butler with paisley suspenders and a matching bowtie. He held a tray of ice-cold beer and a basket of steaming, buffalo-style chicken wings, appearing curt but poised to deliver at the snap of my neatly manicured fingers.

I awoke from my daydream and scanned the library, "Where *is* Gomer?" I asked, referring to the librarian. There was no sign of him anywhere and the place was extremely quiet. A librarian's dream.

"I don't know," Jess said as she performed her own search. "He was here a little while ago."

"We can't wait too long or we'll miss dinner."

"We've got a couple hours before that."

"Yeah, but if we want to hunt through the Mansion House library before then, we best get moving."

"You're right, we need to mingle during dinner and plant our seeds."

"Exactly; now, where is that old goat?"

We waited at least ten minutes at the front desk but there was no sign of him. Finally, I said, "Let's just take it, they've got plenty more."

"I'm not stealing this book," Jess replied, emphatically.

"All right, we'll bring it back when we're finished. That is what you do with a library book anyway, isn't it?"

"Yes, but...."

I grabbed the book out of Jess' hand and headed for the door. She had little choice but to follow. I could feel her contemptuous eyes burning into the back of my head as we walked to her car. I felt no remorse. This book was a connection to Mel, and that gave me certain unalienable rights, at least in my way of thinking.

CHAPTER 15

In addition to being the City Librarian, Harold Smith, the twitchy-eyed and bow-tied pedant, held the title of Sherrill City Historian. It was his job (part time he would quickly remind to garner sympathy for such a "huge undertaking") to manage the thousands of newspaper articles, photographs and other memorabilia regarding the history of the city so that any and all historical events and artifacts could be retrieved with relative ease and accuracy by any curious resident or visitor. He was a stickler for thoroughness, a fanatic about accuracy, an extremist over organization and an absolute freak about tidiness, which were exactly the traits that had gotten him the local government job in the first place ten years ago, as well as a mantle full of Librarian of the Year awards from the tri-county Mid-York Library System. Once he had even won the New York State title, narrowly escaping with the trophy ahead of a young, shapely female librarian from the Westchester Library System (an oversexed harlot, his wife Dorothy had called her) who had done her best to influence the judges with a pearly smile, a plunging neckline and a wealth of homemade baked goods. "There is no substitute for dustless shelves and proper alphabetization," Harold had said during his acceptance speech, his gloating stare aimed directly at his bodacious competitor.

Harold had move to Sherrill over twenty years ago at the age of forty to oversee the City Library, quickly establishing a reputation as an articulate and well read man with an open and apparently shameless agenda of one day commanding the local archives by whatever means necessary. Being politically astute, he took up with the City Historian of the time, a local spinster named Dorothy Talley, who was about his same age. He married her after a three-week whirlwind courtship in a scholarly, if unromantic, ceremony at the City Library. Dorothy's Maid of Honor, her younger sister Abigail, read a passage by her favorite poet, John Milton, while Abigail's own husband of only two months, the Reverend James Newland, presided over the ceremony.

Unbeknownst to Dorothy, her sister Abigail, the Reverend Newland, and the rest of the residents of Sherrill at the time and to this very day, was the fact that Harold Smith was also a student of the teachings of Dr. John W. Mears, a Professor at Hamilton College and ardent antagonist of the Oneida Community in the 1870's. Harold's great uncle had taught alongside Dr. Mears, during which time he established a collection of all of Dr. Mears' published manuscripts on ethics and temperance that ultimately found their way into Harold's eager hands. For whatever reason, a spark ignited inside Harold upon reading the very first line of text, spreading like a wild fire for months as he scoured every page until finally his mind focused like the blue flame of a welder's torch on Dr. Mears' effort to overthrow the Oneida Community. Dr. John W. Mears had led what the papers had referred to as the "Crusade of the Clergy" against the Oneida Community, referring to them as an "intolerable moral strain on the fair name of New York State." In the final years of the Oneida Community, Dr. Mears had invited churches from around the State to a secret convention held at Syracuse University in a call to right a great wrong, as he described it. Harold had an original copy of the invitation and he read it often to remind himself of the war he was waging. *"The great wrong done to society by the institution know as the Oneida Community from its deadly opposition to the principles of Christian morality appears to demand some united counsel and action on the part of teachers of the Gospel and defendants of public and domestic vir-*

tue in this part of the country." The convention had been well attended, a union of Episcopalians, Presbyterians, and Methodists, history proving it to be one of the final arrows launched on the ethical battleground.

To Harold, it was a struggle from which he could not turn his eyes. The immorality of it struck a nerve deep in his Christian spinal chord, and by the time he was twenty-one years old he knew that his purpose in life was to carry on the fight. *Had the Community been truly and finally blotted out in 1881 as so widely claimed and documented?* he often contemplated. Deep in his heart, he hoped that they hadn't and that one day he could be the one to raise the first new sword against them. But in order to be poised for battle, he knew he needed to be closer to the enemy. So, when the opportunity for the Sherrill City Librarian position presented itself, he seized it and set out to infiltrate the local community, keeping his true agenda hidden.

It took nearly ten years of scheming, but Harold finally finagled his wife Dorothy into retiring her post as City Historian and convinced the Sherrill City Commission to hand the title over to him. With unlimited access to hundreds of years of local history, Harold could now fight the fight, researching event records, legal proceedings, family lineage and anything else he desired. He could track the Community and its ancient exploits in complete secrecy. Best of all, he could pry into any and all current activities around the city without raising suspicions in his ongoing effort to ferret out any resurgence of the *lascivious lot.*

Now, he was convinced that all his hard work and diligence was about to pay off. The two visitors to the library he had had today, a young man and woman interested in the salacious side of the Community that he was ever diligent to keep in the forefront of people's minds, had been the latest gust in a flurry of interest that seemed to be blowing harder and steadier with each passing week. Whispers at the post office and at the dry cleaners that hinted suspiciously of a rebirth had been nipping at his assiduous ears for months. When the New York Times reporter suddenly appeared a week ago to do an expose, he knew his intuition could not be wrong–the Oneida Community was back.

Harold smiled as he tried to calm his fluttering heart, his excited fingers dialing the telephone as he watched the young man and woman leave with the stolen government property–the book entitled *Free Love in Utopia*. They would be caught, he would make sure of that, their example serving yet another warning to the Christian community that dominated the Silver City, an alarm that rang loud and clear. *Lasciviousness begets lasciviousness.*

CHAPTER 16

Jess and I had no trouble getting lost in the Mansion House. When we had returned from our auspicious visit to the local library, we found Harriet had gone MIA. Left to our own devices to navigate through the labyrinth of corridors and stairwells, we went in search of the Community Library, as it was called in the literature we now carried like a pirate's hidden treasure map, to further our education on the subject that seemed to occupy a small corner of every mind within a two-mile radius. We had only been in Sherrill—The Silver City—for half a day but hadn't tripped upon a single soul that didn't know of or have something to say about the Communists, the Perfectionists, the free love Utopians formally known as "The Oneida Community." The opinions varied from "a hardworking, industrious group living an alternative lifestyle" (with emphasis always being stressed on the word *alternative*) to blunt statements akin to the city librarian's remark that they were a "lascivious lot." What *was* consistent was that everyone seemed to have an opinion one way or the other. Standing now in another endless hallway clad in rich cherry wainscot paneling and cast iron plumbing overhead, Jess and I hopelessly lost, I began to see that Mel's spin on this place–the moral to her story– could piss off half the population no matter how she wrote it. It was a conundrum, as arcane as the maze in which we now found ourselves.

"Which way now, Columbus?" I said. I had been leading the

way but decided to defer to Jess upon entering a fresh corridor the length of a football field. The place didn't look that complicated from the outside, basically a box with a courtyard in the middle, but I could tell she was as clueless as I was, hoping as Christopher had that the Promised Land would be over the next horizon. Scanning all directions, I saw nothing but rolling white-tipped waves.

"Let's just ask somebody," Jess suggested.

"If there was someone around, I would," I said.

Had we been smart, we would have turned around right then while we could still backtrack over the route that had led us there. But, our adventurous spirit prevailed over our weaker common sense and we pressed on, traversing down a stairway into what could only be described politely in modern homeowner terms as an unfinished basement. A medieval dungeon was a more poetic and accurate description, I thought, and a look Jess and I might have found intriguing if not for the hodgepodge of electrical boxes, metal conduit and white PVC plumbing pipe that overwhelmed the ancient grey stone and clay plaster walls like the cobwebs of a haunted house. I'm sure my father would have noticed how dry it smelled, his do-it-yourself, home-repair mind on constant alert, and that the walls stood solid and straight. What *we* noticed first was that there didn't appear to be a library down there, and that it would be a poor spot for one if there was.

"Wrong turn," Jess said calmly, her patience holding up better than my own.

I started to turn around, saying, "Damn, let's go back..." when a sudden movement further down the narrow passageway to my right caught my eye. It was a man; the man we had met in the dining room when we had arrived late for lunch; the man with the iPod in his pocket who had all but ignored us; the man my imagination was telling me was not a man at all. "Hold on," I said to Jess before chasing after him.

I must have been fifteen yards down the tight, dimly lit corridor before Jess even realized what I was doing. "Where are you going?" I heard her yell.

"To catch a ghost," I replied. "Come on."

I couldn't tell you what sprang from Jess' mouth then, some kind of covert Yonkers P.D. jargon, I imagined. But I can say that hearing her tirade echo off the walls that now encased us made me feel safe knowing a New York City cop was right behind in case there was any trouble up ahead.

I came to a junction and stopped. There was no sign of my ghost and only two choices for proceeding. One was a stairway back up to the first floor–back up to civilization. The second was a very narrow passageway that I would have to duck down to enter, its telescoping walls disappearing into total darkness.

Jess came in behind me and said, "You're going to get us lost."

"We're already lost," I said. I looked at the stairs and then back again at the sinister looking corridor. I knew which one Jess would pick. The question was which one did my ghost pick?

"What did you see?" she asked.

"The iPod man."

"Who?"

"The couple at lunch, didn't you notice the old guy had an iPod in his pocket?"

"I thought it was a hearing aid."

"No, I'm pretty sure it was an iPod. Anyway, I saw him heading down here."

"Are you sure?"

"Positive."

Jess folded her arms, tilted her hips in a disarmingly cute way, and threw the same frown at me that she had when I told her we would have to share a room. She asked, "And did you say something about a ghost?"

I hadn't yet told her of my implausible notion that the kindly old couple we had almost had lunch with, the one with the ice cream fetish, the one that left us holding the bag, the one with the good silver we weren't suppose to use, just might be phantoms. I decided now might be a good time.

I focused on the avenue a ghost would have chosen, staring deep down the dark passageway hoping it would reveal its contents under closer scrutiny. It was too dark and I said, "That's what I said, and I'll bet my left testicle he's down there somewhere."

Jess laughed, "There's a bet I don't want to win." She stepped up along side me and looked into the chasm. "I don't think so," she said, and then stepped back. "He went upstairs, just like we're going to do."

"Oh, come on," I laughed, nervously. "Where's your sense of adventure?"

"Upstairs."

"He's down here, I just know it."

"The ghost?"

I looked back at her, knowing the pose I would find her in, and said, "You're not buying it are you?"

"Nope; whatever you're selling, I'm not buying."

I had to admit, I wasn't totally buying it either. I had never believed in ghosts or goblins and all that, no matter how much Hollywood argued on its behalf. When I was seven, I thought the Great Pumpkin was the real deal, until one of my friends straightened me out, adding that Charlie Brown was not a living and breathing boy who secretly posed for the cartoon drawings, as my mother had led me to believe. After that bubble burst and Santa was later exposed, I vowed never to be fooled again and made a bee line for the more rational adult way of thinking. By eight years of age, I knew that magic acts were parlor tricks and fairy tales were, well, fairy tales. But the nightmares depicting Mel's demise were much harder to resolve as fantasy since they weren't coming from someone else's imagination. I couldn't stamp them fiction and blame my over-active imagination on some Peter Pan dude whose nonsense stories were fed to all us good little girls and boys before we were old enough to know better. These were my stories–*I* was the Peter Pan dude—and it had taken me years to build a box to lock them up in, the hammer and nails for which provided by the good Dr. Sigmund Freud. He convinced me that the nightmares were nothing more than a Freudian slip–my unconscious mind pulling a prank like a soon-to-be expelled frat boy. The old saying that people believe what they want to believe held true for me. Along with a steady diet of scotch, bourbon and beer, I had managed to avoid Casper, The Amazing Kreskin, the thousands of tarot card and palm readers around the world, and my clairvoyant sister; at least until now. Now, it seemed completely possible that Mel may have died exactly as I had dreamed. With the reinforcement of Jess's intuition, I felt a strengthening change of heart tugging at my insides. This time it didn't feel like a Freudian slip and I couldn't help think that perhaps my childhood friend had been wrong. Perhaps the Great Pumpkin really did exist.

I took a deep breath and headed down the dark corridor.

"You're not leaving me here alone," I heard Jess say as I felt her finger wrap around the backside belt loop of my jeans. I was the engine and she was the caboose, two cars linked together, chugging their way into a murky mountainside tunnel with no light at the other end.

CHAPTER 17

Where was Thomas Edison when you needed him?

"Man, it is god-awful dark in here," Jess said. "I can't see a damn thing."

I couldn't see a damn thing either. We were ten paces into the passageway and the light from the junction we had just left reduced to the wattage of a single candle. There was no lighting up ahead and I could barely see my feet in front of me as I crouched down to avoid the steel piping I sensed was still hanging from the ceiling. It might have been Mel that commanded me forward or Jess' unconscious nudging from behind, but I didn't want to turn around, I wanted to see where this passageway led, where the enveloping darkness might turn to light. I knew there was something up there and I had to know what it was.

"A dead end," I said, stopping just in time to prevent breaking my nose on the stone wall in front of me. I stretched my arms out in the near total darkness and felt the walls on either side, thinking perhaps there was a turn we could take. But there were no turns and no openings; nothing but solid wall.

"Its times like these I wish I was a smoker," Jess quipped. "I could light a match."

"Yeah, me too. Doesn't it seem odd that someone would build a long tunnel like this that leads nowhere?"

"I guess. Maybe at one time it led somewhere, but then it was sealed up."

"Could be." I said, thinking about that and other possibilities. "Maybe we missed a turn along the way." I wiggled past Jess in the tight corridor, her finger still locked to my jeans, and assumed the engine position, only now in the reverse direction. "All aboard," I said, just before a round bright light stabbed me in the eyes, blinding me temporarily as I flinched to one side and backward before banging my head against something hard.

"Owe…shit!" I cried as my hands leapt up instinctively to cover my head.

"You folks lost," a voice said from behind the dagger of light.

Instantly, I knew the voice. It was the foul-scented groundskeeper; the guy we *assumed* was the groundskeeper, and he hadn't lost his charm in the hours since our last chat.

"I thought you was a couple kids that snuck in here," he said. "Kids are always sneakin' in here through the back doors and the side doors. I keep tellin'em we need to put better locks on 'em, but don't nobody listen. There's too many for one man to keep his eye on 'em all."

"We were looking for the library," Jess said in an anxious tone. I could feel her trembling as both her hands latched hold of my belt loops. *Some cop*, I thought.

"Ain't no library down here. No books neither. They're all upstairs…in the library."

"We made a wrong turn," I said, wincing as I rubbed my head. "Maybe you could point us in the right direction."

I couldn't see his face, the light was too bright, but an uneasy pause hung in the air as I waited for the man to turn and lead us out. It told me my lie was a lame one, but telling him the truth—that we were chasing a ghost—didn't seem like a good idea either. He would have just thought we were crazy and possibly kicked us out of the place. No, it seemed better to play the dumb tourists and keep our motives well hidden than to appear like the suspicious fact finders that we actually were. Even if it did make us look really stupid. Finally, he lowered the light, walked us back to the junction, and pointed up the stairs, saying, "Library is down the hall, two doors on your right. Can't miss it, it's the big room with all the books."

He was being purposely sarcastic but his face remained straight as a razor, showing no hint of emotion, good or bad. The trusty chain saw, as clean and shiny as it had been in the courtyard, was still at his side making me wonder if he ever went anywhere without it. The man's commanding voice, along with the sight of the grisly tool, made our decision easy. Jess and I followed his suggestion and briskly ascended the stairs, our pent up tension bursting free as soon as we reached the top where we began laughing as we continued our search for the elusive library.

As we walked, I poked Jess in the side and said, "That was some good police work back there. What happened to *protect* and serve?"

"Normally, I can count on my partner *not* to get me into sticky situations," she replied, "like being cornered in a pitch-black hole by some psycho with a chain saw. Without my gun, no less! So excuse me for getting a little edgy."

Jess was right and I couldn't deny it. *I* had gotten us into that little pickle, as my mother would say, by chasing a ghost–a grey haired, iPod toting, flannel-shirted old man who I believed could be a ghost. It was quickly looking very foolish and I vowed to myself right then and there that I would not return to the basement for the remainder of our stay, at least not without a flashlight. It looked too inviting to stay completely away, like prime skeleton-in-the-closet storage space, but I knew I would need forty thousand candlepower and a pocket full of backup batteries if I were to return. I then reluctantly promised Jess we would stay above ground from here on out, realizing as I said it that someone–anyone–could easily go unnoticed down there.

CHAPTER 18

I've never been much of a reader. Business text books mostly, and tax law interpretations. Once in while I could be spotted with an advice book on how to become a millionaire without leaving the comfort of your living room recliner, or even the latest comedy from George Carlin, but that was about it. So, when we finally stepped foot into the Mansion House Community Library, a tall and vast blend of wood craftsmanship and antique charm, I began to feel drowsy as Jess and I gazed upon the thousands of worn and tattered historical vessels lined upon the shelves.

"Wow," Jess said. "I could spend the whole week in here."

"Me too," I said, spotting a long, restful-looking couch that sat at one end, beckoning me with bedroom eyes to come and enjoy it's soft cushions and peach colored pillows. There was even a table next to it where I could set a beer, if only I'd had one. But, like the rest of the mansion seemed to be most of the time, the room was devoid of other people.

Jess didn't hesitate, heading straight to the nearest conclave of books to scan the titles. Three of the four walls were completely filled and there was a small adjacent room that appeared to contain more. Curious, I wandered over to the second room and found a host of children's books, hundreds of them lined along a bookshelf short enough for little hands to reach. It was just a sliver of a room compared to the main library but held enough space for several chairs and a table for doing homework, I imagined. I went back into the main library and walked over to Jess.

"Have you found the free love section yet?" I asked, grinning. The book we had *borrowed* from the city library, the one titled *Free Love in Utopia*, was still in Jess' car and I wasn't feeling ambitious enough to go fetch it. I needed to find another one.

"Not yet, but I'll holler if I do," she answered in halfhearted fashion. I could see Jess was already immersed in the quest, twenty feet under and still plummeting like a wide-eyed deep-sea diver looking for creatures unknown to humanity. *Just like Mel*, I thought to myself as I began scanning the volumes that gave testimony to the human experience. I wouldn't see Jess again until she rose to the surface for a fresh tank of oxygen.

I was surprised by what I found on the shelves. There were scientific periodicals and business textbooks, as well as biographies of other societies and cultures; classic novels and famous American autobiographies. The shelves were not the orgy of free love manuals I was expecting; they were a gathering of some of the finest works and inspiring words from many of the greatest writers to ever put a pen to paper–Dickens, Thackeray, Cooper and Bronte. There was poetry, lots and lots of poetry, in each alcove including Keats, Milton, Longfellow, Whittier and Tennyson, as well as translations of Homer, Virgil and Goethe. It was a school library, a place to learn and grow, and a place where people came for an education that encompassed the whole world. Whoever these people were—this Oneida Community—they certainly valued reading. Seeing the vast array of knowledge amassed upon these black walnut and oak shelves, they most certainly had a hunger for understanding what existed beyond the protective walls of this mansion. Still, perverted as it might sound, I wanted to find out more about free love, and so I continued searching for books about that.

While I was scanning through the titles, Jess had already pulled an armful down and had them stacked next to her on the couch were she sat meticulously examining a maroon and gold stenciled monster any sea-salt-blinded sailor could have mistaken for an anchor. She posed an attractive image sitting there innocently; her silver and black designer-frame glasses propped sophisticatedly on her nose making her look seductively intelligent. The way she was massaging her lower lip with her left hand as she held the book in her right only made me wonder how soft her kiss might feel. She had on a funky, blended-tweed sweater-jacket buttoned half way up and a white-laced camisole underneath revealing just a hint of cleavage as she leaned into her reading. I'm sure she also wore pants and some kind of sensible shoes but I couldn't tell you what. Just as my mind was about to transform her into a wanton librarian, she unexpectedly looked up and caught me staring at her.

"What are you looking at?" she asked, looking me straight in the eye.

I didn't say anything, instead nonchalantly returning my gaze to the shelves as I struggled not to blush, remembering that she was a cop from Yonkers. I was lucky she didn't come over and slug me.

On the second shelf from the top, I finally found what I was searching for (the same book we had taken from the city library) and I pulled it down and opened it up. *Free Love in Utopia: John Humphrey Noyes and the Origin of the Oneida Community* was the title and it was compiled by George Wallingford Noyes who, I discovered after reading the introduction, was the nephew of the group's founder–John Humphrey Noyes. I wondered if this was the same John mentioned by the friendly woman from the dining hall. She had said someone named John had brought the family from Putney and they had called themselves Perfectionists in the beginning. Could this be the guy she was referring to? Was there something in the pages that might help us retrace Mel's steps and lead us to her murderer? I took my find over to the couch where Jess was, pushed some of her books aside, sat down and opened it up. I wasn't sure what I would find but I was anxious and excited to read for the first time in a very long time.

The Mansion House Library
December 1863

Sarah could hear the footsteps marching up the corridor just outside the open library door. *A parade,* she first thought, *but out in the hallway? At this late evening hour?*

Immersed in the latest issue of *Harper's New Monthly Magazine*—a fascinating article entitled "The Religious Life of the Negro Slave" —she reluctantly looked up just as a steady procession of young men were entering the library. She recognized most of them, in face if not by name, and noting the books cradled in their hands, she concluded that they had come in search of empty chairs. She quickly scanned the full quarters and giggled under her breath. *March on, boys,* she thought.

More interested in the blending of superstition and fetishism found in the Christianity of southern slaves than in the plight of a few deskless students, Sarah tucked her hair behind her ears and returned to her reading. She didn't notice the leader eyeing her intently.

"Every seat occupied," the apparent guide of the displaced brigade said with a sigh. Henry, the eldest of the group of sixteen and newest member of the Community, then shook his head. "It has been like this all winter and it's only December. How are we supposed to improve our understanding of geometry and trigonometry if we haven't an adequate place to study?"

"What about the Children's House?" Dexter suggested. Dexter

was the youngest at fourteen, and the shortest, but by no means the shyest. "We could try over there?"

"No," Henry replied, sighing heavily again. "The littlest ones will be sleeping and the others will be practicing their reading and writing at the only table sufficient for our needs. And I'm sure Hannah would greet us with a scowl before we could even lay foot on the porch steps." Then, in a mocking, witchlike voice, he said, "You boys know better than to come marching over here at this time of the night."

Dexter chuckled, as did several of the other boys, but they were swiftly hushed by a chorus of intolerant voices.

Disappointed, but not discouraged, that the attractive woman had not looked up from her magazine to match his gaze, Henry lead the young men out of the library, heading them toward the parlor where he hoped the after-supper Bible study group had already dispersed for the evening.

Walking down the narrow passageway, a train of eager youth trailing behind him, it became evident to Henry that everyone in the Oneida Community—adults and children alike—had been inflicted with a fevered enthusiasm for knowledge greater than he had anticipated. He then recalled the conversation he had had with John just a few days ago, lobbying the group's leader for the purchase of more books. Though the economic times had been hard the past few years, Henry had not had to petition very hard.

After assuring the young man that he would see what he could do to scrape together a few dollars for the pile of texts Henry had his eye on, John added, "We should do all we can to make the Community a University for the education of the whole man. We do not want to make ourselves mere horses and oxen, which the mechanical, solitary labor of common country life tends to do. The legitimate object of labor is to secure leisure—leisure for social, intellectual and artistic cultivation. We all worked hard this past summer so that we could have school this winter. Scripture upholds this practice; *let us labor that we may enter into rest*."

John then put his arm over Henry's shoulder, looking upon him as a son. "The artist," he said, "need not be an idler, a dreamer, or a mere speculator. In truth, the harmony of the two can quicken all kinds of manual labor. By combining the worker and the artist, we can generate the highest level of industrial energy and at the same time be able to keep work subordinate to superior ends."

Henry could not have agreed more. It was this unrestricted–and encouraged–opportunity to study astronomy, arithmetic, geography, grammar, Latin, French, music, literature, the Bible, and many other subjects that had lured Henry to the growing commune in the first place. Not the licentious sexual practices his friends had chided him about upon hearing of his decision to join the Oneida Community. That life-altering decision had also provided him with a job, a home, and a very large family–everything he was missing previously as an unemployed farm hand living out of a knapsack. Though he was frustrated tonight over his inability to find a place to settle down with his books, there wasn't a whisper of regret in his mind.

"Well, the parlor is full too," Dexter said suddenly, pulling Henry away from his thoughts.

Henry stopped in his tracks and stared in disbelief at the clogged room he now stood before. His thoughts wandered back to the library where perhaps the lovely woman he had noticed had finished reading. *I can study tomorrow*, he reasoned.

Undeterred by Henry's earlier rebuff, Dexter offered his standard suggestion candidly, "It's not too late to take a walk over to the Children's House. Maybe Hannah went to bed early."

CHAPTER 19

Jess and I never had a chance to compare notes before dinner. I was reading along, feeling as though I had just begun and thoroughly intrigued with what I was learning about free love in the middle of the nineteenth century, when Jess nudged my shoulder and told me it was almost six o'clock. Surprisingly, I didn't want to go, and she had to take the book from my hands and call me a bookworm before I grudgingly let her drag me out of the library. It was a good thing *she* was watching the time because after we dropped the borrowed books off in our room and then discovered a few new dead ends in the hallways, we arrived in the dinner hall just in time to grab the last two seats at a table with six chairs already filled. The forty-something woman sitting next to me informed us we were having meatloaf.

"You must be that young couple Harry was telling me about," one of our table partners said, a square jawed woman with long black hair slivered with waterfalls of silver dripping over her shoulders. "You're on your honeymoon?"

"Why, yes, we are," I said before Jess could answer. I proceeded right into my courtship story for the third time that day, making it even more elaborate and romantic than I had the time before. Jess was a trooper, sitting attentively through it all with the fake smile of joy I was now accustomed to, the one that everyone expects to see on a new bride in the early stages of marriage. The rest of the table was captivated as well, until the food arrived and we all started passing the serving plates around. These people were hungry, enthusiastically gathering in their share of the steaming fare, leaving my story at the point where I was about to hoist Jess into my arms and carry her out of the factory.

The first person to finish eating was a thin, wiry looking man with a big smile and bad teeth. His short brown hair looked a little greasy and his fingernails a bit rusty. The faded, red flannel shirt he had buttoned tight to his chin looked old (LL Bean circa 1979 maybe?) and I noticed the wristwatch that poked out from his sleeve had stopped ticking at twelve-thirty, leaving me to wonder twelve-thirty of what year? His approximate age was also a mystery; he was one of those people who defy chronology due to the lack of the usual markers like wrinkles and graying hair. But he still *seemed* old. Having dispensed of his slice of meatloaf and all the trimmings, he leaned back in his chair and kicked off the after dinner conversation with a somewhat unexpected question, "You folks swingers?" he asked artlessly.

Jess started choking and I would have, too, had I not just swallowed my last bite of mashed potatoes. The rest of our table acted as if the man had just asked me if I liked the meatloaf, looking at Jess and I with quiet but attentive eyes that were nonetheless eager for our answer.

"Ah, no," I stammered. "We're not into swinging." Just as I said that the thought struck me that, perhaps, these people were and that the man's question was in fact not a question at all, but in truth, an invitation. Even my oftentimes-lewd mind didn't want to go there, but for a brief moment I wished I had answered yes, just to see what Jess would have done. At the moment, she was still coughing and trying to clear her throat with an empty glass of water. I handed her mine, which I hadn't touched yet. After a few sips she settled down.

"Are you all right?" one of the other women sitting at our table asked.

Jess nodded that she was, though her blushing cheeks and watery eyes seemed to indicate otherwise.

"I only ask because we get a lot of pleasure seekers out this way, if you know what I mean," the man said in a loud tone. "And polygamists, too. People seem to think that it's just one big endless orgy around here."

His comment tickled a laugh from the whole room, one woman saying, "Oh, George, you're too funny." I wondered if it had erupted out of sheer embarrassment at the absurdity of the notion or from the titillation of living dangerously by dangling a secret out in the open for strangers like us to see. It brought to mind what the anonymous letter had said—a rebirth of the communists. I imagined Mel sitting in this dining room, seated at this very table, perhaps, and hearing the same joke. I tried to think of what she would have asked.

"Why would people think that?" I asked. It was weak but it was all I could come up with.

"Now there's a long walk off a short pier," the man replied, followed by another chorus of laughter.

I didn't get it but I hoped he would explain. He did, and then some.

"Well," he said, "some folks seem smitten with the idea that the Oneida Community is all about wife sharing and wife swapping. They come here hoping they can get in on the action, you know," he continued with a wink, "have a roll in the fifty foot square bed we got up in the *playroom*." There was another boisterous laugh from the group that was growing more and more energized with each bawdy inference. "Of course, everybody in this room knows its total hogwash, not to mention ancient history."

"You mean there is no fifty foot bed," I joked, trying to play along.

"Nope, never has been, 'cept in some of the more lascivious minds that wander in here from time to time."

There was that word again—lascivious. The city librarian had used it to describe the Oneida Community and I could tell he wasn't being complimentary when he had said it. Others in town had used it as well in similar fashion and I was now seeing it as the pivotal word–ten letters that summed up the very existence of people and beliefs that had built the grand mansion I sat in today– the very place my sister had died in, perhaps, murdered in. Were they lascivious? Weren't they lascivious? That was the sixty-four thousand dollar question that everyone we had encountered had already answered for themselves in very clear black or white terms. There didn't seem to be any gray here and these people certainly didn't appear to agree with the city librarian or the town folk. They saw the experiment, as it was referred to in my afternoon reading, in a different light. I wanted to know more. Did the Community still exist, only in secret now? Was that why the surrounding town gazed upon the hill with such disapproving eyes? I wondered if the original Oneida Community had suffered the same judgmental scorn back in its founding days that had begun a decade before the Civil War and ended more than a decade after.

"So the term *Complex Marriage* isn't just another term for polygamy?" Jess asked, to which she quickly followed with, "I ran across that expression in your library where we were browsing through the wonderful collection of antique books."

"Now you're trying to push me *off* the pier," the man chuckled.

Over the course of the next half hour, through the clearing of spent serving platters and the delivery of dessert–a rainbow mix of jello squares with whipped cream on top–the gathering of men and women proceeded to explain to us the concept that Jess and I had imagined was one of the cornerstones of the Oneida Community. Mel had written the term *Complex Marriage* in her self-addressed email, indicating to us that she had considered it an essential part of her research. Now it served as a glowing marker to begin our dig. Our knowledgeable dining companions made easy work of it.

Jess and I sat mystified like two kids spying on Santa on

Christmas Eve as the Oneida Community's radical innovations in social and sexual theory were explained. "They were not a horde of free lovers as they were often stigmatized in the popular mind," one woman said. "The foundation of their beliefs was biblical; in fact, their social theory was often referred to as Bible Communism," another man said. "They considered themselves married to the entire community rather than to a single monogamous partner, but that of course drew jeers and prejudice from the prudish and the ignorant," a third added.

"Yeah, they took a lot of shit back in the day, as you young people say," George, the comedian of the group, said.

Then Harriet, Harry to her friends, and unnoticed to me up until that moment, began to speak. The rest of the group fell silent, almost bowing in reverence as she said, "John said very eloquently in his very first report from the Community in 1849: The abolishment of sexual exclusiveness is involved in the love-relation required between all believers by the express injunction of Christ and the apostles, and by the whole tenor of the New Testament. 'The new commandment is, that we love one another,' and that not by pairs, as in the world, but *en masse*."

The room nodded in agreement and for a moment, I felt like I was in church listening to a Sunday sermon. Love each other *en masse?* I contemplated the idea as visions of my bedroom-eyed Playboy centerfolds returned. I knew that was probably not what the founder had meant, so I tried to herd the flirty flock out of my mind and stay focused on our objective. I was still wrangling with a few stragglers when Jess spoke up.

"They were creating a Utopia, a heaven on earth," Jess observed.

"In a manner of speaking, yes," Harriet said.

"But how did they manage the community," Jess said, pausing to search her thoughts and clarify her question. "I mean, how did they keep it from turning into the giant orgy they were persistently accused of conducting?"

The room laughed before the more timid eyes returned to Harriet.

"John had rules," she said. "A complete scriptural foundation was clearly laid out in his First Annual Report, which you can find in the library." And with that explanation, she stood up, said her "good nights" to us all and quietly left the dining hall.

After she left, George said, "Harry is the great-granddaughter of one of the original members of the Community and anything she tells you can be taken as gospel."

"Who is John?" I asked. "The man she kept referring to?"

"That would be John Humphrey Noyes," George answered stoutly. "The father and founder of the Oneida Community; the head honcho; the big cheese, as you young people say."

There was more laughter.

"Where can we find his *First Annual Report*—the one Harriet mentioned?" Jess asked in a tone that sounded way to detective'ish to me.

"We love reading about religious cults and strange societies," I quickly added, trying to reinforce our uninformed tourist persona. It didn't go over as I had hoped.

"To use the word *cult* would be a slap in the face," George answered curtly, his bevy of one-liners apparently concluded. "The Oneida Community is a spiritual community deeply rooted in biblical ethics and justification. You need to spend some time in the library, son, before you open your mouth again." He was obviously perturbed by my interpretation and unexpectedly left the room as Harriet had, but without the same cordial sentiment.

George's departure triggered an avalanche of exits, including our own. As Jess and I walked slowly back to our room, I whispered to her, "I think I struck a nerve."

"You sure did," she whispered back, "and before he could tell us where to find that report."

"I'm sure it's in the library somewhere. Don't worry, we'll find it."

We paused in the hallway and let several people pass while we tried to get our bearings. Jess pointed one way just as I pointed in another. Then we both laughed. We needed a navigator and at that moment I'm sure Jess was thinking of Mel just as I was.

"Did you notice the way he said it?" Jess said.

"George?"

"Yes, George. When he said the Oneida Community *is* a spiritual community. He didn't say *was* a spiritual community, he said it *is* a spiritual community."

"You know, you're right, he did," I said. "Slip of the tongue, do you think?"

"Normally, I would say yes, but if we factor in the anonymous letter and Mel's death that followed it, I don't believe normal thinking applies anymore, do you?"

"No, I don't think it does," I replied. I pointed in the direction Jess had offered moments ago and as I followed her deeper into the old place in search of our room, I concluded that we had perhaps uncovered a second suspect–the protective residents of the Mansion House.

CHAPTER 20

As I flopped down onto my side of the king-sized bed in the room Jess and I were sharing, a headless mattress with sausage-link pillows stuffed inside a white, rabbit-ear stenciled bedcover, two thoughts stepped forward like partisan volunteers from a rigid soldier line. The first was really a question: who were all those people with whom we had just shared a two-hour dinner? There must have been over three dozen people there and a lot more than the eight guest rooms Harriet had unveiled to us could have accommodated. Then I remembered Harriet had said there were thirty-five apartments in the Mansion House, a third of which had their own kitchens or kitchenettes. The people hadn't just come out of the woodwork; they lived there year-round, providing a constant stream of ravenous appetites. As that soldier stepped neatly back into the ranks, the second one marched forward–my need to have a drink. The problem was how to sneak into the liquor cabinet while Jess wasn't looking.

"I wonder if it's still warm outside," I said. I went to the window and slid the lower half up. A cool, welcoming breeze caressed my face. It felt like April, chilly and crisp with a hint of mist brought in from what appeared to be a cloudy night sky. "I can't see any stars and it feels like it might rain any second," I said. Actually, I could see a few stars here and there but that didn't fit into my plan.

"Sounds like a perfect night to cuddle up with a good book or two," Jess said. She was curled in the rose-garden chair with her intended reading in hand, her unintentionally fetching glasses perched studiously upon her nose, her abandoned shoes a two-vehicle collision beneath her.

"I love walking in the rain, especially in springtime," I lied. I hated getting wet. "That was quite a dinner they served us; it would be a good idea to burn some of it off, don't you think?"

"You go ahead, I want to get through this first book tonight if I can," Jess answered. She looked up, smiled, and then dove back into the pages.

"Are you sure? We can come right back if it starts to rain."

"No, thanks," she answered as she drifted away into the 1860s.

"Ok, then," I said as I headed for the door. "I won't be gone too long, maybe an hour tops. Unless I get lost or a downpour hits and I have to hole-up somewhere until it stops."

"Ok," she mumbled, seemingly oblivious to my deception.

"Like taking candy from a baby," I said to myself as my feet hit the pavement. I began walking toward the small shopping plaza that we had seen during our sightseeing laps around the city. There would be a bar there, or at least someone who knew where the nearest bar was, and my heart began to sing as I watched more stars appear overhead, joyous in the feeling that my cup was about to spill over.

I hadn't yet reached the plaza when I spotted two young men walking along the sidewalk on the opposite side of the street carrying what appeared to be bowling ball bags. Bowlers, I assumed, heading to the bowling alley, I again assumed, which meant beer! I followed them several blocks expecting to soon see an oasis of neon on the distant horizon, a welcome mat of malted pleasure. My dream was dashed as they disappeared into a large barn-like recreational center that I knew from experience would not cater to my immediate needs. Disappointed and thirst weary, I broke down completely and asked directions from a man in the parking lot. "Keep walking and when you get to the top of the hill, turn your head to the right. You can't miss it," he said. At least I had been heading in the right direction.

It was a good half-mile hike, maybe more, with the better part of it being up a significant hill. It reminded me of the one I used to deliver newspapers on, trudging up its quarter mile for one lousy customer at the top before screaming back down in the red Radio Flyer wagon I sometimes used to haul all the news fit for print. That rickety old wagon made one god-awful racket in the quiet pre-dawn hours. To this day, I still wonder how many sleepy-eyed Putney residents peered out their windows as I rolled by, thinking it might be an alien spacecraft landing or a lost lovesick moose calling to its mate. The ride down always made the hike up worth the trip and, as I reached the top of this hill, the pungent odor of finely brewed lager filling my nostrils, I knew tonight's reward would be just as satisfying.

"Give me a pitcher of your best draft," I said to the bartender, a short and stocky, fifty-something woman who oddly reminded me of a linebacker from my high school football team. She had the same round face and the same curious blue eyes that appeared absorbed in my every move. Her black and pink hair was pulled back into a tight bun and her fingernails were painted blue, matching her eyes quite nicely. She was friendly enough, attending to me quickly, but then there were only three other customers in the place when I walked in. "Just one glass and a whiskey shot, too. Jack Daniels, if you've got it," I added.

She smiled as she delivered my foam-capped half gallon and said in a voice like a box of rocks, "It looks to me like you're a man on a mission." She then poured the whiskey.

Paranoia seized me. How could she know why I was in town? I had always found bartenders to be a bit intuitive but this was downright creepy. I filled my glass and emptied it just as fast. Its refill did not sit in the glass much longer.

"Darlin', it's good to see a man get down to business. I've seen so many pretenders in here lately that I was beginning to wonder when a real drinker would show up again. And low and behold, here you are," she chuckled. "Damn, if I wasn't about to give up hope."

I relaxed as I then realized to what she was referring. I gulped the whiskey shot down, giving her a wink as I did. She was a good bartender, as opposed to a bad bartender, a categorization I had developed after watching a colorized version of 'The Wizard of Oz' and hearing Dorothy ask, "Are you a good witch or a bad witch?" This woman was a good bartender, and I knew I would only need to click my rubber heels together three times and she would cheerfully transport me wherever I wanted to go.

"You know, you look familiar," she said, squinting at me. "Have you been in here before?"

"No, never in my life."

"Well, I know I've seen you before or at least someone who looks like you. It'll come to me, just give me a minute."

She had a determined look on her face and I tried to keep my head moving by looking around the bar so as not to give her a clean look. I had no doubt Mel would have come here, not in hot pursuit of alcoholic mummification, but to talk to the locals and get as many tales as she could on the topic at hand. My sister would have been all business in a place like this, her authentic warmth and childlike curiosity quickly winning them over. I'm sure by nights end, they all went home without a clue that their memory pockets had just been picked.

Jess and I had discussed the possibility of someone noticing my resemblance to Mel but we didn't see it as a big risk since we weren't identical twins. We had agreed that I would not shave during our week in Sherrill, figuring that would be enough camouflage. All I had so far was a chin full of sandpaper. Now I was facing a professional, a recognition expert, a super-sleuth in the art of facial design–a bartender. *God help me.*

"I've just got one of those faces," I said. "I hear it all the time."

"You *are* a cute drop of dew," she said, causing me to laugh openly. "Where ya from?"

If she was anything, she was unashamedly flirtatious. Had she been a few years younger and *not* reminded of my high school football teammate, I might have played along. But one dalliance a night is enough especially considering I had a chaperone expecting me home soon. "The Hamptons," I said, sticking to script I had cooked up that morning.

"Oh," she said with a hint of curiosity and arousal, "rich, too?"

"Well, I guess you could say that. Not like Billy Gates or Howie Hughes," I said, trying to make them sound like they were old buddies. "But, a net worth of a few hundred million isn't too bad." The story grew exponentially from there and soon the chain of Hartwell Spas and Resorts covered the country like yellow dandelions in a grassy green meadow. They were everywhere, I explained, everywhere but Sherrill, New York. This would be an ideal spot for one. It would be a great boon to the local economy, especially the local restaurants and bars, I said. I reminded her that people already traveled here to see the Mansion House and to explore the legend of the Oneida Community. (I said I would love to hear more about them if she had anything to share.) So, why not expand upon it; make it a vacation destination; a getaway-from-the-kids for mom and dad; a place to relax and experience some history. We could call it the 'Utopian Resort and Spa', I suggested, embellishing it with invisible letters etched out in the stale air between us.

She didn't say anything for a minute or two, gazing back at me with a half grin. I imagined her overwhelmed by my genius, but more than likely, she was counting in her mind the freshly massaged and tanned customers lining up at her bar. It was then I noticed her badly faded, logo-embossed tee shirt that proclaimed to all who entered the name of the bar as well as her own name. Unfortunately, between the worn off lettering and some stubborn old condiment stains, it appeared that I was drinking at 'The *ill* Inn', served by a woman named "hell." It wasn't until another patron yelled at her that I determined her name was actually "Shelley."

"So, what do you think Shelley? Is there a future here for a Hartwell Spa and Resort?"

"Hell, yes!" she exclaimed. She then filled my shot glass with whiskey and bought the near-empty house a round. "I knew there was something about you the minute you walked in here," she added.

"So did I," I replied under my breath.

By midnight, it was just Shelley, me, and five exhausted beer pitchers. I had delivered my shtick (along with plenty of free beer) to a dozen thirsty visitors with all the grace and sincerity of a late-night infomercial pitchman on a caffeine buzz, a dream of new prosperity that they gobbled up like ravenous coyotes. Now I could hear the bell toll: *Last call for alcohol.* I downed the shot of whiskey I held affectionately in my hand and asked for one more. Shelley refused me. She was ready to call it a night and I realized then that somehow she had snuck off while I wasn't looking and turned into a bad witch. Her face did look a little green but that may have been from the glow of the light above the cash register that now served as the only light in the place.

"Time to go home, sweetie," she said, wearily.

"Just one more," I pleaded, probably for the fifth time in the last hour. I'm sure I sounded like a whiny kid who wanted to stay up and watch television reruns all night but I didn't care, my pride had been washed away a good hour or two ago.

"No, midnight is it on Monday," she said patting my now-empty hand as it sat lifelessly on the bar. "Come back tomorrow and I'll have a pitcher and a shot sitting right here waiting for you."

"You know something, hell, you sure know how to sweet talk a fella. I'll see you tomorrow." I slapped the bar with my left hand, said good night, and strolled out in the now frigid early spring air where I tried to recall the whereabouts of my car. There wasn't a single vehicle in sight and, after several confused minutes I remembered I had walked there. It was another minute before I started walking in the right direction, down the hill and back to the Mansion House, wishing the entire time that I had had one more drink to help ward off the cold.

CHAPTER 21

"Where are you going?" I ask Mel. She does not answer, only smiles softly, turns and walks away into a misty white fog. I follow her. She is naked, but I don't see her as naked. I am not embarrassed or aroused. She is my sister and that is all I see.

She glides effortlessly in front of me, the swirls of mist caressing her delicate body as her russet mane flutters behind her like an imperial flag. Her head is tilted up slightly; her shoulders are square and her steps deliberate. There is nothing else, only mist and my advancing sister.

"Where are you going?" I ask again. She glances back but only for a moment; her brown eyes sparkle; her smile is unchanged; she continues on.

I find myself calm in this role as follower but that is not my convention. This surprises me. I do not walk in other people's footprints, but somehow Mel commands this from me and I follow, because I must.

The fog parts and suddenly there are gray beams of sunshine everywhere, ghostly fingers from heaven fondling a vast plush lawn that stretches out in all directions, ending at the feet of a large, colorless mansion. There is an abundance of pathways and a sprinkling of young saplings. There are no people. Everything is muted tones of gray, lifeless, but yet I feel a sense of brightness, buoyancy and clarity of sorts. I don't know what to make of it and

I turn to Mel who is now standing next to me. She too has become a palette of hushed grays and now only her face is recognizable to me. Her hair has been cut short and there is a white line down the middle of her head where her flaccid locks part and fall, framing her face like humble window drapes. She is wearing a simple dress, a frock, my mind says, that drips only to her knees where pant legs of the same fabric continue on to the ground, covering her feet. Her jewelry is gone; her earrings, her lapel pins and even the silver choker she has worn as long as I can remember. Mel does not look pretty, not like I want to see her, and this disturbs me. I search her eyes for explanation, for guidance, and my mouth begins to move with an unknown question just as she turns and steps into the painting brushed before me. My eyes follow her and there are people now; lots and lots of people scattered about the grounds in huddles of three and four and five. The men are dressed in dark vested suits with collared white shirts that peek out like v-shaped bibs, bearded and stately. The women are mirror images of my transformed sister, plain and demure but steadfast under my gaze.

There are children running about and, looking deeper into the lawn, I see a group playing croquet and seemingly having a grand time of it. Nearer to the mansion, there is a small orchestra assembled–violins, horns, a flute and a clarinet. Some people are dancing to the music that I believe is playing, but the song does not reach my ears. People are talking all around me but I cannot hear them either, and I look again for my sister who I find wandering among them, observing contently. I already know I am in a dream and that the nightmare will begin at any moment. I hunt carefully and methodically for the red snake that I know is hidden somewhere in this beguiling canvas, stalking. I find nothing. My body begins to swell with anticipation and fear that I will not see its bloody spirit until it has coiled itself around my sister's neck, pulling her into the darkness.

Mel meanders through it all like a carefree butterfly, briefly pausing here and there to look more closely at something or some-one as if gathering pollen from a cluster of daisies and sunflowers. She is happy in her collection and suddenly, unexpectedly, I am happy too. This is how I wake up–happy.

Where the hell am I?

CHAPTER 22

Relax and let your mind find itself.

Staring up at ceilings has evolved into quite a hobby of mine. I'm getting so good at it that I am seriously considering going professional, just as soon as some pubescent internet mogul forms a new league and offers a million dollar signing bonus to the best talent in the land, which, of course, would be me. In the split second it takes a quarterback to spot an open receiver, I can identify the paint color (white, antique white, eggshell, powdered snow or moonrise,) the application technique (wet brush, dry brush, roller or trowel,) the expertise of the painter, or lack thereof (inspiring cloud-like swirls or a vacant tic-tac-toe board.) Even the age of the paint job itself as evidenced by the presence of a number of time and use-induced blemishes such as blistering, burnishing, wrinkling, cracking, flaking, yellowing and mildew.

It usually only takes a few minutes for the capsized boat that is my memory to right itself and then a little longer to bail out all the water, but this time is actually very important to me. It provides a chance to look deep within myself, to search for the meaning of life and, most importantly, for the name of the woman lying next to me.

Harriet? Is her name Harriet?

I can't look over at the woman whose back is facing me. She might wake up right at that moment, turn over, and say, "Good morning, Michael," to which I would reply "Good morning…

ah...." No, first things first–*where the hell am I?*

Relax; let it all trickle back. The painter did a nice job on the ceiling, eggshell is a nice color–white but not too white. The Mansion House, I'm at the Mansion House in Sherrill looking for Mel. No, looking for Mel's killer and Harriet is...*Harriet is...the sweet old lady who greeted us when we arrived yesterday.* My congratulatory smile is short lived. *Oh, shit! Please, God, don't let this be Harriet lying next to me–I'll never touch another drop again!*

Courageously, and very slowly, I looked over and saw it was not Harriet. This woman was too young, her hair too...*not-gray* and, just that quickly, my sails fill with air and my boat was once again cutting through the water as I remembered I was with Jess. I exhaled a sigh of relief and immediately canceled my promise to God.

I peeked under the covers and, just as I had anticipated, I was buck-naked. My next thought was to peek under Jess's covers to ascertain her wardrobe but I quickly thought better of it. She already had me tagged a lush and I didn't want her to brand me a pervert, too. Besides, I could already see she had on some kind of thermal sweatshirt that she probably bought at Macys complete with a pair of matching bottoms. Still, I felt an overwhelming urge to find out for sure. One little peek and...I was right, Macys did indeed sell these sensible pajamas in a set and I replaced her covers gently thinking that she looked good in them.

As I sat up in preparation to get completely up, I noticed a bathrobe draped over a chair that was right next to me. Jess' bathrobe, I concluded, since I had never owned one in my life. I wondered why the chair was not on the other side of the bed where Jess could easily grab the robe when she got up. The dull ache moaning in my temples pushed that question aside and I forcibly finished my rise, immediately stubbing my toe on that same chair which then sent me sprawling to the ground. The thud of my chin hitting the floor created a stir from Jess, so I scrambled for my boxer shorts lying in a heap at the foot of the bed with the rest of yesterday's clothes. *Hang up your clothes when you're finished with them,* my mother's voice echoed in my defrosting mind. With shorts secured, I scampered into the bathroom and shut the door, ever so quietly.

My eyes burned as I flipped on the lone fluorescent bulb fixture in the windowless bathroom, a stark, white-walled gathering of porcelain understatement. It was an unforgiving light, at the complete opposite end of the spectrum from the illusion-inducing hue of a midnight bar. Its invisible, piercing rays scolded me for my poor judgment and disregard for the loyal brain cells I had willingly sent too the gallows. I had no remorse for those fallen comrades, thinking only that I was getting to old for this shit. Then came a second thought that told me that the first thought was beginning to occur more often. I splashed some cold water on my face and decided to stop thinking.

There was an urgent knock on the bathroom door. "Are you going to give anyone else a turn in there?" Jess' gravelly voice said.

"I'll be out in a minute," I yelled back. "Keep your pants on!"

I drained what my overworked liver had been able to process overnight and then traded places with my sleepy-eyed roommate, carefully sidestepping her to avoid any inappropriate body contact as she entered and I exited. I feared there may have already been some of that during the night and I didn't want to add to it, especially when I could no longer have my defense attorney plead intoxication. *If he's too drunk to see, you must set him free.*

I managed to pull on my trashed jeans, a pair of faded blue Levi's with a skosh more room in the seat, and a fresh, white cotton tee shirt from my travel bag before a more spirited Jess emerged from the bathroom. She had only been awake for a minute or two and in the bathroom for half of that, and already she looked in mid-afternoon form, vibrant and alluring even in her pale yellow, thermal PJ's. I looked down at her feet to see if there were slippers sewn on to the ankle-length pants. There was not, but I couldn't help smiling just thinking about it.

"What are you smiling about?" she asked.

Her left hand was perched on her cocked hip. She was taking aim, I thought, getting ready to fire bullets at my disappearing act of last night and I hadn't yet cooked up an alibi. I would pay for it now, I was sure of that. I reached for her bathrobe and threw it across the bed to her, saying, "I thought *you* wanted to sleep on the right side of the bed?"

"I was," she said, with the look I imagined she gave to motorists who claimed they didn't see the stop sign that they had failed to stop at, "until you came in."

Ok, here it comes.

I looked away, grimacing merrily to myself, and hurriedly finished dressing, securing black shoes over black socks and a rusty orange pullover, before grabbing my black leather motorcycle jacket that sat listlessly in the rose-adorned chair. "I'm going down to the kitchen to see what they've got. I'd be happy to bring you back something; a little breakfast in bed for my bride?" I asked, accommodatingly. *Sidetrack her; steer her clear from the scene of the crime.*

"Some orange juice would be good," she replied. Her jaw relaxed and her face brightened just a whisper as she added, "And an onion bagel, lightly toasted, with extra cream cheese."

Evidently, I hadn't done anything too bad last night or she would have read me my Miranda Rights right then and there. Maybe she fell asleep early and had no idea when I came back. You never question a lucky roll of the dice and I left the room, saying cheerfully, "Your wish is my command," before closing the door with a whispered, "Lollipop."

I journeyed my way to the dining hall, making only two wrong turns in the process, probing my memory the entire time for some scrap depicting how I must have jostled Jess to the opposite side of our honeymoon nest. Was I naked before or after the jousting that must have occurred ended? Had I busted a move on her? And, if so, was I naked before or after I did that? If I had been *lascivious* (I was beginning to like this word) she was not showing it, and I decided that it best be laid to rest before it could swell and fester into an ugly, puss-oozing sore.

The Mansion House kitchen had everything Jess had ordered and, after toasting her bagel, along with one of my own, I triumphantly returned to our room through the labyrinth on my very first attempt before proudly laying out our feast on the dresser. Jess appeared to have already showered, sharply attired in blues jeans, a pinkish, collared shirt tucked underneath a lime-green cardigan.

"I hope I didn't toast it too much," I said as Jess took the first bite of her bagel. I had slapped the split halves of the thing together after swabbing enough cream cheese on it to choke a horse. Now the milky white goop was oozing out all over her hands. She licked it off her fingers contently, mumbling, "It's perfect."

This was comfortable, almost uncomfortably comfortable. I had a sudden urge to tell her all about the dream I had that night. It was right then that I realized it *had* been a dream and *not* a nightmare. Mel wasn't dying at the end of it or even in any danger whatsoever. It had started out as a pleasant dream and it had stayed that way–all night! And my lack of sobriety hadn't stopped it. This was a first on both accounts. As I wrestled with the implications, my puzzled expression blooming oddly like a cactus flower, Jess tuned in and asked me what I was thinking.

"I had a dream about Mel," I said, surprised I had just said it so easily.

CHAPTER 23

My sister's best friend wanted to know every gory detail. She had no idea just how gory it might get.

"You had a dream about Mel last night?" Jess asked.

Timidly, I nodded.

"Where was she? What was the dream about?" she asked excitedly. She sat down on the now made-up bed, crossed her legs Indian style and leaned forward like a girl scout preparing for a midnight campfire ghost story. Her expectations were high, I could see that, and the courage that had appeared from nowhere just moments ago began to flutter away. *Me and my big mouth.*

"Well, it really wasn't much of a dream," I said. "I don't remember much."

"Start at the beginning," Jess said, reassuringly. "Who was in the dream?"

Suddenly the room was suffocating me, the walls squeezing in around me. I glanced at the door from the corner of my eye, wishing it would grab me by the collar and pull me out. If only I had a beer in my hand this might be easier, I thought, a frothy-headed German stein the size of Rhode Island. I closed my eyes and all I could see was Mel, my sister, smiling calmly and reaching out to me. She was exactly as I wanted her to be, the picture I kept of her in my mind, smiling her wonderful smile, touching me with her beauty and the unconditional love in her eyes. She was telling me it was all right, that I needed to tell Jess about my dream, about all my dreams. Just that quickly the air was once again filling my lungs and quietly, hesitantly, I began to speak, "Just Mel at first," I said. "But then there were a whole bunch of other people, people I didn't recognize."

"Where was she? Did you recognize the place?"

"I'm not sure, but she wasn't herself."

Jess tilted her head and furrowed her brow as she said, "What do you mean, she wasn't herself?"

I had to think for second. *What did I mean?*

"Well, it was Mel, but it wasn't Mel. She was all decked out in this funky outfit, kind of like the clothes you wear when you get your picture taken at the amusement park. You know, so it looks like you're in an old photo from a wild west saloon or something. Her hair was cut real short and all her jewelry was gone. I almost didn't recognize her at first." It was then that I noticed the picture on the wall of our room, a picture of one of the Utopians, as I was now referring to them. "Like her," I said, pointing at the picture. "She looked just like her."

Jess looked at the picture and I knew by the smile that played across her face that she was beginning to understand my dream, just as I now was.

"Here," I said. "She was here, at the Mansion House. But not as herself from a week ago; she was one of them; one of the Utopians from over a century ago."

The room fell quiet.

"What was she doing?" Jess finally asked.

"She was out on the lawn somewhere just wandering around and watching all the people as they lounged and talked and played...croquet. There were people playing croquet and some others playing instruments in a band of some kind. It was like a party or a celebration."

Jess sprang up off the bed, grabbed one of the books from the dresser that we had commandeered from the library, and vaulted back in an eruption of creaks and squeaks from the mattress springs and the floorboards. Her enthusiastic leap reminded me of the time Mel and I found the Sears Christmas Catalog my mother had hidden behind a stack of old shoe boxes in her mothball-perfumed closet, and had raced back to my room and onto my bed to discover all the new toys created by the brilliant minds of Mattel and Hasbro. It always came in the mail months early and my mother always hid it in the exact same place. If she knew we always found it, she never let on, but I had to believe the dog-eared pages and crayon-circled toys induced at least a little suspicion.

"One of the books I've been reading mentioned how they loved playing croquet," Jess said as she hurriedly flipped through it. She turned the book to toward me, its thick pages drooping down like seagull wings, and pointed to a picture. "See," she said.

I had never seen the picture before, except in my dream. I stared at it, examining each and every face, thinking I might find Mel, as if she were hidden like Waldo. There were a dozen people playing the game, men and women, and a gathering twice that size sitting in the grass along the sidelines watching. The men participating were respectively suited with straw hats or a bowler and the women were just as Mel had looked, simply adorned in pleated knee-length dresses that pant-legged over their shoes and belted at the waist. Some of the women wore single ribbon hats and some had white aprons blanketed over their modest dresses. They weren't smiling, but they didn't look unhappy either–they looked…content.

Jess pulled the book back and said, "They look like they're having so much fun."

"As much fun as croquet can be, I suppose," I replied sarcastically.

"It's not the game so much as it's nice to see a family and neighbors all enjoying something together. They're all dressed up and everyone is involved. I thought about this last night. About how these photos illustrate how well they all got along together despite the disapproving world around them."

"Let me see that again," I said. Jess handed the book back to me and I studied it for a minute as I stood next to the bed. I still didn't see what Jess was referring to. I couldn't help it, I kept looking for Mel. "You see all that in this one picture?" I asked.

She got up on her knees and wiggled to the edge of the bed so she could look at the book with me. "It's not just that picture, there are others as well," she said, before turning the pages to show me surprisingly sharp black and white photographs of men, women and children all gathered together performing a task or having a group photo taken.

"Nobody is smiling," I said. "Didn't they know enough to say *cheese* back then?"

"Actually, they didn't," Jess answered. "Cameras, as *we* think of them, had only been around for a few years when these pictures were taken and I don't think people knew what to do just before the flash went off."

I looked at Jess, puzzled.

"I read it somewhere," she shrugged, before flipping to another picture. "In this shot they're all making traveling bags."

I could feel her eyes upon me as I studied the photograph of some thirty or so adults sitting in a room meticulously working on something dark and fuzzy situated on their laps.

"It's called a bee–a *unitary fever of cheerful industry*, as they referred to it. In this case, a bag bee. They would organize a bee several times a week or more to hoe the fields, harvest the crops, and make bags or to do anything that needed to get done. Notice that there are both men and women working on the bags, side by side in a circle. And do you see the man in the middle? He's reading from the Bible, inspiring the workers."

"Yeah, they were just a bunch of busy little bees, weren't they," I chuckled. Jess didn't notice my pun and I then posed some observations of my own. "What's with the short dresses and pant legs? I'm no history buff, but I thought longs dresses were the thing back then and women wearing pants was forbidden?"

"According to what I've been reading, the Community women were considered equals in property ownership and labor responsibilities. The more fashionable garments of the time, corsets, petticoats and such were not very practical or very comfortable to work in, nor was long hair or wigs that back in those days were measured by the pound. So, several of the women cut off their skirts to knee length and used the discarded material to fashion ankle-length pantalets, as they were called."

"Personally, I would have liked to have seen some leg."

"They weren't trying to turn the men on; they were equipping themselves to work shoulder to shoulder *with* the men. In fact..." Jess took the book back and moved to a page that had a sticky note jutting out before handing it back to me. "Here, read this passage. It's a wonderful summary of their beliefs on men and women working together."

The heading of the passage Jess had pointed to read: "*Circular,* October 8, 1853". "What is the *Circular*?" I asked.

"It was the newspaper they wrote and printed themselves. It appears to have been their way of reporting news within the Community as well as a conduit for expressing their beliefs to the outside world."

"Wow, they had their own newspaper?"

"Yeah, *wow*," Jess said, her eyes widening and encouraging me to read.

I read the paragraph aloud: "We find inspiration working particularly nowadays, in reference to business. At the same time, we feel roused to new earnestness to favor the *mingling of the sexes* in labor. We find that the spirit of the world is deadly opposed to this innovation, and would make it very easy to slip back into the old routine of separate employments for men and women. But the leaven of heavenly principles about labor, resists, from time to time, this backward tendency, and brings forth a new endorsement of the truths contained in the Bible argument on this subject. We believe that the great secret of securing enthusiasm in labor and producing a free, healthy, social equilibrium is contained in the proposition, 'loving companionship and labor, and especially the mingling of the sexes, makes labor attractive'."

Jess said, "A little ahead of their time, don't you think."

Faintly, I nodded in ambiguous agreement as I reread the passage to myself.

"Think about it, Michael," Jess said. "Women wouldn't be allowed to vote for another seventy years–another lifetime, and yet in Sherrill, The Silver City, women were already working and owning equally with the men. While the *outside* world–the modern, moralistic, *non-lascivious* world–wrestled with the issues of slavery and women's suffrage, the Community prospered and grew on a foundation of equality. These people were amazing."

Before I could muster a protest, the bevy of lingerie-adorned beauties lounging seductively in my subconscious were all suddenly wearing smart business suits and designer eyeglasses. I was confused. I wanted my centerfolds back.

"There is a whole section about women and their role in the Community," Jess said, grinning. "You should read it; you might learn something."

"Ha, ha," I replied. "I know all I *want* to know about women."

She got up and walked into the bathroom, still grinning as she said, "Gee, I'm sorry to hear that."

Unwilling to openly admit that my previously iron-clad opinion of women and their role in the world–my world–was again being challenged, I opened the book at another dog ear and attempted to read her handwriting. "What's this note you've got here about *A Maid of Legality*?" I asked.

"A *Raid* of Legality is what it says. Read it."

I did just that. I read that one of the attitudes of the Oneida Communists was that they not allow themselves to fall into legality, which to them meant routine. They believed if they kept in the same track or rut then they would be exposed to the attacks of evil because "the Devil would know just where to find you." Members of the Community were encouraged to change jobs frequently. This relieved the hardship of continuing an occupation after the taste for it has ceased, they believed, and facilitated fresh new ideas and inspiration. The book went on to say that a number of labor-saving innovations had been created during this intercross including one by a young mechanic who, after spending several months working in the kitchen, designed a mop-wringer that the housekeeping crew later conceded they couldn't do without.

"You certainly did a lot of reading last night," I said, lifting my eyes from the pages and into the bathroom through a sliver of space between the slightly opened door and its frame. Jess was primping her hair, preparing to go out, I assumed.

"I can read for hours when the topic is interesting," she replied.

"How long did you stay up?"

"Until the bar closed."

The Oneida Community Farm
July 1866

Every one in the Community loved strawberries, especially Sarah. She would eat them for breakfast, for lunch, and for dessert after supper in a bowl, sprinkling a blanket of juicy red and pink slices over the top of a big scoop of vanilla ice cream. So, when a Bee was called to pick over the one hundred and twenty-five bushels of strawberries that had been harvested from their fields the day before, she was one of the first to volunteer. The fruit needed to be hulled, put into cans and sealed while it was still fresh, requiring the type of well-orchestrated team work that Sarah thrived on. The smell–the fruity and floral sweetness–would be heavenly. The only challenge would be the strawberries them-selves–not gorging herself on them. As she dressed that morning, she promised herself that she would only sample a few from the discarded pile, at least *before* lunch.

Walking toward the barn where the crates of strawberries were stacked high and wide, Sarah heard a man's voice calling to her. She turned and saw a tall, gangly man in a white shirt and dark sleeveless vest chasing after her in a lazy gallop. She smiled, the hem of her simple frock rising almost to her pantaloon-covered knee as she raised her hand to wave. She stopped to wait for him, pushing a lock of her boyish hair behind her ear as a content smile settled upon her pretty, unmade face.

"I thought you were working in the trap shop today," Sarah

said to Edward, her husband of seventeen years. "You were up so early I didn't even get a kiss goodbye."

"I apologize, dear heart," Edward said before greeting his wife with a soft peck on the cheek. His thick beard tickled, but Sarah didn't mind, she loved to be tickled.

After catching his breath, Edward said, "The last of the traps were completed yesterday. They are now on their way to the train station and a train bound for Chicago. And I," he was grinning now, "am bound for a date with my lovely wife."

"Canning strawberries?" Sarah asked.

Edward smiled broadly and said, "I can think of no better way to spend such a splendid summer day than to be by your side doing business as unto the Lord."

With those words, Edward took his wife's arm, laced it into his and led her off to administer to the strawberries.

CHAPTER 24

Jess didn't say another word about my late-night excursion and I wasn't about to inquire as to why. "Never open a can of worms unless you plan on going fishing," my father would say when my mother was in a snit about something. Jess knew all right, but my hope was that the seeds I had strategically planted at the bar last night would already be sprouting roots and that I'd be looking pretty smart by week's end. Even as I gazed out the window into the courtyard, random droplets of rain peppering the glass, I could sense that word of our presence was spreading.

There was a knock at our door.

Jess got up and went to answer it. I stayed at the window.

On the other side of the door stood a cop; a policewoman to be more exact, looking very official in her wrinkle-free blue uniform and gold badge that was pinned affectionately to her breast. She was Jess' height exactly with a light complexion and dark-brown hair clipped up in back. Her hat was tucked snuggly under her left arm while both hands juggled a notepad, a pen and a portable radio. She had a serious look on her face. Dirty Harry's little sister, Dirty Harriet, I thought.

We exchanged pleasantries before the officer said, "You folks the owners of a 2004 Hyundai Sonota, New York State license plate ZLM 4187?"

"I am," Jess said.

"I'll need you to come out to the parking lot and open it for me."

"Why?" I said, stepping up behind Jess as she held the door open. The officer's nametag read "Callahan," and I quickly turned my head to disguise an emerging snicker.

"Is this your husband, ma'am?"

"No, I mean, yes," Jess said, stumbling on the words as if they pained her. "He is."

"He should come along too then."

We followed the officer through the Mansion House maze of corridors before spilling out a door to the back parking lot. She certainly knew her way around the place and I wondered if she had been the first on the scene the day my sister was found dead in her room. I had a god-awful urge to ask her but I fought it off to stay in character.

We were almost to Jess' car when I said, "Did I mention that we were on our honeymoon?"

It would have taken a blowtorch and a monkey wrench to un-screw Jess' twisted face after that little gem and, realizing it was neither the time nor the place for another presentation of our ficti-tious love story, I nonchalantly cowed off to the side while Jess unlocked her car door and popped the trunk. The officer made a beeline for the back seat and the small inanimate object that lay there.

It was over in a flash. Before we knew it, Jess and I were in the back seat of Dirty Harriet Callahan's patrol car on our way *down-town*, to the City of Sherrill Police Station.

"How long can they lock us up for stealing a library book?" I asked.

Jess didn't answer but I could hear her grumbling something to herself, something snarled but indistinguishable. She had her back to me with her head laid limply against the reinforced, bul-letproof window, milky fog appearing and disappearing on the glass with her every breath. It was then that I realized that she had decided to stop speaking to me.

CHAPTER 25

What I was discovering about Sherrill was that you could get anywhere in the city in two or three minutes. The traffic was almost non-existent, and the stoplights few and far between–a good thing if you're running late for a lunch meeting or stumbling back to the Mansion House from a bar in the wee hours of the morning. Not so convenient when you could use a few extra minutes (or hours) to do what my parents and other authority figures had suggested I do for years: *think about what I had done.* What I—what *we*—had done, was swipe a library book and, as we arrived downtown before my seat could even get warm, I had a sinking feeling that hardcover theft might be a felony in the smallest city in New York.

If Jess and I had not been arriving in the back of a police car with emerging concerns over the cleanliness of the jail cells, I would have said the modern red and grey brick City of Sherrill Municipal Building looked warm and inviting. I would have looked for a Starbucks in the small plaza and sniffed the air for the scent of fresh bagels as Officer Callahan lead us into the Police Station. I probably would have even conjured up an image of Andy Griffith as the Police Chief, a friendly, common-sense driven man who would rather you learned your lesson than have you locked up. Instead, I bowed my head, a blank expression loitering across my face, looking and feeling like the criminal I knew I was. The rain had stopped and Jess walked in behind me, still not talking.

"Take a seat right over there," Officer Callahan said before walking up to the front desk where a middle-aged man in a matching uniform greeted her. They talked briefly in hushed tones, inaudible from where Jess and I now sat.

"At least they didn't handcuff us," I whispered to Jess, attempting to lighten her mood.

She scowled at me, which was an improvement over looking at the back of her head.

"The librarian must have blown us in," I said. "Called out the dogs and had us hunted down. I knew old Gomer was a snitch the minute I laid eyes on him."

Suddenly, Jess slugged me in the chest with the back of her clenched fist. "I told you not to take that book," she said, her eyes burning a hole into my skull. "How do you think this going to look on my record back in Yonkers? This could cost me my badge."

"It was a fucking library book!" I said before immediately lowering my tone. "Half the kids in this city probably have overdue books lying under their beds buried beneath a herd of dust bunnies. How can they lock us up for that? This is crazy."

"Its petty larceny and they're not going to lock us up for it," Jess said. "But it's still a criminal offense and most police agencies don't want their cops to have criminal records. They're funny that way."

It was then that I started to *think about what I had done*. Grabbing the book seemed like an ok idea at the time but like most childish mischief conducted by adults, it was now spinning out of control. I could almost see my father shaking his head in disgust. I was already in my thirties and the need for my parent's endorsement still roamed freely in my thoughts like a night watchman. I put my hand on Jess' shoulder and, cringing a little from the fresh bruise on my right pectoral muscle, I told her I was sorry.

"What's done is done," Jess said. "Now let's see if I can wiggle our way out of this."

Jess stood up and walked to the front desk where Officer Callahan was now standing alone filling out a form of some kind while the evidence of our crime, the book, sat ominously on the counter. The other officer was gone, apparently having slipped away while Jess and I *discussed* our situation, providing Jess the opportunity to talk policewoman to policewoman with Dirty Harriet. At least, that was what I assumed Jess was thinking of doing. I leaned forward in my seat, hoping I could hear their conversation, but I couldn't. Then, when Jess pointed back at me, her mouth moving silently while the Officer nodded in agreement, I was sure she had just blown me in as the mastermind of our little caper. *What happened to honor among thieves?*

Jess and Dirty Harriet were laughing now. Had Jess told a funny story? Were the two of them swapping yarns about the agonizing screams they had ignored after locking a young man like me up in a cell with a gang of gay rapists? I was happy to see them getting along so well, feeling a hint of optimism that we could indeed beat this wrap, but at the same time some anxiety over not being in on the joke, or worse, being the brunt of it.

I heard a door open, its squeaky hinges echoing out in the hallway, and then the footsteps and voices of several people approaching from the same direction Jess and I had traversed. *More collared book thieves?*

The sound drew closer and closer until the police station door flew open. Two men entered, both dressed in gray suits and red ties. They glanced at me briefly before walking directly to the front desk where Jess and Officer Callahan shifted their posture to greet them. Jess shook the men's extended hands. After a short, smiling conversation, she led them over to me.

The younger-looking one of the two men stepped right up to me as I stood up and said, "Arlen Bensinger, I'm the Mayor of Sherrill."

Though he appeared to be no older than I was, Arlen carried the look of a seasoned politician. His suit was snuggly tailored, his shoes conservative, and his personal hygiene immaculate right down to his streamlined eyebrows. There wasn't a single brown hair on his head out of place and his chin was so shiny I wondered if he waxed rather than shaved. He looked like he had just come from a salon where he had gotten the works in preparation of hitting the campaign trail; his smile so broad and empty that I felt a compulsive urge to pull out his tax returns for the past ten years and have some fun.

"Mick Hartwell," I said, accepting his hand into mine. He squeezed it tightly, holding it so long I began to wonder if he planned to give it back.

"Good to meet you, Mick," he said heartily. "And this is the Deputy Mayor of Sherrill, Bob Applewhite."

I shook Bob's hand. His grip was lighter then the mayor's, not to mention a bit moist, which could have been one of the reasons he was only the deputy mayor. I also noticed his suit coat didn't sit upon his shoulders quite as evenly as the mayor's and his tie was a much paler red. The wire rim glasses he wore were bent in places where you wouldn't expect them to be bent, his wispy tan hair spraying in so many directions it reminded me of a dandelion clock. He was shorter and smaller then Arlen, almost disappearing behind the mayor as they approached me and it seemed obvious that these more pallid characteristics were a requirement of the lesser position.

"I understand you and your wife are on your honeymoon," Arlen said. "I hope you're enjoying your stay so far."

"It's been great, until this morning," I said, knowing that the Mayor of Sherrill had not left his review of street parking patterns and commercial zoning modifications to lecture Jess and I about the perils of a life as library book bandits. He had undoubtedly heard the cha-ching of our arrival; smelled the Hartwell Spa and Resort chum I had sprinkled around town and was now swimming in for a closer look.

"I found this library book on the back seat of their car," Officer

Callahan said, holding up the evidence like a preacher with a Bible. "It had been reported stolen yesterday."

The mayor took the book from the officer, opened it at the back cover and examined the library card sitting conspicuously in its sleeve. It may have been my own paranoia, but I would have sworn on Mel's grave that there was a hint of recognition on his face when he saw my sister's signature on the card. No doubt he knew of her death, after all he was the mayor of a tiny city that couldn't have too many accidental autoerotic asphyxiations in the course of a four-year term. What I saw though, what I *think* I saw, was something more than just a local official's acknowledgement of an unfortunate incident that had happened on his watch.

Jess spoke up, "As I was telling Officer Callahan, we had gone to the library yesterday and did, in fact, take this book, but only after waiting at the desk for what seemed like an hour. The librarian that had led us to the Oneida Community section had vanished, so we left a note saying we were staying at the Mansion House and that we would bring it back in a few days."

Officer Callahan quickly retorted, "As I told you, Mrs. Hartwell, the librarian said nothing about a note."

"Sounds like a little misunderstanding," Arlen Bensinger said, just as I was expecting him to. "I'll tell you what, we can drive over to the library right now and get you both a library card so you can take this book out all proper and legal."

"Sounds good to us," I said with a smile.

Jess nodded in agreement, as did the deputy mayor. The only person not happy with the sudden verdict was Dirty Harriet, who crumpled the form she had been preparing before disappearing into the bowels of the Police Station in obvious disgust.

Over the course of the next ten minutes, we returned to the library where the librarian and I had a chance to rekindle our affections. We easily secured a temporary library card and then walked the few blocks over to the restaurant where we had had lunch the day before. Not so surprisingly, the mayor offered to buy. He also noted that we were lucky he was at the city offices today. His mayoral post was just a part-time "gig" and normally he would have been in Syracuse working at his regular job as a banker.

How lucky indeed, I thought.

Our waitress hadn't even brought menus to our table yet when the Mayor said, "So, I hear you folks are in the spa and resort business."

I tried my best to look surprised and said, "News travels fast in Sherrill."

"It's a small place," the deputy mayor said; his first words of the day.

"It's really not that small," Arlen quickly interjected as he flashed Bob a look that seemed to say "let me do the talking."

"In fact, it's a perfect spot for a spa...or a resort...or both!"

"It's funny that you should say that, Arlen," I said. "My wife and I have been thinking the exact same thing ever since we arrived yesterday morning. Haven't we, Lollipop."

"Oh, heavens, yes," Jess said. "I think your little Silver City has wonderful potential. In fact, that is why we had gone to the library in the first place, to research the local history."

"We've got lots of that," Arlen chuckled. "Don't we Bob?"

Bob nodded enthusiastically.

"Our patrons tend to be the adventurous type," Jess said. "They love to shop, see the sights and explore the local folklore. Consequently, we spend a great deal of time and money researching the area before we commit to a new project. For our spa to be successful, there needs to be lots of other attractions on the periphery and that's where my husband and I have questions about Sherrill."

"One can only sit in a Jacuzzi with an herbal mudpack on their face for so long," I said, laughing. The mayor and his sidekick *loved* my joke, laughing transparently.

Playing the savvy businesswoman to perfection, Jess continued baiting the hook, "It's a symbiotic relationship that we look for. Our spa will supply customers to shop in your boutiques and visit your wineries. By the same token, your community and its unique appeal will help fill the rooms in our resort and the massage tables in our spa. We both profit by combining forces and the consumer never knows the difference."

"Kind of like the clown fish and the sea anemone," I said, pausing to see if they knew I was kidding. I then laughed and the politicians chimed right in. Jess grinned as if she had just received a lawn trimmer as a birthday gift. She then looked off in search of the waitress who, upon seeing her waving hand, came over with water and menus.

"I hear what you're saying," Arlen said. "And I have to be perfectly honest. You've come to the right place."

Arlen Bensinger, the Mayor of Sherrill, the Silver City, and the smallest City in New York State, then slowly and methodically, like a living brochure, detailed for us the many charms and wonders found in Central New York. As we perused the menus, he excited us with the tempting allure of high stakes gambling at the Native-American-owned casino just minutes away. He took a breath as the waitress took our orders, and then enchanted us with visions of boating, swimming, fishing and waterskiing in the State's thousands of crystal lakes, including the Finger Lakes, which he said the local Indian folklore claimed were formed by God's hand pressing into the land. There were two thousand miles of hiking and skiing trails in the Adirondack Mountains and dozens of beaches along the shores of Lake Ontario, he explained, all "no more than an hour away." As Jess nibbled on her antipasto and I gnawed on a turkey club sandwich, Arlen rattled off the names of museums, theatres, art galleries, antique shops, parks, historical landmarks and even a few churches that were all "no more than an hour away." By the time our waitress inquired about our desire for dessert–the specialty being rhubarb pie–I found myself expecting Arlen to say that Mount Rushmore and the Grand Canyon were just over the hill to the west and "no more than an hour away."

Jess and I both declined the rhubarb pie, although Bob Applewhite appeared quite eager to partake in a slice, before sitting back in our chairs, silently waiting for Arlen to add one more entry to his lengthy list of attractions; an item that was curiously missing during his not-so-impromptu tour–the Oneida Community.

"So, what do you think?" the mayor asked. He looked as proud as a peacock and eager as a beaver, as my father would say.

"There are definitely possibilities here," I said, nodding my head and pursing my lips in a way I thought would exude a state of deep thought. "Don't you agree, Lollipop?"

"Oh, yes, even more so now than we first envisioned," Jess replied. "But...."

Her pause lingered in the air, pulling the deputy mayor away from his pie and the mayor down off his roost. I simply leaned in toward Jess, grinning in a way only she could understand, anxious to hear how she was going to broach the subject of the lascivious lot of free-love Utopians *without* tipping our hand.

"Well," Jess said, "it's just that...we like to position ourselves in places that have something totally unique to offer; something you can't find anywhere else in the world. It could be a natural wonder like Niagara Falls or an extraordinary lost culture like the Aztecs or the Incas. People love exploring things like that and if you've got something no one else has then, bingo, we're halfway home already."

"Niagara Falls *is* only a few hours away," Arlen quickly interjected. "Did you know that?"

"Yes, but we already have a spa and resort there," I said. "In fact, one of our biggest and most profitable, if you'll pardon my audaciousness."

Bob Applewhite finished his pie while the rest of us watched in itchy silence. I felt like I was an eighth grader again, in health class, and our teacher had just asked if anyone could explain the two primary functions of the male penis. Everyone in the class knew the answer, and everyone knew everyone knew the answer, but still nobody raised his or her hand. (I almost had, but I was very happy I hadn't because I would have answered urination and masturbation, which would have been incorrect, not to mention brutally embarrassing.) Now, as Bob pushed away his empty plate and wiped the red rhubarb blood from his chin, I decided to take the same tack and defer the next line of questioning to Jess.

"The Oneida Community was a fascinating group of people that we've been hearing about at the Mansion House," Jess said. "What do you think of a spa and resort with a theme from that era?"

CHAPTER 26

Somewhere in my travels, I learned that people do not always react the way you expect they will. It's not like that with dogs or goldfish. Whenever I throw a bone to my dog, Saxy, the tail-wagging hound is *always* all over it before it hits the ground. Same thing with goldfish, except I swap the bone for fish food and the little orange dudes fly straight to the top of the tank to suck up those tiny corn flakes as if it was their last meal. People are different, as our second lunch in Sherrill was about to prove.

For the past hour, Arlen Bensinger's tail–his Mayoral exuberance–had been banging the backside of his chair nonstop *until* Jess pitched her idea. That was when his smile vanished. He pulled back from the table, folded his arms and let out a frustrated sigh as his face turned suspicious. He then said, "What kind of resorts do you folks run?"

"What do you mean?" I asked.

"Exactly what you think I mean," Arlen said before repeating the question.

Jess and I exchanged puzzled looks. I then glanced at Bob Applewhite who now mirrored Arlen's look of wariness. I really wasn't sure what Arlen was insinuating and it didn't appear that Jess did either. I answered, "The standard resort, you know, relaxing fun in the sun. A little pleasure; a little pampering; and a lot of great food like lobster and rhubarb pie." I aimed my last shot at Bob, hoping to pull him over to our side. It didn't work.

Arlen continued his cross-examination, "What kind of *pleasure*?"

"It was just a figure of speech," I said. "We want our guests to have fun; to have an experience they can't have anywhere else."

"Like *Free Love in Utopia* fun?" Bob asked as Arlen nodded in agreement.

"Oh," I said exaggeratedly, "now I see where you're going." I did finally see where the mayor and deputy mayor were going but I wasn't sure that was where Jess and I wanted to go. They were imagining giant hot tubs full of naked sex mongers, and probably not what Jess had in mind when she had made the suggestion minutes ago. Unsure, I deferred to Jess again since a resort with an Oneida Community theme had been her idea in the first place.

I watched a mischievous look dance across Jess's face as she said, "Well, we've never had anything like that before, but it certainly is an interesting proposition, now that you mention it. What do you think, Mick?"

Jess caught me off guard and I rolled in my seat as I cleared my throat to buy some time while the lingerie models in my thoughts scurried into their shadowy bedrooms. I certainly had no issue with the concept. The question was–did the mayor? I quickly concluded the only way to find out was to play along with Jess. I raised an eyebrow and said, "It certainly would be a *unique* experience and that *is* our trademark." I then joined Jess in her inviting gaze at our lunch companions as they rubbed their hands and bit their lips.

I've heard it suggested that politicians sometimes believe one thing but say something else, but I had never actually seen it happen with my own two eyes until Arlen Bensinger, the Mayor of Sherrill, attempted to field the economic prospect that had just been laid in front of him. Clearly, he was uncomfortable with the idea a mirrored ceiling, satin-sheeted, hedonistic Motel 6 popping up in the heart of his little Silver City but that was not what he ended up saying. After collecting himself while consulting the

"Politics for Dummies" reference guide he had, undoubtedly, committed to memory, he finally said, "We would have to give that some thought, wouldn't we, Bob. But it certainly sounds like one hell of an idea. Just keep in mind there are three other members of the City Commission besides Bob and I, so even if we love the idea, they could shoot it down just like that." He snapped his fingers for affect.

"It would certainly bring some new money into the area," I said.

"Yes, it certainly would do that," Arlen replied.

"What are *your* thoughts on the Oneida Community, Arlen," Jess asked, pointedly. "You don't mind if I call you Arlen, do you?"

The mayor stuttered, saying, "Ah, no...I mean, yes, please do."

A silence then followed. It seemed that Jess' question was seen as nothing more than a passing sneeze, a heart-stopping explosion that is forgotten seconds after it strikes, as Arlen stood up and placed a triplet of tens onto the table. Bob also rose to his feet, as then did Jess and I. After exchanging handshakes and expressing their desires to talk again, they left.

Leaning over toward Jess, I said discreetly, "Another suspect?"

"I don't think the mayor would kill anyone, it would be too harmful to his budding political career," Jess replied, irritated that her question had been ignored.

We sat back down.

"He wouldn't do it himself," I said. "He'd have one of his boys take care of it, like Bob."

"Be serious."

"I'm sorry; the two of them were just so funny. Did you notice them squirming as soon as the Oneida Community was mentioned?"

"Yeah, that was unusual. Everyone else in town talks about it as easy as the weather. What's the bug up their asses?"

"A resurrection perhaps?" I said with a wry grin.

Jess just looked at me. She was thinking about it and then said, "I know I keep saying this but I wish we knew which way Mel was spinning her story about the Community."

"I already know," I said.

"You do! Why didn't you tell me? Did you find her story?"

"No, and I don't know for a fact what she wrote but I know Mel well enough to make an educated guess. And you do, too."

Jess didn't respond initially, but after a few moments she nodded knowingly and said, "You're right, I do know what her spin would have been. Something just like the story she did on my precinct that she called 'Cops on Parade'."

The story was unfolding right before our eyes just as I imagined it had for my sister. The original founders of this community were outcasts in need of a champion, and there was no doubt in my mind how Mel would have written it as I listened to Jess say what I felt in my own heart, "Mel would have made the Utopians look like heroes."

CHAPTER 27

Jess and I had only been in Sherrill for a day and a half but already we were both beginning to side with the Oneida Community. It seemed irrational but then I have always rooted for the underdog and the Community certainly fit the description. Only within the Mansion House had we found kind words from the people we had encountered. Outside, the walls appeared to be surrounded by an army of high-minded moralists and tight-assed prudes that were proving to be an easy target for my sarcastic wit. Still sitting at the restaurant table, Jess was near jovial tears from my barrage of mordant pokes and jabs when another lunch patron approached us.

"Excuse me, I didn't mean to eavesdrop but I heard you talking to the mayor about bringing a business into town and I wondered if I might have a word?"

He was a tall, broad-shouldered man, ten to fifteen years my senior, I guessed by the dusting of grey mixed into his short, black hair, and he wore a navy blue windbreaker over a sky blue button-down shirt that bulged a bit around his middle. His tan khakis had several short black lines drawn haphazardly near the pockets, (accidental pen marks I assumed,) and his brown leather shoes looked heavily worn, ready to be put down. His smile was genuine, and Jess invited him to join us.

I noticed he had a soft voice for such a large man as he said, "The word around town is you folks are in the spa and resort business."

"Yes, we are," I said, extending my hand across the table. "Mick Hartwell, and this is my wife, Jessica."

"But please call me Jess," she quickly interjected as she shook the man's hand. "We were married on Saturday. Now we're on our honeymoon and thoroughly enjoying our visit here."

"It's nice to meet you, Mick and Jess. My name is Charlie Walinski and I think I need to apologize for not introducing myself when I first walked over." He then chuckled in a contagious way that reminded me of Barney Rubble. It immediately set Jess and I at ease. "I'm terrible at introductions, just ask my wife."

Jess said, "Before Mick begins to bore you with the story of our courtship, I want you to know we just love this city. It must be such a wonderful place to live."

"I've lived here my whole life and I can honestly say it is," Charlie said proudly. "Forty-five years and I wouldn't change a day of it!"

I felt a little guilty about the lie I was about to utter but I knew I had to; "I like your attitude, Charlie. If we build here, I want you to come and work for us."

Charlie laughed again, triggering Jess and me to join in.

"So, the rumors I've heard are true?" He asked.

"It is, if it's the one about us building a spa and resort so sweet you'll want to sell your home and move right in!" I replied.

"Well, I didn't catch everything the Mayor told you, but the fact is we've fallen on hard times in recent years here in Sherrill and any boost to the local economy would be a welcome one."

Jess said, "Where do you work, Charlie?"

"I'm an accountant with Oneida Limited, the silverware maker here in Sherrill. We have a whole line of other tableware products, but stainless steel flatware and fine silver dinnerware–silverware–is how most people recognize us. Normally, you would find me there right now, banging away on my calculator, but I've got the week off to spend some time with my kids. The four of them are on some kind of spring break, but as you can see by my presence here, I'm the one who needs the break."

"So you're the ones who make the *good silver*," I said, recalling the altercation with the Mansion House dining hall attendant.

"We are indeed," Charlie said. "The most recognized brand in the country, if not the world, and the official flatware used by Congress."

"Congress? Really?" Jess said.

"I know I'm sounding like a braggart now, and my wife hates it when I do, but we donated a set of Community Silver to Congress back in '87 and they've been using it ever since, at least that's what my Senator keeps telling me so I won't vote for someone else. A specialty steel lobbying group delivered one hundred and eighty place settings to Washington. There was a huge luncheon that kicked off right after everyone in attendance gathered up the existing Japanese flatware and ceremoniously tossed it all into a trash can." Charlie had a big smile on his face as he added, "I wish I could have been there to see that."

"Community Silver?" Jess asked.

"That's what we used to call our silverware back then. It's a reference to the Oneida Community. They're the folks who built the Mansion House where I understand you two are staying. They started making silverware over one hundred and thirty years ago, in 1877 if I remember my employee manual correctly. It grew from there into a household name."

"The free-love Utopians built that multi-million dollar business?" I asked, hoping my intentionally rude remark would reveal which side of the fence Charlie sat on. He responded with another infectious Barney Rumble laugh, which gave Jess and me a clue.

Charlie shook his head as his laugh subsided and said, "They weren't nearly as wild as some people around here would like you to think they were."

"There does seem to be a condemnatory public opinion," Jess said. "That's what we've experienced so far."

"I would call it judgmental," I added. "Some comments we've heard make the Mansion House sound like a 19th century version of Hugh Hefner's Playboy Mansion, complete with silk pajama parties on the front lawn and orgies every Saturday night."

"That's just the hard times talking. People look for answers in lean times and when they can't afford the new car they were planning on buying, they look for a place to vent their frustration. The folks that have lived here a while know exactly what the Community brought to the table, if you'll pardon the pun." Charlie then winked at me, saying, "I get my wife with that one every time."

"They were a big part of the local economy, by the sound of it," Jess said.

"They *were* the local economy for a long time. My dad once told me that back in the 20's and 30's, before the war, almost every household in Sherrill had at lease one family member working at the Limited, as they used to call it. There were twenty-five hundred employees at one time here in Central New York and another fifteen hundred scattered around Mexico, Canada and Northern Ireland. Annual revenues peeked at nearly a half billion dollars at one time or another which enabled them to pay half the city taxes at one point and build an electrical grid that the city now operates to provide the residents with cheap hydro power supplied by the State. Not bad for a bunch of lascivious Communists," he said with another wink.

Everyone here likes that word lascivious.

"Geez, Jess, maybe we could be part of the Community. It sounds profitable," I said. I then turned to Charlie and said tongue-in-cheek, "Are they still accepting membership applications?"

"Well, the original Community broke up around 1880 and I'm afraid all that's left is that big house on the hill that rented you a room and a thousand and one stories," Charlie replied. "And only about four hundred of us left working in the area for the company now."

"That's terrible," Jess said. "What happened?"

"It was a bunch of things that I promised my wife I won't rant about to strangers, but in a nutshell it was overseas competition and a sluggish U.S. economy. Then, we lost millions in sales when the airline industry removed flatware from planes after the terrorist attacks on the World Trade Center. Just one more straw to an already overburdened camel's back."

"Maybe we could start a new Community," Jess said.

Charlie's ensuing laugh echoed through the empty restaurant, triggering a giggle from the lone waitress prepping tables for dinner. I got a sense it wasn't because he thought the idea ridiculous. Unlike his other outbursts, this one had a nervous edge to it, as did his eyes as they drifted out the window and into the rain that had just started up again for the first time since we had come in. I thought of the anonymous letter to Mel's editor warning of a rebirth of the Communists. Had it been sent by Charlie? Or, perhaps, Charlie was *part* of the rebirth? He did say that people look for answers during lean times. Could a new, modern day Oneida Community revitalize the struggling Sherrill, bring back the luster to the Silver City? How would Mel's story have helped or hurt? There were still a lot of unanswered questions and even though the afternoon had provided a wealth of new information, the murder's trail was still invisible. I was feeling antsy. It was definitely time for a beer.

CHAPTER 28

The mood in the City of Sherrill Mayor's office was light considering the mayor, Arlen Bensinger, had just called an emergency meeting at a time when he and the others gathered would normally be sitting down to dinner with their families. During his tenure in office, Arlen's handpicked advisors, unofficial as they were, had all come to learn that Arlen was a worrier and, more times than not, his exaggerated fretting was not worthy of their own perspiration. His motives were ninety-nine percent political and so his *emergency* meetings tended to be "damage control exercises," as he himself liked to call them, aimed at appeasing riled voters concerned over the rising price of a dog license or a parking ticket. Today they arrived as usual, thinking they could easily settle Arlen down and get back home before their meals got cold. They were about to discover that this meeting fell into the one percent category that would soon have them all sweating.

Bob Applewhite, the deputy mayor, had made the phone calls only minutes ago and sat at the round, walnut-veneered table tucked snuggly into one corner of the mayor's modest office with the Reverend James Newland on his right and the City Historian, Harold Smith to his left. The mayor, who had been admiring the photographs of George W. Bush and Ronald Reagan that adorned his credenza when his confidants arrived, joined them by taking the last remaining seat directly across from Bob.

"We have another situation," Arlen said in a serious tone.

Harold and Reverend Newland both turned to Bob and, upon seeing his somber expression, instantly realized that this wasn't just another instance of Arlen crying wolf.

"Another reporter?" Harold asked.

"No, worse," Bob replied. "A married pair of Donald Trump wannabes, some Gen-X couple with more money than they know what to do with. They tripped over Sherrill on their way to God knows where, and now they've got their wallet poised to set up a spa and resort with an Oneida Community theme. They've been staying at the Mansion House where I'm sure the staff and residents have been filling their heads with all kinds of wild ideas."

"Have you spoken to them?" Reverend Newland asked. "The young couple, I mean."

"Bob and I met with them earlier today after they had been brought into the police station for taking a library book," Arlen said. He then glared at Harold, as he said, "Which I don't think was necessary *or* advantageous."

"I was just doing my job," Harold said, indignantly.

"Your job is to keep the records in order, not piss off the tourists," Arlen snapped.

Harold shot back, "We don't need *their* kind here."

"And what kind is that, Harold?" Bob asked.

Harold was quick and adamant with his reply, saying, "Decadent bed hoppers; a salacious horde of immoral thrill seekers. Lascivious is what they are; the whole lot of them."

"Harold, we've discussed this before," Bob said. "Not everyone who visits here fits into that category and we can't treat them all as if they did."

The Reverend calmly interjected, saying, "We *do* have an obligation to the community to maintain the highest level of Christian morality that we possibly can. Turning a blind eye to lascivious behavior would be a sin worse than the perversion itself."

"I don't think Bob is suggesting we turn a blind eye," Arlen said. "He and I both understand that Sherrill is ninety-three percent Christian and that we need to be attentive to their concerns. But we also have many small business owners who like the tourist traffic and they have a voice, too."

"A vote you mean," Harold retorted.

Arlen's face grew flush with anger as he said, "Look, I don't have to justify to you...."

The Reverend cut him off, saying, "Simmer down, gentleman. We are all on the same side here–God's side. We can manage these two lustful strays just as we handled that reporter."

The room fell silent momentarily as the four men reflected on the woman reporter's death that had occurred the previous week. Her accidental death brought immediate attention to her presence, which up until then had been a well-guarded secret, sending a wave of gossip rippling through the city as to why she had been there in the first place. Arlen had called an emergency meeting the next morning and they had been working on damage control ever since, squelching the rumor mill as best they could. The word around town was that the reporter had taken a real shine to the Oneida Community and was preparing a very flattering expose. "Such blasphemy would have caused the licentious locust to descend upon our fields in unprecedented numbers," the Reverend Newland had stated firmly at the time. His posture today was beginning to take on the same look of consternation.

"We didn't really handle that situation, as much as we got lucky," Bob said.

"It was a terrible tragedy," Arlen said. He had met Mel once for lunch where they had talked about the city mostly and its struggling economy. She was about his age and a good listener, he recalled. Mel had reminded him a little of his wife, who had been a journalism major in college with plans of pursing a writing career before meeting Arlen and venturing into the baby manufacturing business. A father of three youngsters, Arlen took the news of Mel's death hard not only because it happened in his city, but because he had honestly liked her–more than he had admitted to anyone.

"Yes, it truly was," The Reverend added. "But that woman would have led the devil to our doorstep, however good her intentions may have been."

Arlen and Bob nodded in concurrence.

Harold was still clearly agitated as he said, "I told you it was a bad idea to send that anonymous letter to the newspaper. The press never sides with the church. According to them, we're always on a witch hunt. They would have berated and mocked us just as they had the clergy that went after the original Oneida Community."

"We had no reason to believe that any reporter in their right mind would not make a beeline for the sex element of a story when it's clearly available," Bob said. "That's what sells newspapers in today's world. I'll bet you dollars to donuts that her editor would have made her spice her story up before he printed it, if she hadn't sexed it up already."

"Well, we'll never know," Arlen said. "The police chief told me the laptop Harriet Kinney said she had seen the reporter with came up missing. He also said the woman's editor has called him several times asking that they keep an eye open for it because she had never sent him a copy of her story."

"It was probably grabbed by one of the kids who are always wandering through the Mansion House," Bob suggested, "or one of the housekeepers."

"A story exposing that lascivious lot would have been a good thing, if you ask me," Harold said, his eyes twitching nervously.

"Maybe," Bob said, undecidedly.

The Reverend James Newland then rose to his feet and stepped away from the table. He was a towering man, solid as a redwood tree with a chiseled face and riveting grayish blue eyes that could steal attention like a flash of lightening whenever he took to the pulpit. A sermon was swelling within him now as he turned to the men and said in a thunderous voice, "Then Jesus was led by the Spirit into the desert to be tempted by the devil!"

"The Lord is challenging us, testing our will and commitment to his words. Jesus knew what to do and, hence, so do we," his voice then erupted again, "Away from me, Satan! For it is written; 'Worship the Lord your God, and serve only Him.'"

The lights remained on in mayor's office well into the wee hours of the night.

CHAPTER 29

Under the premise that we needed to continue digging for evidence of an Oneida Community reborn, I convinced Jess to ride up the big hill I had hiked up and down the night before to grab a drink and see what other mosquitoes might be out looking for a spot of blood. So far, the day had proved very fruitful and I was feeling quite proud of myself for all the hard work I could only vaguely remember from my not-so-secret late-night prowl. I had no doubt that Jess gave me credit for baiting our hook so nicely, but I wasn't going to hold my breath waiting for her to openly acknowledge it. The fact that she had so agreeably consented to a beer run was enough applause for my ego and as we pulled up to the bar, its warm neon glow beckoning me to slip into its embrace, I looked at Jess and felt another urge to share a little more with her.

It was only about four in the afternoon and the place nearly deserted, except for Shelley, the owner, who was standing at attention behind the bar like a Buckingham Palace Guard, her right arm poised on the beer tap, cocked and ready to pour. *Her libatious sixth sense must have tipped my arrival.*

"I was hoping you'd be back, Mick," she said with a big smile. "Same flavor as yesterday?"

I glanced at Jess tentatively and upon receiving an indifferent nod, I told Shelley to pour away. We sat down at the bar.

"And you've brought your wife today," Shelley said as she delivered a white-capped pitcher of beer and two frosted mugs. "I've heard a *god-awful* lot about you, Jess." Then she laughed.

Shelley's friendly little jab told me that somewhere during the course of last night's intoxicant-fueled conversation with her I must have mentioned Jess' frequent use of the term *god-awful*. Sitting there now as I was at Shelley's mercy, I only hoped that I had told her how endearing I thought that habit was. I also prayed that I hadn't said anything embarrassing that might now suddenly spring from Shelley's mouth like the bare breasts of a party girl during Mardi Gras.

"Oh, really," Jess said, raising an eyebrow. "What has he been telling you?"

As it turns out, Shelley, the middle-aged flirt with the pink and black hair, was a hopeless romantic at heart. She told Jess how I cherished her smile and lusted for her body, comparing it to that of Venus, the Goddess of Love. I was at full blush by the time she finished with a remark about how I had said her intelligence made me tingle all over. All the while Shelley's voice resonated in a longing envy that had me twisting in my seat as if I were sitting on a sleeping porcupine. I began to wonder how much I had drunk and if Jess believed any of it. *So much for bartender-patron privilege.*

When Shelley left us to retrieve bar snacks for the soon to arrive happy-hour crowd, I leaned toward Jess and began some disorganized damage control.

"I was just playing my role as the goo-goo eyed husband," I said, before apologizing for getting a little carried away.

Jess took a sip from her beer, looming at me from the corner of her eye.

"That's not to say I don't honestly think you have a nice figure, because I do, I mean...." I stopped, noticing she was now eyeing me in the mirror behind the bar. She was grinning–looking right through me–and before I could say another word, she put the thawing mug to her lips, this time pulling a little longer at its golden innards. She wasn't buying a word of it.

I then filled my glass a second time and did what any red-blooded man would do when he has put his foot in his mouth–I acted nonchalant about the whole thing.

Ending my torment, Jess said, "Relax, I'm not going to hold you to any of it."

"Well, at least I didn't tell her about your nickname, Lollipop," I laughed nervously. I then followed her advice, settling into my bar stool eager for my face to de-blush. It did, about fifteen minutes later just as a familiar face walked in. Charlie Walinski spotted us immediately and strolled right over.

"Long time, no see," he said. He ordered a shot of whiskey from Shelley, declining my offer to share our beer with him.

"I can't stay but a minute," he said hurriedly before downing his drink. "I'm taking the wife and kids over to my mother-in-law's for the evening. She's a sweet old lady but her thirteen cats drive me up the wall. I can't move a muscle without stepping or sitting on one of them."

"What are you doing here then?" Jess asked.

"My wife sent me over for a quick attitude realignment," he said and then he was gone, though his laugh lingered like the smell of my mother's baked bread.

"That means we won't get a chance to cross examine him tonight," I said.

Jess sighed, "Yeah, I wanted to ask him more about how the Community got into the silverware business."

"He can't be the only one around here that knows the history," I said. "We need to scope out the City Historian, whoever that might be."

"That would be me."

I turned to my right and, looking past Jess, I saw a woman–maybe ten or so years younger than my mother—sitting a few stools over with a martini glass in her hand. She had a vibrant look about her, which I noticed right away, appearing slim and shapely in a black jogging outfit. Her shoulder-length stylish haircut looked youthful, though, not inappropriate for her age. Her small comfortable smile glowed with a subtle confidence and ease. She had that aura of friendliness, an oasis to tourists like Jess and I, reminding me of the one lone relative that I actually *enjoyed* talking to at our annual family reunion–cousin what's her name.

"Well, I used to be anyway," the woman added, "up until the first of the year when my husband took over the job." She threw her purse over her shoulder and with martini in hand, slid over one chair and sat down next to Jess, saying, "Hi, I'm Dorothy Smith and I'll bet you two are the wealthy entrepreneurs the whole town is buzzing about."

Jess and I tried to appear humble as we introduced ourselves and fed Dorothy our shtick about a spa and resort venture in Sherrill. It was the third time that day that we had recited it for an audience and I noticed that both our performances were starting to wane. I was frustrated and Jess looked it, too. Sherrill was interested in our money all right, just as any struggling city would be, but so far, the encounters hadn't unearthed a single clue about Mel's death–a few flimsy suspects, but not solid leads. I wasn't even close to quitting yet, but there was an urgency building, nagging at me from the back of my brain to push harder, to ask more pointed questions.

I decided to stir the pot, asking, "What's the bug up everyone's ass about the Oneida Community?"

Dorothy didn't flinch, giving me the impression she had been asked this very question a few times before. She stared thoughtfully at the two olives suspended in her glass and then replied, "Would you like the long version or the short version?"

"How about the short version to start with," Jess said. "And then we'll let you know about the long version."

"Sex," Dorothy said. "It's all about sex."

The Mansion House
October 1867

The liberated maple leaves blanketed the quadrangle in a dazzling, patchwork-quilt display of crimson and gold. *Fallen stars*, she thought as she watched a rebellious band deliver a spirited, swirling dance provoked by the evening's gusting breeze. The air smelled of autumn, cool and crisp. The orange sun was going down, its watchful eye closing, bidding goodnight to the East Coast of America.

Admiring the ebbing day through her third floor bedroom window, she could feel her heart trembling. She noticed a young man striding across the yard in confident, purposeful steps. Her heart quickened another beat, though she thought it impossible. He paused, peering up at her window, a knowing smile breaking through the resolute surface. Any doubts she had vanished as he continued on his mission, disappearing beneath her feet as she gazed down upon the sea of glittering stars.

A long, anxious moment passed. Then, steady footsteps in the hallway outside her unlocked door, quiet at first, but growing louder with each tick of the clock she kept on her dresser. It was nearing seven as the possessor approached. They would have an hour, perhaps two. *Would that be enough?* She thought. *Somehow*, she attempted to convince herself, *it would have to be.*

Never had Sarah felt as intoxicated as the evening she first met Henry several months ago. He was only nineteen, fourteen years her junior, but held the carriage of a much older and experienced man. Tall, with dark features and a settled face that belied his years, Henry's eager black eyes had captured her the moment she had entered the Great Hall, never leaving her own as he laid his talents as a violinist before her during a night of music and theatrical skits. Enchanted, she watched him play all night, knowing completely that the thrusts of his bow offered much more than the fevered notes from the sweltering strings of his instrument.

Sarah loved music, a passion she had been unable to share with her husband, Edward. She played the piano, though not very well, she would readily concede, but admired anyone who had unraveled its mystery. Clearly, Henry had and with it held the key to Sarah's secret heart.

She watched the doorknob turn, her anxious lips quivering as the young man stepped through the threshold, illuminated only by the soft amber flame of the hurricane lantern resting quietly beside the empty bed. In a whisper, the two shadows fused and the walls of light flickered, excited by the suddenly churning air. Tentative fingers floated across flushed cheeks, fervent eyes probed for something they had both long for but had never seen. *Utopia.*

Bridling his youthful spirit, she pulled him in, kissing him for the first time, long and deep, filling herself hungrily. She then reached up, took his hand from her face and led him to the bed where she had him sit on the white beddings she had washed in lavender soap that very morning. Slowly, she unbuttoned her dress, unwrapping herself before him, offering herself to him just as he had from the orchestral stage so many days and aching nights ago.

"Slowly," she whispered as their song began. "Adagio, adagio."

She slid her hands down his arching back and dug them into his burning flesh, quieting the tempo of his slender hips into her own. *I will teach you, my darling,* Sarah thought, *you must only listen and obey.*

As the lantern's flame danced wildly in Henry's widened eyes, his short, moaning breathes leaping from his lips, Sarah knew he was uncontrollable. He was possessed–possessed by her–and so she would let him take what he wanted, this first time. Overcome by Henry's melody, Sarah emptied her mind and let her soaring body sing with his.

"Yes," she moaned, "Vivace! Vivace!"

Later, lying by his side, she wiped a tiny bead of sweat from Henry's brow. He was everything she had imagined and she wanted nothing more than to fall asleep in his arms. But Sarah knew that was forbidden. John had been very specific about that during one of his recent talks published in the Community newspaper and, besides, she had already committed one sin by allowing her young lover to spill his seed. She dared not risk another by spending the night with him.

"You'll have to go soon," Sarah said.

"I know," Henry replied unhappily. "John's says that we should leave the table while our appetite is still good, but I don't want to."

Sarah smiled and burrowed deeper into his smooth chest. She didn't want him to leave either, exciting her and worrying her at the same time. She had not shared her sleep with a man for several years, not even her husband. The Community held that for the sake of love it was best that the sexes should sleep apart and so she had kept her own room for some time. "Over familiarity dulls the edge of sexual passion," she recalled John commenting on the matter. Surprisingly, Sarah had found the practice liberating, but the thought of Henry slipping from her grasp tonight pulled jaggedly at her core.

With Henry's pulse rushing loudly beneath her ear, Sarah squeezed him tightly, wishing only that she could weave him into the sheets now soaked in his musky scent, crafting a warming embrace to cover her forever. *Was this overpowering ache what John contemptuously called "special love?"* she thought? A "good woman" in the covenanted Community did not hold one man in such favor over any other the way she now coveted Henry. A Community woman did not allow such passion to circumvent her scriptural obligation–her duty to conform to the expected practices of the group–to love everyone equally. Sarah had seen how the "marriage spirit" brought jealousies, causing some women to lose their equilibrium. *Would she die inside if another woman touched Henry the way she just had?*

With a deep sigh, Sarah closed her eyes and listened anxiously to Henry's slowly calming heart. In less than an hour, she would have to send him away.

CHAPTER 30

Dorothy Smith, the former City of Sherrill Historian, certainly knew her history. After I had requested the long-version answer to my question (her short answer only served to raise my curiosity more, which I'm sure was her intention), Dorothy went on to explain what she called the "sexual system" practiced by the Oneida Community in the mid 1800's. The more she told Jess and me, the more it sounded like she was describing a commune of hippies in the 1960's, a rebellious band of flower children living in San Francisco during the Summer of Love. It sounded like a love-in.

But the people of the Oneida Community lived during the Civil War, when the debate over slavery and the power of the national government rose to a hideous, blood-spilling level. I couldn't recall anything from my high school history classes about an alternative lifestyle movement in America that rejected existing marriage and sex-role practices for a religious based substitute. According to Dorothy, as opposed to my high school faculty, Pre-Civil War America was one of major social transition much deeper than the depth officially taught to teenagers. In New York alone, there were the polygamous Mormons, the Shakers (who practiced celibacy), and the Oneida Community, where the theory of "Complex Marriage" originated. These groups and others, Dorothy said, comprised the white water of religious and social diversity that tipped and tossed the righteous boat of mainstream society, nearly capsizing it.

"I'm not sure if I understand it, this *Complex Marriage* thing," I said. "I work better with examples, so if you'll indulge me for a moment, let me pose a what-if scenario, and this is strictly hypothetical, you understand."

"Ok," Dorothy replied, with a tentative grin, "strictly hypothetical."

Jess had a nervous look as well, but I knew she was as interested as I was as to how this marriage theory worked, so she kept quiet.

I said, "Let say it's 1860-whatever and Jess and I have just joined the ranks of the Oneida Community. We're already married, but we enter the group agreeing to abide by all the rules and regulations set forth by Mr. John Humphrey Noyes, the founder, including the Complex Marriage thing. Now we're sitting at dinner the first night with the whole clan and wondering what we're suppose to do next. Do we just wink at another Community member, pair up, and disappear into the depths of the Mansion House to mate like giant pandas in a Chinese zoo?"

Dorothy laughed and said, "Heavens, no. You've been reading too much of that free love rhetoric the biographers are so preoccupied with. Sexual relations were much more controlled than that."

I felt a little let down, showing my disappointment as I said, "So, if I see a hottie in a satin hoop skirt I can't bust a move on her right then and there?"

"Well, you could, but John would probably kick you out," Dorothy replied.

"Was he in charge of hooking couples up?" Jess asked, perceptively.

Dorothy hesitated, giving me the impression this was a sensitive subject, before saying, "I've read things that lean both ways on that issue but there's enough evidence to suggest he presented the loudest and most authoritative voice."

"Ok," I said. "For argument sake, let's say John gives me the green light–his full approval and blessing to woo the object of my affection."

Jess jumped in, saying with a hint of jealousy, "Or gives me the go ahead to dally with a young gentleman."

I must have reacted disapprovingly, because both women gave me a look as if I had just told them they were not smart enough to vote.

"It did work both ways," Dorothy said. "Women had equal status in the Community. They owned property, worked shoulder to shoulder with the men, and had the right to voice their opinions even if it was criticism of the men."

Outnumbered two to one, I said, "I stand corrected. If Jess or I, or *both*, start courting someone else, what happens to *our* marriage?"

"Nothing, really," Dorothy said. "Your marriage prior to joining the Community was a legality of the outside world, if I dare call it that. In the Community, each member was married to all members and sexual intercourse was considered a method of ordinary conversation."

"Like discussing the weather?" I asked, "Or the firmness of the scrabbled eggs at breakfast?"

"That was the theory," Dorothy answered.

"But that sounds like free love to me," Jess said. "And defenders of the Community we've met don't seem to like that characterization."

"It's the word *free* that clouds the issue and sets the fur to flying," Dorothy said. "Complex Marriage was a lot of things, but it was anything *but* free."

I was confused, scrunching my face as I said, "I can sleep with my wife and other women at the same time...but not freely?"

"First of all, as new members, John wouldn't just hook you up with anybody and everybody. The pairing had to be mutually concentual as well as innocuous to the harmony of the group."

"You mean harmless in terms of stirring up jealousy?" Jess

asked.

"That *was* a big challenge for many of the initial converts to the Community who were previously unaware of the unorthodox sexual practices that existed. Many people deserted John in the beginning, at first attracted by his religious beliefs but then repulsed by his theory of marriage, Biblical Communist as he sometimes referred to it, a concept widely believed to be immoral in every sense of the word. The goal of the Community was for all the members to love each other both passionately and physically without the exclusiveness of pairs as with a traditional marriage or coupling. John believed that to overcome human selfishness, one had to submit to the will of God and that faithful Christians should relinquish restricting marital ties. So, as long as the motives of the man and woman requesting approval were in alignment with that—they weren't looking to get engaged or "go steady" — then they got the green light, as you say."

"I think most men would be fairly happy with that rule," I said. "No strings attached sex!"

"Yes, I would agree with you there," Dorothy said. "But I don't think you'd have been real keen on some of the other rules, which is where the part about the system not being free comes into play."

"One of the big concerns in the Oneida Community was uncontrolled pregnancies, propagation as it was commonly referred to in those times. There were no birth control pills back in the mid-1800's or devices as we have now, so abstinence and coitus interruptus were the primary methods of the time. John and his flock were not about to abstain, and John himself believed vehemently that ejaculating after withdrawal from the woman was a waste of a man's seed and vital powers. So, and this is the part you'll like, Mick," Dorothy said with a wry grin, "John instituted the practice of what he called 'Male Continence'. Coitus reservatus–birth control by self-control. The male was not allowed to achieve orgasm—before, during or after sex, unless of course the woman *was* trying to get pregnant."

"I'm out!" I yelped. Dorothy was right. The Community's sexual system *was* anything but free and I conveyed my impression by groaning, "That's too big a price for me."

"But the woman could have all the orgasms she wanted?" Jess asked.

Dorothy took on a thoughtful look and said, "You know, I never thought about it that way before but, yes, I guess the woman could have all she wanted."

"You wouldn't have lasted five minutes," Jess said, laughing at me.

"Self-control is a lot easier said than done," I said as I tried to imagine doing it myself. *No orgasms? That would be like intentionally shaking a bottle of soda over and over for years but never removing the cap. Sooner or later you know what would happen.*

Dorothy said, "It's funny that you should say that because that became another challenge for them–controlling the younger people's unbridled passions. Youthful hormones raced just as fast then as they do today."

Just then, Shelley the bartender interrupted, asking if we all needed another round. I quickly replied yes before Jess could utter a word. With a fresh martini loaded up with double olives in her hand, Dorothy continued with her off-the-cuff symposium, speaking like a well-seasoned professor at an Ivy League college with Jess and me her completely captivated students.

"Before I get into *how* the Community harnessed the young adults, I think it is important to understand why it was considered necessary in the first place. The Oneida Community was, in part, an experiment in eugenic breeding. They planned their pregnancies as much for hereditary control as for the quantity of children being born. Times were hard back then and additional mouths to feed only made it tougher, just like it does today for many families. So, learning self-control— 'Male Continence'–the ability to suppress ejaculation was essential to controlling the quality and size of the population. Believe it or not, it worked quite well. The Community survived the hard times and prospered, more so than any of the other seventy-some social experiments that existed in America in the nineteenth century."

"The pressure was all on the men, by the sound of it," I said. "It gives a whole new meaning to the phrase *taking one for the team.*"

Dorothy said, "That was one of the key responsibilities the men had in the Community; self-control for the good of the group; birth control, plain and simple, not to mention an effective approach to suppress the spread of sexually-transmitted disease; a *strength of will* condom."

"A poor man's condom would be a better description," I said.

"It sounds like a mature approach to me," Jess said. She then raised her glass and tinged it against Dorothy's in a solidarity salute.

"Well, to be honest," I said. "If I'm a young man in that Community looking to pop my cherry, the last thing on my mind is holding back the pop."

"Is he always this reserved?" Dorothy laughed, looking at Jess.

"No," Jess replied as she pulled away the half-full pitcher of beer. Her eyes spewed fire at me as she said, "Only when he drinks too much before dinner."

"I'm sorry, Dorothy," I said. "Let me rephrase that. A man's primal urge is to procreate, which means spreading his seed. Our bodies aren't built to hold it in, we'd explode!"

"Oh, please!" Jess sighed. "That is the most god-awful excuse I've ever heard. I'd be willing to bet there isn't one documented case in the history of the world where a man exploded from an excessive accumulation of unspent sperm."

"Willy Williams, August 14, 2002," I said.

"Who?" The two women chimed.

"Willy Williams. He was a kid I knew growing up. He took over my paper route when I was twelve and never gave it up until he died at the age of twenty-six. The official cause of death was testicular cancer, but I happen to know that Willy died a virgin and everybody knows the side effects of that. So, read between the lines, ladies."

The two of them erupted into laughter. They knew my story was bullshit, but it gave me an opportunity to slip past Jess' guard and retrieve the beer pitcher.

Jess and Dorothy eventually calmed before Dorothy said, "In all fairness to you, Mick, the Community openly confessed that self-control was not an easy thing to do. It was an acquired skill that required training and practice."

"Training?" I asked.

"Practice?" Jess added, blushing.

Dorothy's eyes, which had been engaging and direct since introducing herself to us, suddenly turned away as a shy smile stole across her face. It appeared that she found the subject as embarrassing as we did, but after a moment, she explained it nonetheless.

"They felt the best way to transition the young adults from the hot blood of virginity to the quiet freedom of Complex Marriage was to have the older, more spiritual members of the Community who had already mastered carnal constraint teach them."

Jess looked shocked as she said, "Sex education?"

"Literally," Dorothy said.

"Wow," I said. "And I always thought the kids who were home-schooled got screwed, no pun intended."

Dorothy added, "The men would introduce the practice of Male Continence to the young adult women and the women would train the young men."

Jess' face flashed with excitement as she turned to me and said, "The women got to train the young men? I guess I was born a hundred years too late."

"Not necessarily," Dorothy grinned, before the two women broke into laughter once again.

There was a pause in the conversation as we all sipped our drinks. This Oneida Community had grown more complicated with every turn and I wondered what Mel had thought of it all. She was shy when it came to sex, turning beet red whenever I told a dirty joke or asked a boyfriend of hers if he had seen her yet in her black, patent-leather dominatrix outfit. She didn't have a dress like that or the French maid costume with the ruffled panties that I often jokingly inquired about in mixed company, at least not that I knew of. How had she handled it?

"Where did you learn about all this?" Jess asked.

"There have been countless books written about the Oneida Community," Dorothy replied. "I've read most of them, some two or three times each. Then in 1993, a huge manuscript compiled by George Wallingford Noyes, the founder's nephew, was made available for scholarly review. It shed a whole new light on the inner workings of the Community. It contained all kinds of wonderful stuff–original letters, diaries, documents and bits from the newspaper that they published regularly for years."

"A hundred years later? Why was it kept under wraps for so long?" Jess asked.

"The story goes that back in the 1940s some senior executives at Oneida Limited were more than a bit uncomfortable with the full details of the Community being published. So, they put some sort of legal kibosh on George's manuscript that prevented him from publishing it. Then they burned all kinds of irreplaceable Community documentation, everything they thought damaging. I guess they figured it would prevent more manuscripts from being created."

"Oneida Limited, the silverware manufacturer?" I asked.

"The one and only," Dorothy answered. "The Oneida Community started that company over a hundred years ago."

Jess said, "Yes, we've heard about them. We met someone who works there–Charlie Walinski."

"He's an accountant with the company," I added. "Do you

know him?"

Dorothy laughed, "That Charlie is such a story teller. He bends the ear of everyone who wanders through here. He doesn't work for Oneida, never has. In fact, I think he's out of work right now. He lost his job as janitor at the high school a few months back because he kept trying to mop up the girls' locker room shower–while the girls were still in there!"

"He also told us he had a wife and four kids," Jess said.

Dorothy said, "That part is true, but she packed up the kids and left him years ago. She got tired of him losing jobs and chasing after every woman in town. He comes across like a sweet guy, and that laugh is hysterical, don't you think? But he's at the mercy of his own *dick*-tatorship, if you know what I mean."

"You mean he's a pervert," Jess said.

"Well, I don't like to brand people too harshly," Dorothy said although her expression told Jess she agreed.

I said, "He was just in here, before you came in. But he only stayed a minute."

"Yeah, I saw him leaving when I pulled into the parking lot," Dorothy said, disparagingly. "He was trolling, checking out the bar to see who was here. He does that all the time, more so when he is unemployed, which seems to be every few months. He's lived here for seven or eight years, I think, but he's harmless, all talk."

Damn! I began to wonder if all the things he had told us about the silverware giant were true–the story about their once *being* the local economy and the bit about Congress using their flatware. I said, "Should we believe anything Charlie said to us?"

"Yes, he keeps his historical facts pretty straight," Dorothy said. "He's a nut about local history. When he starts including himself in the story is when you know he's pulling your leg."

"I'm staying away from him," Jess said.

Suddenly, a ghastly vision of Mel jumped into the forefront of my mind. The red creature that had become the symbol of her murder was around her neck and her hand was reaching out to me, her eyes a blaze of terror. A shadowy figure pulled at the snake, squeezing it tighter and tighter, but I couldn't see a face. Was it Charlie? Was Mel trying to tell me it was Charlie Walinski, the village pervert? The lying bastard Charlie that had lured Jess and me into his make believe world. Had he done the same with Mel? Paranoia or not, he just climbed onto my top-ten suspect list, with a bullet.

"Oh, God, look at the time. It's past seven already." Dorothy said, looking at her watch. "My husband got called over to City Hall for a powwow with the mayor just as we were sitting down to dinner and I promised I'd warm it up as soon as he got back. So, it was a pleasure talking with you both but now I've got to run."

She was out the door before Jess or I could say anything more than goodbye.

"I wonder who her husband is?" Jess asked.

"Somebody important, by the sound of it," I replied.

CHAPTER 31

There was no way for Dorothy Smith to know when her husband, Harold, would be home for dinner. Harold refused to carry a cell phone and growled impatiently at her whenever she called him at work, a trait she neither adored nor hated, instead painting it a pale white in her mind so that it went relatively unnoticed. She knew better than to call the mayor's office and ask for him, so when she got home she placed his plate of roast beef, potatoes and cooked carrots in the microwave and preset the timer. That way she was armed and ready, prepared to hit the cook button as soon as she heard his car pulling into the driveway. This would please him, she thought. She then sat down and finished her own meal knowing that Harold liked to eat alone, especially after an emergency meeting with the mayor.

Harold would be wound tight when he got home. Someone to avoid, Dorothy had learned. One false word and he would explode like Mount Vesuvius, spewing righteous lava all over her and the neighbors next door with his thunderous preacher voice, as she secretly called it. It was that Reverend Newland that revved Harold up, Dorothy had decided years ago. The Reverend's rabid attitude–"serve the Lord or be damned to hell"–had spooned perfectly with Harold's stiff moral posture right from the beginning. Whenever the two of them got together, Dorothy knew her night would include a double serving of Jesus with a side order of Matthew, Mark, Luke and John.

Dorothy was religious but just not *that* religious. She went to church every Sunday, routinely joining her one and only sister, Abigail, the Reverend's wife, in the front row where they could enjoy the full flavor of the Reverend's sermons that never failed to stir the congregation. He was a powerful speaker, the Reverend James Newland, a crusader without a crusade, Dorothy thought, but she loved him nonetheless. He was her brother-in-law, her little sister's husband, so how could she not love him?

Harold was another story. Dorothy wasn't sure she loved him now, or if she had ever really loved him. He had rescued her from a life alone twenty years ago. Shouldn't that be enough to love someone? As she sat in their kitchen alone now, she didn't know the answer.

When she had first met Harold, she was only months away from her fortieth birthday. She was terrified of being that old with no husband and no children, with the prospect of finding a good husband slim at best. In a little place like Sherrill, most everyone was already married and the few single men her age were all ex-husbands of friends. Her *younger* sister, Abigail, had just gotten married to the handsome, young Reverend Newland, triggering the already boisterous clock in her head to tick that much louder. Then, out of the blue, Harold had arrived in town, seemingly with a fistful of roses already in hand and love for her in his eyes. The sudden attention took her completely by surprise, but then she was in a vulnerable state, ravenous for marriage, which to her was synonymous with love, and so she had succumbed to it in a single beat of her aching heart.

It was a good marriage, economically comfortable and socially accepted, but then she knew nothing different. Harold did his thing and Dorothy did hers, and every few months they did it together. They tried for children but they never came and somewhere in her mid-forties she pushed that yearning to the back of her mind with the other whitewashed thoughts she didn't want to have anymore.

Sitting in her warm, cozy home Dorothy knew life could be worse. That was how she got through the days, remembering to stay on the sunny side, always on the sunny side, as her mother used to sing to her and Abigail. She had lived through worse but those times were gone and the secrets they contained buried along with them. With her meal finished, Dorothy sipped her tea and thanked God once again that Harold had not discovered her past. He would have left her, she thought, but not before placing her immoral soul in the town square for all to assault with tomatoes of scorn. She then said a prayer that he would never find out what she had done so many years ago, a quiet plea to protect her secret. Then Dorothy Smith asked God to protect her sister Abigail's secret as well.

CHAPTER 32

I was all-talked-out for the day. We had grappled with the city police, hobnobbed with the mayor and his sidekick, cavorted with the tall-tale-teller Charlie Walinski, and tipped a few with Dorothy Smith, who at this moment appeared to know more about the Oneida Community than anyone else we had met. It had been a very long day, a routine one for my sister Mel, I suppose, posing questions and recording answers was her life, but I was used to a primarily solitary existence behind a desk and a computer screen. After ten hours of verbal rumba, my head was numb and my voice was hoarse.

Jess suggested we just grab a burger here at the bar and then call it a night. She was tired, too, and her idea sounded good to me so that's what we did.

We were back in our room at the Mansion House an hour later, collapsed on the bed.

"Don't worry," I said. "I'll stay on my side tonight."

"You better," Jess replied.

I wanted to ask her what would happen if I didn't, but I was too tired to ask even that simple question. Besides, my mind was on Mel.

They say that when someone close to you dies, you don't begin to mourn right away. It takes the heart and the brain time to process the loss and then, like the thunder that follows a flash of lightning, it strikes, sending a shock wave rippling through your body. They also say there's not a damn thing you can do about it. Mourning has to run its own course and trying to dam it up or divert it will only strengthen its surge. I had never thought much about that analogy, about what it really meant, but I was thinking about it now. I could feel something churning inside; something tugging at my sense of well being, pulling me down, and it scared me. It had been days since her funeral and I was here with her best friend trying to unmask her killer, yet it was only now sinking in– Mel was gone. She was really and truly gone.

"So, what do you think, Detective Hartwell," I said, unable to close my eyes for fear of what I might see. "Are we making any progress?"

"We're certainly learning a lot," she replied.

"Yes, that's true. But that's not really why we're here, is it."

"Not exactly, but we've only been here two days. We knew the guilty party wouldn't greet us as we drove up."

"I know, I just thought…."

"Thought we'd have more clues by now?"

I sighed and then said, "Yeah, something like that."

Jess said, "Charlie Walinski is worth pursuing. I'm going to call my colleague in Yonkers in the morning and have him do a background check on that little fibber."

"You mean your boyfriend?"

"I never said he was my boyfriend."

"Are you saying he's not?

"That's none of your business," she said, tersely. "We used to share a beat in Yonkers."

"Which one, the horizontal bop?" I quipped, regretting it the second in hit the airwaves.

Out of nowhere, Jess swung her fist like a tomahawk chop and nailed me in the chest, right where she had bruised me the day before.

"Damn!" I cried, sitting up quickly. "Stop doing that!"

"You need to be retrained," she said. "Like one of Pavlov's

dogs. When you say something sarcastic to me I'm going to slug you and, hopefully, after a while you'll begin to make the connection–sarcasm equals pain."

"What are you, a fucking psychologist, too?"

"I took a few courses in college and a few more during my police training. It takes a good deal of study to understand the criminal mind," she grinned, "and the behavior of people like you."

"Is that what you've been doing?" I asked. "Studying my behavior?"

"Casually," she replied. "So don't draw any conclusions from it."

It was too late, I already had.

I said, "Do you think we should call Charlie's wife?"

"And say *what* exactly?"

"I don't know, maybe, *do you think your husband is capable of murder?*"

"First of all, I don't think she would answer that question and, second, she would be on the phone minutes later asking her friends here in Sherrill who we were and what the hell we were doing."

"And our cover would be blown," I said, quickly realizing her point.

"If he's got any criminal history–violence or sex related–we'll know it tomorrow or Thursday at the latest."

"He works fast, this friend of yours."

"Fast enough," was all Jess said.

CHAPTER 33

Seven years ago, opportunity knocked on Charlie Walinski's door and he didn't hesitate to answer it. A silverware factory in Sherrill, New York was hiring line workers at a pay rate that was twice anything Charlie had ever made before and he had an inside connection, he told his wife. Sherrill was the perfect little city, he explained, with reasonable housing costs, good schools and friendly neighbors. Oneida Limited, the company that was hiring, had been in business for over a hundred years and there was no way they would go belly up now, not a global brand like that. He conceded that he had been wrong before, gambling on new startup companies or old ones in the midst of bankruptcy and reorganization that in the end had all laid him off within months of his signing on. He apologized profusely to his trusting wife, tearfully, for having moved the family so many times, but this time it would be different. It would be a fresh start, he said, a new beginning. They could pack their four preschoolers into the van, and leave their old troubles behind, stacked up at the curb for the garbage pickers to squabble over. Just one more chance, he pleaded to his wife. Just one more chance to get it right and this time she would have everything she had ever dreamed of. She wouldn't be sorry, he had said.

Cheryl Walinski bought the whole story, just as she always had, coming to Sherrill with her husband and children, eager to become a Limited wife, as Charlie described it. The wives of

Oneida Limited executives had maids to help with the housecleaning and nannies to care for the children, he said. He was part of a training program that put him on a three-year track to a corner office with his own secretary. He had to learn the business from the ground up first, he said, and that was why he would start on the line polishing forks and spoons.

The first few months in Sherrill were wonderful for the Walinski family. The city was really just a little village and the people were even friendlier than Charlie had described. The neighborhood was full of children for her kids to play with and mothers to invite to coffee, and Cheryl quickly slipped into the illusion that the old problems with Charlie were over. When her debit card was rejected at the supermarket forcing her to leave her cart full of groceries still sitting embarrassingly in the checkout line, she went home hating herself for falling for it again. *Fool me once, shame on you; fool me twice...*she thought to herself. Fool me a dozen times and I should be shot in the head, she tearfully concluded. She recognized the symptoms all too well and she cornered Charlie that night and screamed the truth out of him.

The only honest part of Charlie's charade was his having a contact at Oneida Limited. An old high-school buddy worked in the factory and, going on rumor, had contacted Charlie and told him to "get his ass up here" because they were going to be hiring a new shift of fifty or more workers. The two men had stayed in casual contact over the years via email, alerting each other about new work opportunities and the latest and greatest internet pornography sites. Believing his friend was Charlie's first mistake.

Charlie didn't bother to confirm Oneida's intentions; instead he based his decision on faith and, to some degree, laziness. Charlie was Catholic, serving mass as an alter boy for most of his teenage years, and had been taught that the Lord will provide. He couldn't tell his wife the truth that he didn't have a job with the Limited yet, because she didn't have the faith he had, or so he told himself. He was sure that if they moved there he could secure a job with Oneida and Cheryl would never know the difference. She didn't know half of what he did and this would be no different, he convinced himself. Thinking his wife wouldn't find out was Charlie's second mistake.

Within a week of discovering Charlie's little secret and that he was actual working as janitor at a brewery miles away, Cheryl stuffed the kids and their meager belongings into their van, and left Charlie for her parents' home in Florida. In the time since then Charlie had never heard from her, not even to say if she was going to file for divorce. Never once had he tried to contact his kids, instead trying desperately to get a job with Oneida Limited, believing that once he did he could win Cheryl back again. They were still married as far as he was concerned.

Charlie was on the waiting list at Oneida Limited, several hundred names down the page, when they announced the closing of the Sherrill factory and the elimination of five hundred jobs just a few months ago. That was Charlie's third mistake, thinking that some companies were immune to the bad economic times.

With nowhere else to go, Charlie stayed in Sherrill, immersing himself in the local history (his favorite subject was the Oneida Community) and acquainting himself with everyone in town, especially the women. He suitably transformed his self-image into that of an eligible bachelor, perhaps the best catch in town, if he did say so himself. The rest of the populous did not agree. To most folks, *especially* the women, he was a letch and a bore, a perception developed through years of unwelcome flirtations and countless firings over pornography downloading at work. He now lived in a small apartment just inside the city limits, filled with old furniture, girlie magazines, and what he referred to as his "collectibles."

After his wife left, Charlie's desire to amass seemingly worthless items–junk–worsened, as did his need to sit at his computer searching for porn at all hours of the day and night. The counselor his wife had dragged him to in the early years of their marriage had said he had Obsessive-Compulsive Disorder, at the time referring Charlie to a specialist whose card he tossed away within minutes of leaving the counselor's office. He didn't have OCD, he concluded; he was a collector and had plenty of valuable pieces to prove it. Old boom-boxes with cassette decks were among his favorites. He amassed hundreds that now filled every closet and shelf in his apartment by visiting dumps, flea markets and local neighborhood garage sales. Another item he coveted, and an odd one at that, was clergy apparel–robes, stoles, hoods and sash cords. That urge had started the first time Charlie had walked out onto the alter dressed in his alter boy cassock as Sunday Mass was about to begin. He felt different standing up there in front of everyone–special–and ever since that day, the simple act of putting on a delicately embroidered, velvet-lined robe would lift his spirits like nothing else could. Charlie had even thought about joining the clergy once, but he knew he could not handle celibacy.

Charlie kept his priestly garment collection in a cedar chest in the storage garage he shared with a friend. He didn't like sharing the space, exposing all his valuable pieces to the sticky fingers of another human being, but he couldn't afford the monthly charge all by himself.

Tonight, Charlie was at his computer as he always was on Tuesday night, preparing for an online date with a woman named Nikki. Charlie liked to call it a date (Nikki called it an appointment), but it was really just Charlie watching Nikki slowly undress and fondle herself as he frantically typed suggestions to her with one hand on his keyboard and the other in his pants, all for the same price as two front-row tickets to a Bruce Springsteen concert. Online dating was the one luxury he could afford, Charlie told himself.

Charlie had been "dating" Nikki exclusively for nearly a month, a departure from his normal habit of "juggling several chicks" as he would often brag to the male patrons of Shelley's bar, completely mesmerized by her schoolgirl looks and forbidden fetish illusions. As he logged onto her website and gazed upon her already naked body–curves of golden flesh writhing like a giant anaconda in the swamps of the Amazon–his eyes darted to the long silk scarf wrapped tightly around her neck. It was the red scarf; the one she had used during their first time, and it was digging into her satiny skin, squeezing her lungs dry just as Charlie was unzipping his fly.

CHAPTER 34

"That's the one," Mel's trembling voice says. "There!"

I follow the invisible line of her glassy, wide-eyed gaze and see only a sea of people frozen like mannequins in a department store window, empty smiles and lifeless eyes unrecognizable to my own.

"Can't you see, Michael," she says with a growing panic leeching from her words as she backs away, cowering from the crowd, slipping away from me.

"Who?" I cry, desperately scanning the faces that now suddenly all look alike. "Which one?"

I return to Mel, pleading for the answer. She is fading away now, colorless, like the way she looked in the coffin at her funeral. Not like my sister. Like a dead person.

"There," she whispers as her pale, grey face disappears into blackness.

I turn back and see nothing but a thousand mirrors and my own reflection looking back at me.

When I woke up I was still dressed and Jess was lying next to me. She had her clothes on as well and was on her self-assigned right side of the bed. We had fallen asleep while talking, I concluded, and now it was nearly two in the morning according to the blue glow of my travel clock. I was wide-awake. I did not kill my sister, and I wanted to go back to sleep so I could tell her that. But I was afraid. Afraid the words would not come out. Afraid the menacing red serpent would kill her again; choke the life from her helpless body while I stood watching and doing nothing to stop it, again.

Between a rock and hard place, I got up, draped my half of the blankets over Jess, went to the chair, and sat down. Out of habit, I reached down into the cushion in search of lost coins–buried treasure, my father had called it when he had taught me the trick as a young boy. I pulled out a pink hairclip with a few dark hairs dangling limply from the metal clasp. *No gold this time.* I pushed the doubloon back down to where I had found it.

"I'm sorry, Mel," I whispered at the ceiling. I should have done something last week as I was doing something now. Why hadn't I? She was my sister–my twin. We had shared my mother's belly and then we had shared a common soul that I would never—could never—acknowledge. Why was I such a pathetic brother? I held my head in my hands and rubbed my face hard hoping an answer would magically appear like the winning prize in some million-dollar scratch-off game. If only I could have a do-over.

My second night in the Silver City turned out to be a long one.

CHAPTER 35

Jess was a peaceful sleeper. She didn't toss and turn like a restless child or grumble and belch like an old man. After five hours of observation, I could honestly say she didn't fart in her sleep either. She lay on her back all night, with her head tilted ever so slightly to her left, a faint crooked smile pinned to her face. I would have thought her an angel if it were not for the balled up fist resting on her hip, an ominous reminder that had me unconsciously rubbing the bruise on my chest. Perhaps it was the cop in her, trained to be ready in a split second. Maybe she was battling the bad guys in her sleep or getting ready to slug me again. She had better dreams than I did, I imagined, the kind of dreams *I* only dreamed about.

I could have read more about the Oneida Community, there were plenty of books scattered about our room, but I couldn't stop looking at Jess. Somehow, over the past few days, she had captured my eye but it was more than that. She had a deeper hold on me and I found myself that night needing to figure out what it was. *Was I falling in love with her?* I contemplated. I could have answered that but I had never been in love before, at least not the kind of which Air Supply sang. I was quite familiar with the Barry White "Your Sweetness Is My Weakness" kind of love, but I think that qualified as more lust than love, but then, I shouldn't speak for Barry. But looking over at Jess, I knew that wasn't it. I honestly didn't know what it was and by the time the clock read 7:00 a.m., I still hadn't figured it out. What I *had* determined was that Jess had intriguingly odd-shaped ears with rather bulbous lobules, and incredibly thick hair that never seemed to rumple.

At the suggestion of my protesting stomach, I threw on my coat and left our room in search of breakfast. My rubber-soled shoes echoed loudly in the tranquil, hardwood floor hallways as I headed for the kitchen, the faint odor of cow manure twitching my nose as I tried to quiet my steps to conceal my journey. Nobody awake but the local farmers and their herds, I concluded, thinking they must leave some windows open in here at night in the spring to enjoy the "fresh" aroma of country living.

I found the kitchen without any problem but it was locked-up tight and after waiting ten minutes, I gave up on waiting for the help to arrive. I thought about returning to the room and borrowing Jess' car keys, but I decided a walk would be good, remembering how the waitress at the restaurant we had been frequenting had bragged about the blueberry muffins. I would burn off a half-hour or so getting there and back, and by then Jess would be awake, or at least ready to be awakened, if I was feeling courageous.

It took me a little longer than I had anticipated walking to the center of Sherrill where the restaurant sat promisingly back away from the road, flanked by maple trees covered with tiny green leaf buds. I enjoyed it nonetheless. It was a pleasantly warm morning for April, quiet and sunny with the hopeful scent of spring in the air. I leisurely strolled back to the Mansion House with my face pointed upward, thinking this would be the start of my summer tan. It wasn't until I saw the old place in the distance, sitting on its little hill like a crown atop a king's head, that I noticed something in the air. Rather, there was something *missing* in the air–the smell of cow manure. If the odor was coming from the nearby farms as I had first thought then surely I would smell it outside in the open air just as I had in the hallways of the Mansion House. But I didn't and that meant that either the wind had changed direction or it must have been coming from *inside* the Mansion House; from one of the other rooms, perhaps? Why would someone have cow manure in his or her room? A farmer lived in the Mansion House, in one of the apartments, I reasoned. Or a hired hand? That would make more sense because a farmer would live on his farm, right?

With a few hundred yards yet to go, I suddenly remembered where I had experienced the manure odor before. It had been on Monday when I was standing in the courtyard with Jess looking up at the dormer windows. Mel's image had startled me just before the creepy groundskeeper appeared out of nowhere with his crypt keeper charm and menacing chainsaw. *Wind change, my ass!* In a flash, I tucked the bag of muffins and juice under my arm like a football, and sprinted back to the room where I prayed Jess was still sleeping peacefully.

The room Harriet, Harry to her friends, had escorted us to several days ago was empty. No, it was void of human inhabitation. All the books were still scattered about, along with luggage and some dirty clothes, but Jess was gone. She wasn't in the bathroom or in the closet and she wasn't hiding under the bed. I looked. Nothing appeared out of place or missing, except, as I looked down on the carpeted floor I noticed the clear outline of muddy boot marks. I looked at my own shoes. Clean as a whistle. I looked for Jess' shoes and didn't see them anywhere. As I scanned the floor, I knew the footprints couldn't belong to her, they were way too big. I wiped at the mud with my finger and took a whiff. Cow manure without a doubt. *The groundskeeper!*

In a panic, I fled the room and marched down the hallway not even knowing where I was headed. There must be a garage or a shed of some kind where he kept all the equipment and tools required to maintain this place, I thought. The most likely spot would be out back somewhere, out of the public eye, just like where my father's sheet metal vault was, keeping his thirty-year-old mower safe from vandals and antique collectors. That would be the first place to look for the groundskeeper, I concluded, as I turned down a corridor that I was sure would lead me to a back exit. I was wrong, coming to a dead end near the library. I cursed myself and then retraced my hurried steps before choosing another corridor that looked encouraging. It was another dead end. *Son of a bitch! This is a god-awful time for a brain cramp.*

Finally, I found myself near the front entrance and I opted to go outside. Hell, even I could find my way to the back of the property by walking *around* the building, I reasoned. And, I could run!

Sure enough, there was shed, a big shed. One might even have called it a small barn and the barn door was open. Pathetically winded and wheezing, I went inside without knocking and shuddered at what I saw.

The walls were laden with all form of sharpened steel: sickles, saws, picks and shovels; pruners, shears, clippers and snips; knives, machetes, axes and all sorts of other exotic odd-shaped blades. It was a Gothic hardware store, a landscaper's paradise and a gardener's Christmas list all in one, but a nightmare for a jumpy friend in search of a missing companion. Staring at this weird fortification of terror, I concluded that this guy was either a twisted Johnny Appleseed or Jack the Ripper, or a really bizarre combination of the two.

"Jess!" I yelled and waited. No answer. *Maybe she was bound and gagged!* I screamed her name several more times, thinking that if she heard me she could kick something to lead me to her. But other than my panicked pleas, the barn remained deathly silent. Not even the scurry of a frightened mouse.

Then I noticed the smell. The place reeked of manure; the source of which I discovered was several large drums of brown water. None of them had a lid and each had a stick protruding out the top like the kind you would use to stir a can of paint, only much longer and thicker. I peered into one of the cans, grabbed the stick and began to stir the murky water, bracing myself for a floating head or an errant eyeball. *Please, Jess, don't be in here....*

The rancid odor thickened as I churned the water with nothing rising to the surface but what I assumed were clumps of cow dung. *Some kind of poison? Or a mind-numbing drug? He drugged her and then quietly carried her off!*

My eyes began to tear and just as I started to back away, a vise-like hand gripped my shoulder and pulled me around. *Christ!*

"You don't want to be stirrin' the tea," the groundskeeper said. "Gotta let it steep for a few days and then it'll be ready for drinkin'."

I froze for a moment not knowing what to say, first looking for the chainsaw, but then looking past him to see if Jess might have followed him in. His hands were empty; Jess nowhere in sight. With my initial surprise yielding to my overall distress, I muttered something ridiculously irrelevant, "You drink this stuff, this...?"

"Manure tea is what most folks call it," he replied. "The plants drink it, though I'll take a sip now and again to make sure it's ripe. Springtime is growin' time and the roots will be hollarin' for it soon enough."

"Oh," I managed to mutter. We then traded places, sliding by each other as if we had leprosy. I felt more comfortable with nothing between me and the door, and it was then that I noticed the table full of chains and an assortment of nasty metal contraptions. Focusing more closely, I recognized the objects and pushed back my fear, calmly asking, "What do you use the animal traps for?"

"Trappin' animals," the man said with a steely gaze that sent a chill down my spine. "Get all kinds of vermin around here."

Is that what he thought Jess and I were–vermin? I stared back at him, my jaw tightening as my head began to pound from the demolition derby of thoughts colliding in my brain. Should I confront him now, force him to spill his guts all over the rotting timbered floor? Or should I play it cagey and back him into a corner somehow? The two of us squared off in a showdown, locked onto one another's eyes like two gunslingers at high noon, our fingers twitching on imaginary pistols waiting for the other man to make his move, the crows in the trees outside cackling like an angry mob thirsty for blood.

Finally, one plan emerged from the smoke and chaos of my mind. It came from my auditor training, and it had me take a step back and regroup before the water got muddied with my own zeal. It was what I had done during audits when I knew I had somebody by the balls but I didn't have irrefutable proof. I wanted to squeeze him, the groundskeeper with his you-got-nothing-on-me smirk, I wanted to squeeze him hard, but I knew that might allow him to slip away squealing like a greased pig. Keeping my eye on the man, I slowly backpedaled out of the shed, flipped open my cell phone and dialed for information as I stood blocking the shed door. "Sherrill Police Department," I said to the automated assistant. As I waited for the number I could hear a faint tapping sound. Annoyingly, it would stop and then start again but I couldn't determine where it was coming from. Then, as I heard the automated system forwarding my call, the noise got louder and it suddenly stuck me–it was the sound of bones cracking! My arm went limp by my side, along with the phone in my hand, and I stepped deeper into the shed doorway to peer cautiously inside. The groundskeeper was gone! I frantically scanned the interior searching for another exit but I could find nothing. There must be a secret entrance to this shed, I thought, or a secret chamber–a dungeon! I went outside and briskly walked the perimeter of the building, all the while the maddening whack-whack-whack ripping at my ears. *Where are you, you little bastard!*

There must be a trap door *inside* the shed because he couldn't have gotten past me without me seeing him, I concluded, even while I was punching the buttons on my phone, calling for backup.

Then I remember my call, cursing myself as I discovered I had inadvertently closed my cell phone, hanging up on the police as I did. I looked back at the Mansion House in disgust and that's when I saw Jess, rapping against the window to get my attention. She had a plate full of bagels in her hand, holding them up as if to say, "Breakfast is ready."

Her bones looked perfectly fine.

CHAPTER 36

The time was drawing near.

Homer Tubb knew what he had to do and with his uninvited visitor finally gone, he set about his preparation by first slipping into the rawhide apron hanging in the l-shaped cove in the corner of the shed his grandfather had built as a dressing chamber. Homer had found it to be an advantageous hiding spot when he was younger, nearly invisible to the untrained eye with its weathered lumber blending so perfectly with the surrounding walls that it looked as if it *were* part of the wall. He never asked his grandfather if he had done it for that purpose, but Homer didn't care. It had worked its clever magic today as it had some many times before and his curious pest was gone. Now he could focus on his work.

The strapping workbench that sat along the wall of the shed had a short line of tools awaiting his attention–an axe for chopping, a curved saw attached to a long pole for trimming branches and several lengths of slender rope in need of repair. Homer was an excellent rope maker, a skill taught to him by his now-deceased uncle, braiding his own from hemp or nylon and occasionally using cotton to create colorful strands of jump rope for the children of the Mansion House. They always asked for red, which he obligingly kept in plentiful supply.

Homer was careful with his rope, always being sure to twist strong so that it did not break when called to task. A broken rope was failure to Homer, and failure was unacceptable.

The crows stirred up once again, their steady "caw, caw, caw" a brewing thunderstorm that quickly reminded Homer of his task. He went to work on the axe, grinding it tenderly against the stone wheel he turned with a foot pedal. "I hear you, you black devils," he whispered, knowing the time was near. "Have faith, judgment day is only a prayer away."

CHAPTER 37

Arlen Bensinger now had three silk ties to take to the cleaners. One of them was his absolute favorite, a burgundy red Armani accentuated with a pattern of grey and brown circles that he had just put on that morning. It went perfectly with his charcoal grey pinstripe suit, his prevalent choice on Wednesdays when important meetings at the office routinely filled his schedule, but now he had to remove it and select a replacement. Harried, he pulled another red tie from the dynasty of red power ties residing in his closet and expertly knotted it so it dropped perfectly just past his belt buckle. He needed to be at work in thirty-five minutes, at the bank in Syracuse where he had been recently promoted to Branch Manager. The drive from Sherrill would take forty minutes on a good day and he was going to be late. He was not happy about it.

Emma, his two-and-a-half-month-old daughter had just sucked down the bottle of breast milk Arlen had warmed for her that morning as if she hadn't eaten in a week, only to then promptly spit it all up on him for the third day in a row. A perfect record for the week so far, Arlen complained to his wife Betsy as he returned to the kitchen neatly retailored. She smiled blankly but kept her sleepy eyes riveted on the stove where a pan of bacon and French toast sat sparking and fizzing like a campfire in a rain shower.

"You going to work, Daddy?" one of their three-year-old twin boys, Ethan, asked.

"Yup," Arlen replied, thinking to himself, *Thank God.*

"Can we go, too?" Andrew, the other half of the set, asked.

I would rather have my fingers snipped off one at a time by an un-hinged gangster than take you kids to work with me, Arlen thought. He said, "No, they don't allow little boys at the bank. Sorry, Sport."

Andrew and Ethan didn't really care; they were too busy fighting over the squeeze bottle of imitation maple syrup as their mother began serving the breakfast goods. It was a typical morning in the Bensinger home, a nice, modern colonial built a year ago in the only new development in Sherrill, and Arlen knew from experience that things would be spraying wildly, like Emma's breakfast, at any minute. He quickly kissed his wife on the cheek and fled with his leather briefcase in hand.

Arlen Bensinger enjoyed his daily rides into Syracuse. They provided him time to shift from home mode to work mode, two existences that had evolved into two completely divergent realities, he'd realized in the last few years. "It's like I'm living two different lives," he often lamented to one of his unmarried colleagues. "I manage million dollar deals by day and change dirty diapers by night," he would complain. "When did I lose control over my life?"

Arlen sometimes wondered how he had gotten to where he was, and more often, where he was going. Career wise, he was happy in the banking business, content for the moment with his recent promotion, confident that his stock there would rise even higher in the years ahead. His role as the Mayor of Sherrill was just part-time and paid very little but he garnered satisfaction from helping the community, the nice buzz from the position of power it held a small fringe benefit he had not anticipated.

Home life for Arlen was another story altogether. He and Betsy didn't talk much anymore, not like they did before the twins when they would spend their evenings cuddled together on the couch sharing a bottle of wine and dreams about the future. It was impossible to share intimate moments now with one, two or three kids clutched to his legs or pulling at his arms, screaming they were hungry or didn't feel good or that their brother hit them in the head with a Tonka truck. When a quiet moment did present itself, the silence would put the exhausted Arlen and his wife to sleep; seizing the moment to renew their strength knowing they had survived a small battle, but wary of the long war ahead.

Will our sex life ever heat up again, Arlen found himself thinking after ten minutes on the road to Syracuse. If it's true what they say that, on average, men think about sex every six seconds then Arlen Bensinger was one of the guys boosting that statistic. He thought about sex *every* second or so it seemed sometimes. He and Betsy had not made love since Emma was born (the hand job his wife had given him a month ago didn't count) and if this time was going to be like the last time, when the twins were born, he knew he was in for a long dry spell.

"Never do your poachin' in your own backyard," one of Arlen's buddies had advised him during a boy's night out the week before. A bunch of them were sitting at Shelley's bar getting wasted on tequila shooters when he ceremoniously lifted his glass to proclaim that "Mr. Johnson is no longer under management's control and, effective immediately, will be pursuing alternative forms of recreational release." When asked who the lucky woman he planned to have an affair with was, Arlen had replied, "The next woman to walk through that door." As fate would have it, the next person to step through the front door of Shelley's bar and restaurant was an attractive young reporter named Melissa Gibson. She was a bit more than Arlen was expecting, but after his friends began placing bets on his failure, he knew he couldn't back down. He introduced himself that night and, much to the surprise of his friends, secured a lunch date for the following day.

Arlen's palms began to sweat as he recalled the events of the prior week. He should have listened to his friend's advice. Betsy would have crucified him for sure if she found out what he had

done before fleeing with all three kids under her arms. The ensuing gossip and humiliation would have certainly derailed his
budding political career in the Silver City, if not all of Central New
York. He would have become a cliché—a divorced father paying
child support like the pathetic Charlie Walinski, the sorry soul
roaming the streets like a bear in heat.

Talking to Melissa Gibson, Mel, as she told him to call her, had
been so easy he couldn't help walking away from their first lunch
in love, a lustful crush he told himself at the time, but helplessly
infatuated just the same. She was smart, beautiful and sexy, turning every head in town when she had arrived a week ago Monday.
Vibrantly alive, that's what Arlen had noticed the most, the very
essence of what his wife *used* to be. He hated himself for thinking
of Betsy that way, like a nonsexual plain Jane that stirred nothing
within him just like many of the wives of the other bank employees he had met at the office parties and picnics. Melissa Gibson
was exciting, and listening to her talk about the Oneida Community and its sexual practices only electrified his moth-balled desires all the more. Her enthusiasm intoxicated Arlen, eventually
clouding his judgment as he interpreted her friendliness as an
open invitation to something more.

Arlen Bensinger had been wrong about Melissa Gibson, the
Times reporter sent to Sherrill to profile the Oneida Community,
wrong about her interest in him and he had nearly paid dearly for
it. Bob Applewhite was right, he had gotten lucky, they all had, he
thought to himself. He also knew it was a terrible way to think of
that young woman's death, a cold-hearted eulogy of sorts, but
there was nothing he could do for her now. He noticed the sign for
his exit off the expressway approaching and he told himself to get
his head back into his banking business.

"Oh shit," he said after he had parked his car, noticing several
tiny stain spots on his necktie, maple syrup he assumed. "Those
little...." He reached for a napkin he kept stocked in his glove
compartment, but there were none. He had used them all up on

the way back from McDonald's the night before when his son Andrew had tried to bounce his Happy Meal off the car window like a basketball. It splashed rather than bounced, much to Andrew's delight, and looking into the back seat, Arlen could still see several posthumous French fries stuck between the seats, laughing at him.

As he marched into the cold granite building, a thought appeared—a connection really, two independent thoughts coming together. Melissa Gibson had told him that during her research she had read that the Oneida Community believed that children needed more than their own parents to guide them and so made it the duty of the entire Community family to care for the children. "Wouldn't that be nice," Arlen had commented when she had told him of the Children's House that was once part of the Mansion House, a wing devoted to various-aged children, from babies to twelve year olds. Later that same day a good friend of his, a Sherrill resident with several children as well, had told him in confidence that some of the young parents in town were thinking of forming an informal, secret day care and asked Arlen if he and his wife might be interested. Had they gotten the idea from reading about the Community? Why hadn't he made the connection before? Were the rumors about a secret revival of the Community actually true and this was a thread to it? He knew where the last question had originated from and as he set his briefcase down on his desk, he told Mr. Johnson to sit down and shut up. He had a long day in front of him—several client meetings, an interview with a college kid looking for an intern job and a stack of paperwork a mile high. There was no time for erotic daydreaming every six seconds, that was pointless, his business mode self told him. Even his lunchtime was spoken for—an hour of phone calls to contacts who he hoped would give him the skinny on the company known as Hartwell Spa and Resort.

CHAPTER 38

As we sat down at an unoccupied table in the dining hall, Jess asked, "Were you and Homer getting better acquainted?"

"Who?" I replied.

"The groundskeeper; his name is Homer."

"How did you find that out?"

"I asked him."

"When did you do that, this morning?"

"Yes. I ran into him in the kitchen when I was scrounging for bagels. Here," she said pushing one of the cream-cheesed wheels in front of me, "I made one for you."

"Thanks," I said. "I got you a muffin." I pulled the two muffins out of the bag I'd forgotten I had tucked under my arm. They looked like blue-blooded road kill.

Jess tried hard not to laugh but she did anyway, just a little. "What kind were they?"

"Blueberry; I got them at the restaurant in town but on the way back I kind of had a brain twitch and, obviously, assassinated them."

"A brain twitch?"

"I thought the groundskeeper, Homer, was stalking you," I said, half-embarrassed and half still suspicious of the man. "I ran back thinking you might need to be rescued."

Jess smiled and her eyes twinkled as she said, "That's very

gallant of you, but why would you think that?"

"I thought I smelled the guy in the hallway before I went into town for the muffins but it didn't register until I was coming back. It was that cow manure smell. The same odor that hung in the air the first time we ran into him, in the courtyard, remember? He's got a truck load of that shit in his shed out back. He said it was fertilizer for the plants, *manure tea* he called it. He's probably using it to slowly poison people, if you ask me."

"You weren't kidding about that brain twitch, were you?" Jess chuckled.

"It feels like one now, but at the time...."

"Well, obviously, I'm fine," Jess said. "And since your heart was in the right place, even though your mind wasn't, I'll give you a few points for the knight-in-shining-armor bit anyway."

"Thanks," I chuckled. "But there's still the matter of some muddy footprints in our room. How do you explain that?"

"Muddy footprints?"

Before I could explain, we were interrupted by a familiar voice, "Are you kids enjoying your stay here?"

It was the nameless woman with her male companion in tow, the old ghosts. I hadn't heard them come in and then, poof, they were standing right next to our table. I scanned the dining hall as if I might find a doorway from another dimension, noticing only that the rest of the room was deserted.

"Yes, we are," Jess answered politely, "please, sit down."

"Why, thank you, but only for minute. We've got a million things to do today as I'm sure you do as well."

"Well," I said, realizing that we *didn't* have a plan for the day or the rest of the week, for that matter. Jess and I were flying by the seat of our pants, as they say, hoping the clouds would part sometime soon and show us where to land.

"We're footloose and fancy free today," Jess said, bailing me out. "Maybe you could tell us about the Perfectionists you mentioned the last time we spoke. We'd love to learn more about them."

"What a *perfect* suggestion," the woman said, laughing over her little pun. "First, we'll need a history lesson and I *love* giving history lessons. Perfectionism, you must first understand, was an offshoot of Methodism, which in the 1700s had formed its own unique doctrine of Christian perfection under the guidance of an Englishman named Wesley. Wesleyan Methodism, as it was sometimes referred, attempted to lead believers into a state of righteousness, which was often described as freedom from sins committed through conscious choice. It was not absolute perfection, it allowed for unintentional sins and character defects. Methodists then and today believe that Jesus Christ was the only one capable of absolute perfection so they gave their congregation a little slack to work with. And that slack is exactly what put John Humphrey Noyes, the founder of the Oneida Community, at a fork in the road that eventually led him into trouble."

"He didn't believe people could be perfect?" I asked.

"No," the woman replied, "just the opposite. John thought it completely illogical that a Perfectionist church did *not* expect or require sinlessness of its members. At the time, John was himself a pastor, earning his license to preach at Yale where his study of Perfectionism and its true nature lead to his proclamation that anyone who commits sin is *of the devil*."

"I'll bet that made him a popular guy," Jess said, grinning.

"It didn't," the woman said. "In fact, his fellow students and professors labeled him crazy. Shortly thereafter he was forced to resign his license and *invited* to leave the college altogether. He lost everything, including his first love who deserted him to marry another man. Eventually, he rebuilt his life, marrying and then establishing a small group of followers in Putney, Vermont, which he later fled after being indicted on two counts of adultery that nearly got him lynched. He ended up here in Sherrill around 1848, joining a farm owned by a loyalist of the Putney group."

"Is that when they started making silverware?" Jess asked.

"Oh, heavens no, dear, that started some years later. They farmed at first, and then made silk and animal traps to support themselves. They were hard workers, you had to be, or suffer criticism from the group. There were no slackers in the Community."

I said, "It sounds like this Noyes fella was a man on the run."

The woman said, "I think the people of Putney just wanted him to leave and, once he did, they didn't chase after him. All John really wanted was an honest chance to experiment with *his* idea of Perfectionism."

Jess asked, "Which was?"

"The end of disease and death–the literal kingdom of heaven and earth."

"Utopia," I said mockingly.

"He wasn't crazy," the woman said authoritatively, reminding me of my psychology professor in college who would loudly direct our class away from conjecture with a disapproving scowl. "John was attempting to overcome the religious and social disorder of the time by establishing a common set of religious values that would put him and his followers in the right relations with God. And, to be successful, John believed that men and women needed to live together harmoniously within a structure different from the "dog-eat-dog" capitalism that was spreading across America at that time."

"Bible Communism," Jess said. "I've read about that."

"Share and share alike," I added.

"In every sense of the word," the woman said, looking very pleased with her quick-learning students.

She certainly made it sound valiant—one man against the world, trying to save the common man from himself.

The woman must have read my mind before she said, "I know what you're thinking. The man was delusional and thought he was Christ, the second coming or something."

I raised my eyebrows and said, "You have to admit that it does sound a little...."

"As I said, he wasn't crazy," the woman interrupted calmly. I could tell she had seen skeptical responses before and was ready for it. She continued, saying, "John and the Community were very much grounded; they were *jiggy with it*, as you young people say. Women in the Community owned property and had a voice in things years before the rest of the country could say that. The children were cared for in a common area with nurses and teachers very much like a modern day care facility. And, smoking was prohibited inside the Mansion House one hundred and fifty years before it became a law for the rest of society. Their hard work paved the way for the spiritually and financially rich community you are sitting amidst today. No, John didn't think he was Jesus or God, and he certainly wasn't crazy either."

"Sounds like a man ahead of his time," Jess said.

The woman didn't openly respond to Jess's comment, smiling modestly instead and nodding her head faintly.

"It's too bad he's not still around," I said. "From what we've heard, the local economy could use a boost."

"Yes, maybe a revival of the Community would springboard Sherrill into a new dawn of prosperity," Jess added.

The woman laughed nervously and shuddered as she said, "Oh, my heavens, it would be 1879 all over again and the Episcopalians, the Presbyterians, and the Methodists would probably burn this old place to the ground."

"Would the rest of the local community really feel that threatened?" Jess asked.

The elderly woman paused as she put her hand thoughtfully to her chin. "Perhaps I'm exaggerating. I'm sure many people nowadays are only concerned with having considerate neighbors, which in the beginning was the way it was the 1800s. People who knew the Oneida Community knew them to be good neighbors–quiet, kind and compassionate. The Community also hired local people to work for them and paid wages equal to or better than most other businesses. The scrutiny came from the ignorant and the self-righteous, led by clergymen threatened by the ideology and a little jealous of the Community's success, if you ask me. But then again, John did push the envelope, as you young people say, so there might be more than a few in this city who would be quick to answer a new alarm if it sounded."

"What would they do?" Jess asked. "What *could* they do?"

"Anything is possible," she said before turning to her companion, who hadn't said a word the entire time. "We've learned that, haven't we, Dear?"

The old man nodded.

Anything? I thought. *Even murder?*

I lowered my voice and leaned into the table feeling like a spy on a secret mission passing along a code word to ask the question I had wanted to ask since Jess and I had arrived on Monday, "We've heard some rumors that the Community is back, born again right here in Sherrill. Do you know anything about that?"

The woman smiled knowingly.

Was that a yes? I think it was a yes.

Before I could pursue it further, the woman and her companion stood up, bid us a good morning and strolled out of the dining hall just as they had the last time, looking proud and relaxed as if they owned the place.

"A big fat article in the New York Times praising the Oneida Community's beliefs would be a very loud alarm, wouldn't it," Jess said.

"I think the alarm went off soon after Mel arrived," I replied.

The Mansion House
April 1870

The upper sitting room was one of John's favorite places in the Mansion. Off-limits to touring guests, it was secluded and comfortable with a balcony designed to look like state rooms on a Hudson River steamship. Two long, narrow windows filled one wall, standing like sentries, their white, flowing drapery filtering the sunlight that welcomed visitors in the early afternoon, keeping it warm until well past sundown. "It will be a fine sanctuary for serious discussion," John had said to the architect as they were laying out the building's design only a few years ago. As the dinner hour approached, John sat enjoying his refuge's pleasant surroundings while studying the young man's disappointed face, anticipating the question that he knew was forthcoming.

"But why was my application vetoed?" Henry said. His head was cocked to one side as if a different viewing angle might provide him a better understanding. "Why was I ruled unfit?"

Henry had not been the first to request a meeting over this subject and so John did not pause long before answering.

"You know, Henry, that we have always had a keen appetite for having children," John began. "One we have had to suppress until our financial security improved. Deliberate additions to our numbers are now feasible due to our hard work and diligence."

"And twenty years of continence, of course," John added with a knowing smile.

Henry did not return the facial applause. He was listening attentively, but somewhat anxiously, and so he didn't catch the humor in John's opening. His mind was on Sarah. Devastated by the rejection of his application, she had pleaded with Henry to talk to John, to attempt to convince John to reverse the decision. To do so, Henry knew he would first need to understand its grounds, and being well acquainted with John's oratory prowess from the many talks and meetings he conducted daily, Henry knew he would need to be patient. He shifted in his chair, searching for a comfortable position.

"The matter of the mating between those who have volunteered resulted from extensive study by the committee," John said. "Good health and sound character, beauty of form and complexion, strength of mind and body, all these rudiments were considered."

"But I have these qualities and more," Henry insisted. "I am as strong as an ox in both body and spirit and I...."

John interrupted him with a calm wave of his hand. He then finished his criteria list, emphasizing the final three words with an authoritative inflection that he wanted his young follower to hear. "Amiability of disposition."

So that was it, Henry thought, *my strong will had ruffled his feathers. Well, we shall see.* Unwilling to concede, Henry persisted.

"Sarah wishes to carry my baby and you yourself have said that childbearing should be a voluntary affair, one in which the choice of the mother should be respected."

John knew all about Henry and Sarah and their forbidden "special love." John knew everything that went on in the Mansion House and he was not going to allow their exclusive marriage of the spirit to flourish. He said calmly but sternly, "From your point of view, you are correct. Our principles accord to women a just and righteous freedom in this particular, but mating done by promiscuous scrambling such as yours removes the principled hand of science from our goal of controlled propagation. Darwin has been dealing out the law of Stirpiculture by wholesale to the scientifics, and the phrenologists and popular physiologists have retailed it to the masses until everybody is under conviction about it. It is wonderful to see how unanimous the acknowledgment has become that we ought to be doing for man what has been done for horses, swine and potatoes. The history of Abraham and the Jews is a splendid example of Stirpiculture, with Christ and Paul as specimens of the result. The very definition of the word Stirpiculture–race-culture–exemplifies what we wish to achieve here in the Community. History still shows that all good that has yet been accomplished in the world has resulted from providential direction in the matter of parentage."

Holding Sarah in his arms later that evening, Henry professed his love for her and vowed to never give her up. "John is wrong," Henry said tearfully. "The Community is wrong and one day I will make them see that."

Sarah soothed her fretful young lover with affirming whispers and delicate kisses, all the while hiding her own torn heart. She could not tell Henry that the committee had paired her, along with several other women, with John, the patriarch of the Community. Though each of the others had felt honored at the privilege of having John as the father of her child, Sarah was not as certain. She knew whose baby she wanted but duty was calling to her, coloring her thoughts, commanding her to leave her romantic notions behind–to leave Henry behind. She believed in the Community and had thrived in its embrace for many years. Betraying John now by continuing with Henry would jeopardize everything and Sarah was not sure she had the strength to do that. Staring into Henry's longing eyes, neither did she have the strength to send him away.

"Do you know what the outside world is calling this, this eugenic breeding experiment?" Henry asked, his eyes wild with condemnation. "Barnyard ethics! He has gone too far this time, Sarah. And I am not the only one who believes so."

Had John gone too far? Sarah wondered. Along with siring her child, he had requested that she give up her music–her lifeline to Henry–and assume a role writing for the Community newspaper, his request hitting her like the death of a cherished friend. *How could she give up her music?*

"Shhh," Sarah said, pulling him into a tight embrace. "No more of this tonight." *No more thoughts of my commitment to John–to the Community–not tonight. Tonight, I will fill my love's heart with song one last time and hope that it is enough. He will have to understand and, perhaps, one day, forgive me.*

CHAPTER 39

Long before Abigail Talley had become Abigail Newland, wife of the good Reverend James Newland, she had been affectionately known around Sherrill as "Curious Abbey Talley" or sometimes simply by the acronym "Cat." The story goes that when she was three and a half, Abbey had asked her mother where babies came from. It was a standard question for most inquisitive youngsters, and Mrs. Talley fielded it cleanly and fairly honestly, saying that babies grew in the mother's stomach and then when it was time, popped out of the bottom through a special tunnel. "You mean like I do on the slide at the playground and you catch me?" Abbey had asked, excitedly. Mrs. Talley had confirmed Abbey's analogy with a nod, preoccupied at the time with a kitchen full of pies for a bake sale that morning. She would discover her youngest daughter later that day camped out beneath a table in the church basement, lifting the dress of an appalled pregnant woman who had just sat down with a cup of coffee and a slice of apple pie. Later, when asked what she was doing, Abbey had told her mother she just wanted to tell the baby not to be scared and that she would catch her at the bottom. "That's what you always tell *me*, Mommy," Abbey had said, candidly. That morning, "Cat" was born.

From that moment on the questions and answers of earthly living were just appetizers to Curious Abbey Talley. Hands-on experience was the main course; the reason one sat down at the table in the first place, she reasoned. By the time she had neared her 28th birthday, "Cat" had ordered and enjoyed almost everything on life's menu. She had dallied with boys (and a few girls) before moving up to men (and a few women). She experimented with alcohol, marijuana and other recreational drugs, as she called them, and hitchhiked around the globe several times. Her mother's death and a tearful appeal from her older sister Dorothy finally convinced her to trade in her cowboy boots and backpack for a pair of sensible shoes and a layered-bob haircut.

Sherrill was not prepared for the wild and worldly, late twenties' Abigail Talley anymore than they were for the nearly four-year-old "Cat," but after a few long months of steady tutelage from her big sister Dorothy, Abbey eventually calmed and settled in, becoming a Real Estate Broker with a local firm specializing in commercial property. A few years later, with several impulsive indiscretions protectively concealed by her sister Dorothy, Curious Abbey Talley met and married the handsome young Reverend James Newland, pastor of the local Methodist Church. The wedding marked the end of "Cat" and the beginning of Mrs. Reverend James Newland, a title and persona Abbey took very seriously. She could still recall the look of joy on her father's teary-eyed face as she walked down the isle after the ceremony under the sheltering arm of her new husband, and the loving gaze of her big sister, whose own face appeared rinsed of worry for the very first time. It was a fresh start for Abbey, a new life that she stepped into with the same vigor that had carried her and her single change of clothes around the world. Now, some twenty years later, she was happy and content, a warm puddle of relief still lingering inside her nearly a week after the woman known as Mrs. Reverend James Newland had nearly drowned of fear. Dorothy had saved her once again and Abbey reminded herself how lucky she was and how much she loved her sister.

"I should have my column for the newsletter ready this afternoon, dear," Reverend James Newland said to his wife as he sat down to enjoy the lunch she had just prepared for them both. He smiled and said, "I know how you like to get it out by Thursday morning."

"You've got plenty of time, James," Abbey replied. "So please don't rush. You know how disjointed you sound when you rush."

Abigail, as her husband insisted on calling her, had assumed the role of editor of the Church's weekly newsletter shortly after the two married, along with the duties of unofficial Church secretary, Sunday school teacher, adult Bible study coordinator, Choir director, church decoration arranger and bake sale planner, among other things. She fed James, bought his clothes, prepped and preened him before each mass, always stood beside him before the congregation in both body and spirit, and, most importantly, loved him with all her heart. He was a man whose passion for life rivaled her own and he had accepted her past without reservation, referring to her as "one of the lost sheep whose shepherds had led them astray." Abbey had told him from the very beginning of her physical and emotional wanderings, that is, all but one. She could never raise one secret to her lips. "It would cut your husband too deep," Dorothy had warned. Abbey had listened to her sister all those years ago only to watch in frozen horror a week ago as her past suddenly resurfaced and fluttered about Sherrill like a vengeful ghost. The risk of its exposure seemed tiny now, fading further with each passing day after the sad death of the visiting woman reporter, but the scare had made her wonder if she had made the right decision.

"I think you're going to love this one," the Reverend said. ""I've been inspired in a way that has been long in coming."

"A little fire and brimstone?" Abbey grinned.

"The good Lord has chosen to send us a test, placing temptation upon our table," he replied, his eyes widening as he spoke. "He now awaits our response."

"Temptation?" Abbey asked, warily.

"Yes, a wealthy young couple intrigued by the Oneida Community is considering building a spa and resort of some kind here in Sherrill. They have rented a room at the Mansion House and are now spreading inveiglement all about the city, placing well-conceived traps of promised wealth and prosperity into the minds of the beleaguered. It is now that we must shine the light of God as brightly as ever to illuminate the shadow of Satan that most certainly hides behind these visitors." He paused and took a sip of his coffee, as if digesting his resolve before saying, "This week's piece will be a lengthy one, my dearest Abigail, so be sure to tell the other contributors to be direct, but brief."

"I have already collected the other offerings and I still have a full page for you, my love."

"Splendid! I shall get it to you within the next few hours and we can distribute it tonight at Bible Study. *The Lord's word runs swiftly*. In the meantime, might I ask a small favor?"

Abbey just smiled. Her husband knew the answer to that already.

The Reverend said, "These visitors, the ones who tempt us today, I must imagine are searching for suitable property to erect their misguided alter. I would ask that you go and offer your assistance and glean what you can from their intentions. Show them what property is available. Determine if they are as serious about using an Oneida Community theme as the mayor and our brother-in-law so vehemently fear. Bring them by the church afterward. We must first understand the Devil's plan if we are to cast him out once and for all."

Mrs. Reverend Abigail Newland readily agreed to pay the young couple a visit. She realized right at that moment that her youthful fascination with the Oneida Community would be like a Judas kiss upon her husband's cheek. She had indeed made the right decision years ago to keep her one secret hidden, just as her sister had begged her to.

CHAPTER 40

The old mansion felt cold that morning.

Jess and I arrived back at our room only to find the bed neatly made, our dirty laundry gone and a small place card sitting on the bureau announcing that Candice was our housekeeper and that all tips should be given directly to her. I then noticed the three pennies I had dumped in a water glass were gone, concluding that Candice had indeed received her tip directly. The carpeting had also been picked clean, the victim of a Hoover upright, no doubt, as evidenced by the sporadic spinning brush marks that clearly did not extend under the bed or under the chair. *As an auditor, I'm trained to notice these things.*

With no evidence to support my claim of Homer's raid on our room, I decided to let it slide, heaving a frustrated sigh as I went to use the facilities. I noticed Jess reaching for the phone as I shut the door behind me. "Are you calling your *friend* in Yonkers?" I asked loudly. "What was his name again?" She hadn't mentioned his name before and this was my fairly obvious way of tricking her into telling me.

"Be quiet!" She snapped. "I'm on the phone."

"Ok, I'll just call him Yonker-dude then."

By the time I had wrapped up my affairs in the bathroom and returned to the room, Jess was already off the phone, cozy in the chair and nose deep into one of the books we'd gotten from the library. She interrupted her reading long enough to tell me that her "contact" at the Yonkers Police Department was on the case and that we would have Charlie Walinski's complete profile sometime tomorrow morning. "We'll need to find a fax machine though," she said, "if we want to see the full report."

"Just have him break it down to the jiggady-jig," I replied, "if the guy is a perp or not."

Jess peered at me over the top of her book.

"I just want to know if the guy has a violent history. I don't care about his traffic tickets or overdue child support payments."

Jess nodded and said, "Tomorrow."

The sudden agitation I was feeling had snuck up on me. Was it because we were close to discovering Mel's murderer? Would the report from Yonkers be a Shakespearian tragedy of epic proportions–domestic abuse, assault and battery, child molestation and rape? I paced around the room wondering why the local police hadn't interrogated this…this…sister killer.

"I think you need to relax," Jess said, after watching me fume for fifteen minutes. "Take a warm bath or a hot shower."

"I don't take baths and I've already showered this morning," I retorted, lying about the shower part just as I had to my mother all through high school. I drank beer to relax, or whiskey, tequila or rum (not necessarily in that order). "Let's go up to Shelley's place for lunch. I've got a few more questions I'd like to ask her."

"Like, *when does happy hour start*?" Jess asked. "Or, *can I get a discount if I buy two pitchers of beer instead of one*?"

"No!" Was all I could say. I didn't have any questions for Shelley and Jess knew it. I just needed a drink or two or three and she knew that, too. *Stuck between Jess and a hard place.*

The phone rang.

"Man, that Yonker-dude is quick," I quipped. "I feel bad for his girlfriend."

Jess flung a smirk at me and picked up the receiver on the second ring. It was Harriet. We had a visitor waiting for us in the lobby.

CHAPTER 41

According to Abigail Newland, real estate broker extra-ordinaire (her words), the City of Sherrill was founded in 1916 through a special act of the New York State Legislature. Sherrill had been a village up until then, but the community wanted a commission and manager-style government, "like the big cities," Abbey explained, which at the time was unconstitutional under General Village Law. The Governor approved and Sherrill became the only municipality in the state with a city charter under the jurisdiction of the town it resided in.

"Once a trend setter, always a trend setter," I said, referring to how years before the Oneida Community had made it vogue to go against the grain.

The Reverend's wife described the local residents as predominately white, with a sprinkling of African American and Native American families here and there, and a median household income of around fifty thousand dollars, nearly ten percent above the national average, she proudly claimed. Sherrill property held its value, Abbey told us repeatedly throughout our tour of the area. "The schools are great, the water is abundant and clean and the electricity is cheap, making it an excellent investment opportunity." Then, just that quickly, the saleswoman wind she had been sailing in shifted, spinning her in the opposite direction, and suddenly she was explaining to us that unfortunately Sherrill had very little room for further development. "One hundred years of good jobs and low utility costs have filled our little basket to the brim and I'm not sure we can carry anymore," Abbey said with a frown I took as false.

"What about some of the old buildings that the silverware maker isn't using anymore?" Jess asked. "We heard they've shut down a lot of their manufacturing here in Sherrill. Maybe we could renovate?"

"None of it is on the market, not that I know of anyway," Abbey quickly replied. "And of what's there, I can't see any of it being transformed into what you have in mind if it *was* for sale; at least not without spending a fortune, anyway." She then abruptly turned her car at the next intersection, squealing the tires in the process, sped us past several aluminum-sided residential blocks and into an open pasture divorced only by the road, saying, "There's lots of old farm land for sale just outside the city limits. Let me show you some of that."

"Who said we didn't have a fortune to spend?" I chuckled. "Did you tell somebody that, Lollipop?"

Ignoring my term of endearment, Jess said, "We'd rather be near the heart so we can be part of the pulse of the city, you know what I mean?"

"Yes," Abbey said limply, surrendering it seemed. "I do." She pulled into the next driveway and turned around, heading back into the Silver City. An awkward silence enveloped the plush leather interior of Abbey's four-door, luxury sedan as the three of us adjusted our respective battle plans.

It was obvious to me that Abigail Newland was trying to literally railroad us out of town, encouraged by her husband, I imagined, the Reverend Newland. Conspicuously, she hadn't asked us much about the details of our plan to build in Sherrill, reinforcing my belief that she already knew about our idea and that she had her own hidden agenda of how to deal with it. A direct line of questioning had worked well with Dorothy Smith, so I decided to stick with that.

Leaning forward from the back seat, I asked Abbey, "What do you think of a spa and resort with an Oneida Community theme?"

The poor woman flinched, pulling at the steering wheel so erratically that it nearly sent us spinning into a ditch. I had my answer, along with a crick in my neck.

What was rather funny about this whole situation was that Jess and I had no idea of what our proposed Community theme was. We had never considered the details such as décor, staff attire, activities or menu. Hell, we hadn't even agreed on a name for the place, let alone have a clue as to what it might look like. We just kept throwing the suggestion out there like one of those inkblots that psychiatrists use and let the locals interpret it as they would. So far, it seemed everyone saw a woman's vagina or the head of penis or, based on some reactions, both! *Interesting, as Freud would have said.*

After a moment, a more composed Abbey said, "That would certainly make for a colorful brochure."

I wasn't sure what *she* was envisioning, not the naked Playboy centerfolds that I pictured on my tri-fold advertisement I'm sure, but I played along, saying, "Yes, it would."

Jess asked, "You're familiar with the local business atmosphere, Abbey, do you think a spa and resort would do well in this area?"

The once extinct "Cat" suddenly appeared, her face lighting up as she said, "I think it would be amazing to have something like that here. I used to visit spas all the time in my other life so I would be there everyday. You'd make a pretty penny from me alone."

"I'm sure we could work out a nice lifetime membership deal," I chuckled.

"Are there already spas around here that you go to?" Jess asked.

"No, I'm sorry to say. I did some traveling in Europe in my younger days and practically lived in the spas over there. And in hostels and communes and flophouses," she said, casually. "I was a bit of wild child in my teens and twenties. I hope that doesn't spoil the conservative image it's taken me years to establish." She added a disarming smile to the end of her comment.

"Not at all," I said. "In fact, Jess was a bit of a gypsy herself some years ago; singing in the streets for spare change before I came along and tossed a Benjamin into her hat with my phone number on it."

"She called me that very same evening," I whispered to Abbey.

Jess just sighed, turned her head to the window and watched Sherrill saunter by as we made our way back toward the Mansion House.

At the main intersection that we had now come to know so well, Abbey made an unexpected turn and shortly thereafter we were pulling into the parking lot of a cedar-sided church with a rising bell tower that reminded me of the old top hats men used to wear in black and white movies. You could see everyone in Sherrill from up there, I imagined. *Maybe that was the point.*

"My husband wanted so much to meet the two of you that he asked me to bring you by when we were finished with our little tour," Abbey said as she unbuckled her seatbelt. "I hope you don't mind."

"Sure," I said, feeling my stomach knot like it did fifteen years ago when I was sent to the principal's office for putting laxative in our French teacher's coffee. Why would the Reverend want to meet us? Did he need a new organ for the choir? Or some new, energy-efficient, stained glass replacement windows like they sell on television perhaps? Remembering the pre-numbered offering envelopes I received from our church each year while growing up in Putney, the word 'donation' started ringing in my ear.

"How long have you two been married?" Jess asked as she and Abbey entered the church. I held the door open.

"It'll be twenty-one years in August," Abbey replied. "Time

does fly, doesn't it?"

"We've been married all of five days," I said, just to cement our cover story. I thought about going into the paper-mill-rescue bit but stopped as I vaguely remembered reciting a different lie earlier. *Something about gypsies?*

The Reverend James Newland was standing at the alter waiting for us, looking reticent but accepting, as if we were coming forward to confess our sins. I could feel my stomach tighten.

Introductions were made and glances were exchanged, and then nothing but the faint song of an unseen bird echoing from the rafters above.

"There's a bluebird nest in the bell tower," the Reverend said. "With four eggs that I believe should be hatching very soon. Birds are a wonderful gift from God."

The Reverend was a few inches taller than me, which I found slightly intimidating, and looked solidly built beneath the flowing black robe that stretched from the base of his thick neck down to the carpeted floor. A bright red sash-like adornment cascaded over his shoulders, falling almost to his knees, emblazoned with the word "Rejoice" on one side and a white dove in flight on the other. His hair was short, tidy and still as black as the day he was born, I guessed, making me wonder if he used that anti-graying formula my father was always threatening to apply one day. Oddly, I noticed that I couldn't see his shoes, and I found myself imagining his naked toes wiggling behind the curtain of his robe, clutching at the soft shag beneath us.

"Yes, they are," Jess said, as we all looked up in an apathetic attempt to spot the accused.

"I understand you and your husband are considering building a nest here in Sherrill," The Reverend said. "Tell me about it."

"A spa and resort, actually," Jess said. "A nest for travelers and vacationers, I guess you could say."

"And nothing for yourselves?" The Reverend asked.

"We have enough homes already," I said, smiling at the opportunity he had just unwittingly provided. "One in the Hamptons; another in Palm Springs; and of course the villa in Milan. Jess would never forgive me if I forget to mention Milan."

The Reverend turned toward his wife and said, "You lived in Milan for a spell, didn't you Abigail? Perhaps you might know the area."

"That was some years ago, Dear," Abbey replied. "Where in the city is your villa?"

I started to mumble something about the south side before Jess bailed me out by pointing at the tapestries hanging about the pulpit and commenting how beautiful they were. She then proceeded to steer the conversation around the entire alter and its decorations before we once again found ourselves under the spell of the invisible bluebird.

As I stood trapped in the awkwardness of the moment, the chirping suddenly dissolved as if some hidden force had just turned off the volume. I felt my head slowly pan to the Reverend's red sash. The frayed edges were morphing into two serpent heads right before my very eyes, their devilish tongues hissing at me, their diamond eyes sparkling with eerie delight. Without warning, the suddenly lively snakes leapt out at me, attempting to strike as I stepped away in shock, right onto Jess' foot. Her startled cry snapped me out of the trance.

"I'm sorry," I said, throwing my arm around her as much to hold her up as to apologize. "What were you saying, Reverend?"

"Are you practicing Christians?" he asked, pointedly.

I looked back at his stoic face, his posture looking rigidly erect like an army sergeant. The sash was once again just a limp garment. I hesitated before saying, "Yes, we go to church."

Jess then added, "We were married in a church just this past Saturday. St. Joseph's in fact. The Reverend did a wonderful job. My mother was crying like a baby, it was so lovely, she said."

The Reverend said, "Then I am sure you will understand when I speak for the community and express our concern over the type of resort you plan to build here. I understand you are considering something that embraces the ancient Oneida Community, a group that has long been forgotten along with memories of the Civil War, I dare say. It's nothing more than an interesting topic to read about by the fire on a cold winter evening, really." He then began a slow walk down the center isle of the church as he talked and we followed like herd sheep, listening to every pious word. "We are a devout community here in Sherrill, where neighbors care about neighbors, residents and business owners alike. It is a safe place for our parents to retire and for our children to grow because we have diligently worked our souls into a fertile soil in which God's word can thrive."

I could feel the sermon rising within the Reverend James Newland as he expounded on the evils of the Oneida Community as we neared the church vestibule. His voice had grown deeper and louder with each step, he words resonating off the gold plated plagues depicting Jesus' crucifixion that lined the noble walls as if Jesus himself were speaking them. But I wasn't listening to a passionately religious man speak; I was hearing a murderer cover his cowardly heart with scripture and ethical obligation. His red cloth band was no longer slithering but that didn't matter, I had already judged him and was now imagining a gallows as our walk ended and we stood at the door where we had entered. My sister was dead but I could feel her nudging me toward her killer.

Jess was looking at me now, her face twisted with confusion over the anger that undoubtedly was leeching out of my pores; a swelling crescendo to match the Reverend's now booming baritone. "Christian morality is at stake," he said. "The concupiscent debauchery buried by those who first stood against it must remain in its tomb forever. Now it is our burden to bear. Our legacy is as keepers of that chamber, protectors of the lost souls and weak minded, and we accept God's assignment earnestly."

The silence returned like a heavy rain. Even the bluebird had hushed, hiding from the fury of the Reverend's words in the rafters somewhere, just as Jess wanted to I was sure as she looked at my tightened jaw and piercing gaze in uncomprehending alarm.

I took a step toward the Reverend, my fists clenching hard as my mind raced with the visions of Mel screaming my name. Just as the heel of my shoe hit the floor, I felt a tug on my body that stopped me cold. Jess had latched onto my arm and was steering me out the door as she said, "We understand, Reverend. And thank you, Abbey, for your time. You've both been very helpful." She didn't let go until we were standing in front of Abbey's car.

Jess stared me down, shaking her head in tiny back and forth motions. Finally, she said, "Would you like to tell me what the hell is going on in that head of yours? You were about to pick a fight with a priest?"

I looked away, realizing what I had almost done and knowing that I wasn't sure how to explain myself. Could I trust this latest vision? Should I trust it? *Fuck, I don't know.* I took a deep breath and proceeded to dodge the question in my usual fashion.

"A pastor," I said.

"What?"

"Technically, he's not a priest," I said, as the cool, non-baptized, outdoor air began to clear my head. "He would have to be Catholic to be a priest, I believe. I could be wrong, though. And where did St. Joseph's come from? Is that where you go to church in Yonkers? With your cop *friend*?"

"Don't start," was all she said, before heaving a guttural sigh.

Abbey soon reappeared, unwittingly rescuing me from further interrogation and, without a word, drove us back to the Mansion House. I gazed blankly out the window the entire time, watching the little city being tucked into twilight, feeling like a foreigner who didn't know the language or the customs. I ached for the familiar surroundings of home. Had this been a foolhardy exercise all along? Two blind mice looking for a phantom with a fine silver carving knife? I didn't have an answer but I knew if I was to continue, to somehow unmask a murderer and avenge my sister's death, I would have to tell Jess about my dreams; tell her about the red demon that was haunting me; confess to her somehow so that we might wrestle the beast together.

I was seeing a fresh killer with every new sunrise and that was what was spooking me—big time. It was as if my nightmares were slowly creeping into the daylight hours and I felt helpless to stop them. Was the Reverend truly my sister's killer? Or were the visions that have plagued me for twenty years just screwing with my head? Just thinking about it brought on a tremor the likes of which I hadn't felt in a long time and I squeezed my insides hard to hide my shaking from Jess as best I could. There was only one sanctuary left and I knew right then where I would be spending the night. *Hopefully, Shelley is in the mood to stay open late tonight.*

CHAPTER 42

When Jessica Hartwell was mad, you knew it. After our meeting with the Reverend Newland and his wife, the air turned chilly in the car as Jess fumed and I withdrew. Thankfully, it was a short drive back to the Mansion House so I didn't have to listen long to the annoying rat-a-tat-tat of her thumb against the door handle or her convulsive sighs of frustration. She then slammed the car door in the Mansion House parking lot loud enough to trip house alarms within a two-mile radius and then again with the door to our room, followed last, but not least, by the bathroom door just as I was laying my coat on the bed. I timidly put my ear to the semi-glossed wood panel and heard the shower fizz on and then several muffled whacks that I imagined were her unbuttoned garment buttons hitting the wall as she flung off her clothes in disgust.

"If you need help washing your back, let me know," I shouted through the door, "or some extra towels." There was no reply.

She knew I had the twin telepathy; it was the only explanation. She had seen it in Mel and I could only imagine I had taken on the same haunted glow during my Sybil impersonation at the church. Now, she was angry that I wasn't sharing the premonitions the way Mel had probably shared with her—the ones about me. She had suspected it all along, right from the very beginning when she had asked me about it pointblank back in Putney. My answer hadn't fooled her then and I wasn't fooling her now.

Instead of facing her and confessing, I zipped my coat back up and walked the mile to Shelley's bar thinking the whole time about what a chicken-shit I was.

CHAPTER 43

After careful and in-depth examination of the subject, I had concluded that a person's sense of time gets lost somewhere between the fifth and sixth beer consumed in the first few hours of an evening spent glued to a barstool. My field tests have never been sanctioned by any authoritative body or scrutinized by lab-coated intellectuals for the proper environmental conditions, however, being a scientist of sorts–an intoxicologist, if you will–I remain confident my findings have evidentiary merit. Nothing in writing, mind you, but then many of the best theories concerning modern man have never made it to paper, of that I am sure.

Wednesday night was a perfect night for further research and after deciding it would be best to leave Jess alone in the shower (since she hadn't, nor was she about to invite me to join her), I found my own soothing spray a modest hike away in the form of a beer tap. Things were hopping at Shelley's place at the top of the hill. It was as if there was a full moon and the werewolves of the sleepy little Silver City had finally come out to play. Needless to say, my fangs were as blood thirsty as anyone's.

The clock on the wall faded away midway through my second pitcher of German ale like the memory of my fourteenth lay, fortifying my hypothesis about the human internal chronometer and placing me in a vacuum of cheerful apathy.

Somewhere along the way, I found myself holding a pool cue, asking a rather portly college-aged kid if combos were allowed, while eyeing a pair of twenty-dollar bills that sat flirtatiously on the shoulder of a smallish pool table I speculated was originally built for midgets. "They are," he said, and so I did, stuffing half of my prize into my pocket while buying a round with the other for the now-dwindled, mid-week crowd. I was in the zone, as they say, a man possessed with geometric supremacy and a crisp, delicate stroke. At least, when compared to the competition. As I stood there basking in my victory, I saw a familiar figure enter the bar and watched curiously, as the dapperly dressed man headed my way.

"If anyone had asked me, I would have guessed that Bob Applewhite would be tucking you into bed right about now, Mr. Mayor." I quipped, wondering if his pajamas also came complete with gold cuff links and a red power tie.

Mayor Arlen Bensinger pretended to laugh before asking, "Has anyone called winners?"

"Nope," I said. "Do you play?"

"Would you like to find out?" he quickly replied.

I let the mayor prepare the rack for my break, reminding him to place the eight ball in the middle, before I dropped two balls–a solid and a stripe–on my first, ear-flinching shot. He declined my offer to buy him a drink as I paced back and forth assessing the table, saying it would be bad for his image. I signaled to Shelley for a soda anyway, not wanting to miss my chance to bribe a local official.

"And playing pool with a lascivious tourist at this late hour isn't," I said, before dropping the one ball into a corner pocket.

"Well, I think the good folks of Sherrill will forgive me just this once," he said, a little too smugly, "being that I'm on official business and all."

"Oh, yeah?" I said, pulling away from the pool table to engage him fully. He had the look of a man on a mission, determined, with his shoulders squared and his chin turned up slightly like a boxer taunting to a punch. His haughty body language tripped my sarcasm and I asked, "Have you come out to meet with the common man; listen to his woes and tell him how hard you're working to make things better?"

"No," he said, with a wry grin. "I've come here tonight to ask you who you really are and why you came to Sherrill."

CHAPTER 44

Wednesday night was Harold Smith's favorite night of the week.

As the coffee machine gurgled happily in the background percolating a fresh pot of decaf, Dorothy Smith pulled two mugs from the stainless steel dish strainer next to the sink and set them out on the counter of her spotless kitchen. She was a neat freak just like her husband, Harold, who was sitting in the dining room relishing the newsletter they had received that evening at Reverend Newland's weekly Bible study class. It had been a superb class, Harold thought, one he had been anxiously awaiting for many years–a call to arms against the lascivious lot.

Dorothy poured the brew and obligingly joined him, helping herself to the cream and sugar that sat on the table between them. Harold's eyes were anxiously twitching as he took a cautious sip, a warning to Dorothy of a sermon bubbling within her husband much like her trusted Mr. Coffee. She referred to his outbursts often to her sister Abigail, calling them fits of spontaneous combustion that she feared would one day literally set him ablaze. "His face turns beat red and his voice pops and cracks like damp kindling wood," she would laugh. "It's a good thing I quit smoking, or I might accidentally spark a fire!" Abigail Newland didn't care to listen to Harold's amateur rants, as she called them; she had her hands full with her husband. *At least he is a professional*, she often thought to herself when comparing the Reverend's public sermons to Harold's private ones.

"The title of this week's piece by Reverend James is perfect," Harold said, excitedly. "'You can't walk with God and still hold hands with the Devil.' It's perfect, absolutely perfect."

Dorothy was already beginning to tune her husband out. She was listening only enough to count the number of times he had said the word "perfect," a solitary game she secretly invented years ago after discovering Harold's habit of repeating certain words during lengthy tirades about one thing or another. If she heard the term "lascivious" once, she had heard it a million times from his lips, and counting was one way she kept her exasperation in check. Day dreaming was the other way, but she was too tired for that tonight.

Harold was reading from the opening paragraph of the Reverend's essay as he said, "We must show determination to honor the Lord even in the presence of the heathen people...no man can serve two masters." He looked up at his wife, smiling ear to ear and said, "The Reverend was in perfect form tonight, wouldn't you say dear?"

"Perfect," Dorothy grinned.

Harold continued quoting the piece, "One cannot expect to reap the cream of this world *and* heaven besides...a true disciple lives in the heart of God's land, not on the border's edge...put to death therefore, whatever belongs to your earthy nature; sexual immorality, impurity, lust, evil desires, greed, which is idolatry." He paused, as if chewing on the words before swallowing and then said, "I think that last part is from Colossians. And a perfectly scripted line it is. I shall have to look it up tonight."

"That sounds a bit harsh," Dorothy said, knowing Harold would take it as a challenge to his view.

In his best preacher-like voice, Harold said, "The eternal God is your refuge and underneath are the everlasting arms. He will drive out your enemy before you, saying, 'Destroy him!'"

"But that young couple seems so nice, I don't see why you and

Reverend James need to brand them the enemy so you can get all of Sherrill against them," Dorothy said. She was mentally drained from the Bible study that had lasted twice as long as normal and her annoyance with her husband's recap was beginning to bleed through her normally tolerant exterior, word counting or not. "I don't think a nice little spa with an Oneida Community theme is such a bad idea. Honestly, Harold, I think you've worked yourself into a snit about nothing. John Humphrey Noyes and his followers have been dead for over a hundred years. Are you worried they will rise from the grave?"

Harold looked his wife straight in the eye and said with firm assurance, "Other seed fell among thorns, which grew up and choked the plants." He added that that was a quote from Matthew 13 before walking into the kitchen to deposit his half-empty cup in the sink. He then slipped away, leaving Dorothy with only the sounds of his footsteps ascending the staircase and his fading voice proclaiming, "Lead us not into temptation, but deliver us from evil."

Dorothy's stomach began to flutter nervously just as it had a week ago. Twenty years had passed without worry of being exposed and then suddenly back-to-back alarms ringing in her ears louder than the steeple bells of Reverend Newland's church. If only Harold had arrived on his white horse a year earlier then she would have nothing to fear from the ghosts of the Oneida Community. If only her mother hadn't died when she had and her sister had stayed in Europe. *What peculiar music the hand of fate does play sometimes,* Dorothy Smith thought to herself.

An impulsive surge of anger washed over her, anger toward Abigail, but it didn't last but for a moment. Abigail was her little sister, like her daughter almost, and Dorothy had never been able to hold a sour thought about her for any longer than it took her to sigh. This night would be no different, and as she exhaled a deep breath, she smiled to herself as she remembered the devilish proposition young Abbey had made shortly after her return home all those years ago and the impish look in her eyes as she had said, "I can resist anything, except temptation."

Dorothy still wondered how Abbey had talked her into such a lascivious act, as her husband would say. She told herself it was because of the frustration over her own life at the time, which had become routine and dull. In more honest moments, she knew the jealously she had developed toward Abbey's carefree lifestyle and the whole "Cat" persona had played a part in clouding her judgment. Finishing her coffee, she knew it made little difference now. *If only it hadn't involved the Oneida Community*, she thought, *my Harold and the good Reverend would care little, if at all.*

She glanced at the Reverend's newsletter, which Harold had left sitting on the table. Feeling a twinge of sympathy for the visitors she remembered only as Jess and Mick, she thought, "Those poor kids; such a nice couple, too."

CHAPTER 45

My glass was empty and Mel refused me another drink.

"Who died and made you King?" I said, my eyes wide with a 'don't fuck with me look' that I had perfected in the playgrounds of Putney, Vermont. Mel was standing behind a bar, Shelley's bar by the look of it, and she was wearing the same clothes my mother had her dressed in for her funeral. She looked much better in them now, being alive and all, but that didn't alter my irritation as I said, "Pour one more and there's a nice tip waiting on the other side."

"Queen, actually, and you've had enough," my sister said. "Besides, you've got work to do." She then turned her head away, fixing her eyes on the far half of the room. I followed her gaze only to find a dance floor crowded with people dancing merrily to rock music that was suddenly blaring wildly, though I couldn't distinguish the song. The mayor was there and he was dancing with Dirty Harriet, the policewoman. The Reverend Newland partnered with his sister-in-law Dorothy Smith, while her sister Abigail was doing the Funky Chicken with the old librarian Harold Smith. Looking deeper into the odd sight, I spotted Charlie Walinski pawing at an unfamiliar young woman; George, the Mansion House comedian, and the reception lady (Harry to her friends) were kicking up their heals in gay delight; and the whole gang of cooks and waitresses from the local restaurant were performing some kind of country line dance. Even Homer was in the fray, awkwardly bumping through the mass of frolicking flesh like the silver ball in a pinball machine.

I turned back to my sister, hoping to get an explanation, but she was gone. I scanned the place looking for her but she was no-where in sight. Then, I noticed my glass was once again filled with beer and there was a freshly poured pitcher sitting next to it, it's frothy head spitting wonderful juices into the air just beneath my nose. I smiled at it, reaching out with my hand just as the music stopped. My head slowly swiveled toward the gathering that was now motionless, everyone completely dressed in black.

Just then, their tight circle began to part and there in the mid-dle stood Mel with her eyes closed and her hands clasped. It was her coffin pose and I felt my chest collapse as the air fled my lungs in shock. My sudden recoil toppled the beer at my side and I stared at its death in disbelief, watching the fluid sparkle as it ran off the edge of the bar knowing it took my only escape with it.

The music began to rise up and now the dancers were alive again, ensnaring my sister as they weaved all around her. She was a mannequin, beautiful but lifeless, with puddles of blackness at her feet–blood, my mind said–being trampled by the zombie frenzy. I couldn't move, I couldn't blink, my entire body locked in terror. I screamed in silence, pleading and protesting. The per-formers ignored me, enveloping my sister in an ever-tightening embrace. Then, a deep crimson color emerged; the mayor's tie, the librarian's suspenders and the Reverend's stole. Each was a stark contrast to the black canvas in front of me and I could only gaze back in horror. There were other objects, too, hazy to my eye but unmistakably red, clutched in hands and draped over shoulders like a waterfall of blood.

I awoke with a start and punched the alarm clock that Jess must have set to the local radio station. It took me a moment and one ruckus chorus from the gravel-voiced lead singer to realize it was AC/DC singing "Highway to Hell."

It was Thursday and nearly ten o'clock. The morning was half-gone and I was alone in the Mansion House square I shared with my currently AWOL roommate, shaking uncontrollably.

I showered in preparation of the day ahead, admiring my chin, cheek and upper lip hair growth in the steamy bathroom mirror for several minutes before clipping my toe nails with a shaky hand and soothing my throbbing head with a few aspirin and a cold washcloth. By the time I was dressed, my quaking body had calmed. I sat down on the bed with one of the Oneida Community volumes, wondering when Jess would return and feeling like the jilted lover of a one-night stand.

What little recollection I had of the night before was murky at best and my desire to review it even worse, so I decided not to even try. Instead, I set the book in my lap and let it open by itself, thinking the self-exposed section would be where Jess had left off her reading. I could circumvent her impending reprimand with some quick study we could then share, I reasoned. It was wishful thinking, I knew that, but it was all I could come up with on short notice.

"Bible Argument?" I asked aloud, reading the page heading, "defining the relations of the sexes in the kingdom of heaven." I leafed forward and found that the text was part of the Community's First Annual Report of 1849, a lengthy document outlining their beliefs, which, it said, were based on scripture. Fascinated to the point of forgetting all about my nightmare, I read on until well past one, at which time Jess walked in with a brown paper bag that smelled suspiciously like Chinese food. My cottony mouth began to water. *Was she in the mood to share?*

"I had begun to think you'd run off with Homer," I said.

"A viable alternative," I heard her mumble as she set the groceries on the bed. She then retrieved a towel from the bathroom, spread it out over the top of the comforter, sat down and carefully unpacked several overstuffed, steam-leaking, juice-oozing white cardboard containers. "There's Kung Pao chicken in one, pork fried rice in another and some vegetable chow mein as well." She then tossed some chopsticks in front of me and proceeded to attack one of the cartons without another word.

I looked at the food hungrily and then at the chopsticks gloomily and said, "I can't work those things worth beans. You didn't happen to grab a fork, did you?"

She shook her head and kept eating.

"It's kind of ironic, don't you think, that we'd be sitting here, of all places, with all this food and no silverware," I said. I tried to muster a laugh to go along with it but it just sounded like a cat with a fur ball. Determined to persevere, I wrestled with the utensils as best I could and somehow managed to satisfy my complaining stomach. At meal end, I thanked Jess and helped clean up our mess, knowing that each small step I took was one giant leap toward getting back in her good graces.

Over the next hour, I described to Jess, in a one-sided conversation that had me pacing the room while she sat in the chair, what I had just read. How, according to the scripture sited by the Community's report, God will reign over the Kingdom of Heaven on Earth, supplanting all human governments. "It reminds me of John Lennon's song 'Imagine,' you know, the part about no countries," I said. "Although, now that I think about it, he suggested we imagine there's no religion, which doesn't correlate too well to a 'Bible Argument' I suppose." Jess' expression didn't change, leading me to conclude that she either wasn't into John Lennon or was suppressing more anger than I originally thought.

There were also paragraphs discussing the fall of Adam and Eve and its consequence–sexual shame, I explained. "When Adam and Eve were still innocent they, like little children, were not ashamed of their sexual organs–God's workmanship–the most perfect instruments of love and unity. The Oneida Community believed, according to the report, that 'to be ashamed of sexual conjunction is to be ashamed of the image of the glory of God–the physical symbol of life dwelling in life.'" I concluded that the report presented some interesting points supporting their *free love* ideas, and then asked Jess if she had read the report herself.

"Yes, I read it," she said flatly, breaking her silence. "And basically what they're suggesting is that we love one another the way Christ wanted us to–one big happy family."

"Exactly," I said trying to superglue our broken bond. "That's what I got from it, too."

Uneasy silence ensued. I stood still and watched her fidget in the chair.

Looking straight at me for the first time that morning, Jess asked, "Would you like to know why I got Chinese food for lunch?"

I had no idea why she thought I would care, but I played along and said I did.

"Well," Jess said in a tone reminiscent of my mother's, "I ended up having to trek ten miles to the next town and back because the waitress at the restaurant we *had* been enjoying all week purposely ignored me for over thirty minutes. When I asked her what the problem was, she told me to take a hike."

All I could muster was a contorted look of bewilderment.

"So, now might be a good time to explain to me what you did last night and why," she added, before folding her arms over her chest and locking her jaw.

CHAPTER 46

Bob Applewhite, Sherrill's Deputy Mayor, had had a busy Thursday morning interviewing candidates for an open sales position at the medium-sized textile manufacturer in Syracuse where he held the position of Human Resource Manager, so when Arlen Bensinger called with an offer to buy him lunch, he readily accepted. The bank where Sherrill's mayor worked was only a few miles away providing for frequent get-togethers to talk city business like the one Bob anticipated after he hung up the phone. When he walked into the sandwich shop and saw Arlen's face, he instantly knew his assumption had been wrong.

"You look like you've seen a ghost?" Bob chuckled.

"Not exactly," Arlen replied. "I'll explain it all after we sit down."

The two men waited their turn in line, received their orders on a damp orange plastic tray and sat down at a small table in the corner of the restaurant, conspicuously away from the other patrons. Bob unwrapped his sandwich, pulled open the tiny bag of potato chips that came free with every meal, and was taking a sip of his Diet Coke when he noticed Arlen hadn't touched his lunch yet. The Mayor was just staring off into the distance.

"Are you going to keep me in suspense all afternoon?" Bob said just before taking a bite of his ham and cheese on wheat bread.

"I'm in deep shit, Bob," Arlen said in a hushed tone.

Bob chewed thoughtfully as he recalled Arlen's past cries of wolf. He was easily excitable, Bob knew that all too well, and sometimes as jumpy as a frog in biology class. Every so often though, Arlen had been justified in his concerns, enough times in fact to make Bob a little nervous to ask his next question. He swallowed and said, "Could you be a little more specific?"

Speaking quietly, Arlen said, "do you remember that couple that we met with a few days ago that said they were thinking of building a resort spa in Sherrill? Hartwell Spa and Resort?"

"Yeah."

"There's no such animal. The whole story is a ruse."

Bob put his sandwich down and said, "A scam? What the hell for?"

"The guy is the brother of that reporter who died at the Mansion House last week. Her name was Melissa Gibson and she accidentally killed herself."

"I know who you're talking about Arlen. I live in Sherrill, too, remember?"

"I'm sorry, it's just this whole thing has got me spooked."

Bob wiped his chin and said, "Let's back up a bit. How do you know their business, the Hartwell Spa and Resort chain, doesn't exist?"

"I had a buddy of mine do some digging and he couldn't find a single scrap of paper with that name on it."

"Well, maybe it's a private company under a different name?"

Arlen shook his head. "I went to the source and asked point-blank. Sure enough, the whole thing is just a ploy to cover the real reason they're here."

"You talked to them? When?"

"I confronted Mick, Michael actually, last night over at Shelley's place. He confirmed that he was the Gibson woman's brother in what turned out to be a very enlightening evening. The guy likes to drink. And when he drinks, he talks. The woman he is with is not really his wife, either, although he claimed Jessica

Hartwell is her real name. She's a cop from New York City."

Bob said, "A cop? From New York? Why the hell would she come all the way up here?"

Arlen pushed himself back in his chair, paused, and then said gravely, "She's a friend of Melissa Gibson and she came here to investigate her murder."

"Murder?!"

"Shhh," Arlen said, with a scornful gaze.

Bob said in near whisper, "It was ruled accidental, autoerotic asphyxiation, as I recall."

"Yeah, but they believe the police report is wrong so they came to Sherrill to snoop around. They're on their own though. The woman took a week's vacation time so *officially* she's not here. He's just some tax auditor taking a few extra bereavement days."

"Just a couple of amateur detectives," Bob said as his face relaxed and a smile emerged. "And here everyone was working themselves into a lather worrying over an Oneida Community theme park." His appetite revived, Bob chuckled as he returned to his lunch. After several bites, he noticed Arlen still hadn't started in on his pastrami on rye.

"Relax, Arlen, and eat your meal; our boys in Sherrill did a thorough job, they always do. These Perry Mason wannabes aren't going to find anything different. The whole thing was an unfortunate accident."

Arlen's face remained a pale white as he said, "You don't understand. I was there that night."

"Where?" Bob asked, still chewing.

"At the Mansion House the night she died," Arlen whispered. "I was in Melissa Gibson's room."

CHAPTER 47

Cornered twice in a twelve-hour span did not play well with my ego.

"Why didn't you make something up?" Jess barked after I told her as much as I could remember about my encounter with the Mayor. "You should have told him his information was wrong–anything to keep our cover intact!"

"I know, I know, I should have lied through my teeth," I said, hoping that agreeing with her would calm her down as my arms flailed spastically like a pet bird whose wings have been clipped. (The poor thing thinks it can still fly, but it can't. That was me.) "He caught me by surprise and I panicked, I guess."

"You guess?" Jess replied. She was pacing the floor now, her eyes wild with rage, a lit fuse only a second or two away from exploding. I slowly backed up toward the exit door thinking a quick escape might be my only chance for survival. "You guess?" she repeated with more emphasis as her gaze sent a chill up my spine.

"He just kept pounding and pounding on me, saying *this* didn't add up and *that* didn't jive, and no one on the planet had ever heard of Hartwell Spa and Resort," I said, pleading my case. "I tried to keep quiet, tried to throw him a few bones, but the more I gave him, the hungrier he got. Next thing I knew, our whole charade had caved in."

"You mean YOU caved in!"

"I don't see what good it does us now to point fingers," I said, knowing that the best defense is a good offense. As a backup plan, I began to carefully search for the doorknob behind me.

Jess was shaking her head in frustrated disbelief. "Pounding and pounding you," she said with a six-inch thick layer of sarcasm. "It sounds more like *you* were pounding and pounding the beers to the point of severing all communications between your brain and the rest of your inebriated organs; *Mr. Motor-mouth* with nobody at the wheel."

She was right. I couldn't deny it. My drinking had once again put me—*us*—in a pickle, and for one of the few times in my life, I felt guilty about it. Maybe because this time it was about Mel and about Jess. I'd let them both down. There was no way for me to wiggle around that, not with macho resolve, false Alzheimer's claims or patented quips from old college roommates. The dream I had had that night had summed it up perfectly in a way I could only now understand: I could keep reaching for the booze or reach out to Mel…or the nearest equivalent–Jess.

Just then, a piece of paper slid under the door and got stuck under my shoe. As I bent down to pick it up, I heard the faint sound of tiptoeing footsteps disappearing down the hallway outside our room. I looked at the sheet, turning it over once briefly to view both sides, before opening the door. The corridor was empty. *Quick little bugger, whoever it was.* I closed the door and began to read the delivery.

"What is it?" Jess asked.

"It looks to be a parish newsletter from the Sherrill Methodist Church," I said, scanning the headlines and bylines. "Most of which is an editorial by Reverend Newland." I read the first paragraph of Newland's piece and, after feeling a sudden nausea, handed the thing over to Jess. I then went into the bathroom and leaned on the sink. Five minutes later, I resurfaced to see if Jess was still standing.

"He's talking about us, isn't he," I said.

"That would be my guess," Jess replied. "And it certainly explains my reception at the restaurant today." She went to the chair and collapsed in it, her hands falling down at her sides, her head turned upward as she sighed heavily and said, "How did this go so god-awful sour so god-awful fast."

"God-awful if I know," I said.

She shook her head at me, grimacing, before exhaling an even deeper sigh. "We're fucked," she said. It was the first time I had ever heard Jessica Hartwell swear aloud.

CHAPTER 48

For the remainder of Thursday afternoon, our fourth day in Sherrill, Jess and I laid low in our room at the Mansion House and contemplated our next move. The Mayor now knew of our misguided agenda, as he had called it standing beside the pool table that night, as, in all likelihood, did the rest of the civic staff of the smallest city in New York State, including the police department. We would find no loose government lips now, not that we would have before, but at least then there was an outside chance of it, however outrageous that fantasy had been. A good slice of the community would also be pitted against us as the infamous newsletter circulated, the Reverend Newland had seen to that. Consequently, we were not eager to venture out to watch that wildfire spread. Needless to say, the situation looked bleak and Jess and I, defeated.

"They're probably gathering out in front right now," I said, "an outraged mob of farmers and shopkeepers with pitchforks and torches screaming for Harriet to hand us over before they burn the place to the ground."

Jess wasn't amused. "I don't understand how you can joke about this," she snarled. "What little chance we had of finding out the truth about Mel's death is gone and you don't even care." She paused and turned away, her head slumping down, tears falling to the floor like raindrops. "You don't even look upset," she said, her lips quivering now as she wrapped her arms around herself, desperately trying to hold it together. "Do you feel anything at all!?"

I used to, I wanted to say, *a long time ago.* But I didn't. Somehow in the past five days, I discovered that even though my sister was gone, I could still feel her presence. I still cared. Right at that moment, I knew I had never really stopped caring. Mel was the one I needed to explain myself to, not my father. I decided to tell Jess everything, hoping that my sister was listening.

Knowing that what I was about to say could quickly spin out of control, I said, "I've been watching Mel die my whole life. Somewhere along the way I guess I grew numb to it." I then turned away and went to the window. Outside, birds littered the leafless trees. My only desire was to be one of them so I could fly away and leave Michael Gibson behind.

With heartache and apprehension choking her words, Jess turned toward me and asked, "What are you talking about?"

"I've had premonitions about Mel for as long as I can remember," I said, still enviously watching the crows and the sparrows appear and disappear in the sky. "They're nightmares mostly, with all kinds of tragic endings for the leading lady, the star of my productions–the one and only Melissa Gibson."

"Then you did feel her," Jess said, her eyes clearing just a bit. "I always thought you did, but I couldn't be sure."

"I still do, but in a different way," I said. "I've never known life without feeling Mel watching over me; at least, until last week when I woke up that morning and knew she was already dead."

"The morning after the night she died?"

"That would be the one," I replied gravely.

"But the police report said her body wasn't discovered until that afternoon. How could you know?"

I turned around, looked her right in the eyes and said, "I knew."

I could see by her expression she wasn't going to argue the point. Jess had told me that Mel had confided to her the premonitions she had about me, challenging my own denial of similar abilities at the time, and so this revelation was no shock to her, just an overdue confirmation. Looking into Jess's eyes, I saw what I had only hoped to find—acceptance.

"Well," Jess said, wiping her eyes. "There was nothing you could have done. She was...."

"Wait," I interrupted, "there's more." I paused, clearing my suddenly congested throat before taking a deep breath. *The point of no return.* "The day she died I had a premonition, a day dream if you will, while I was at work. I had them sometimes like that, in the middle of the day. It doesn't happen often but when the broadcast is a little too vivid, I find a bar and black out the screen. That day I had a nasty one. Mel was screaming to me for help, pleading with me, reaching out to me and I just stood there, frozen like a fucking statue. There was something wrapped around her neck, a snake, I think, bright red against the blackness of a phantom who was choking her, killing her right before my eyes."

Jess sat listening, horrified by what she was hearing.

Continuing, I said, "I fled to the nearest tavern with my tail between my legs and several hours later had forgotten all about it. The next morning when I woke up, I knew she was gone."

"You didn't call her first, to see if she was all right?" Jess asked, disbelievingly.

I hung my head and mumbled that I hadn't.

"But why? Mel was your sister, your twin. She would have dropped everything in a heartbeat to protect *you!*" Her rising anger had dried all her tears. She leaped out of the chair and stormed toward the door.

"Don't go," I pleaded. She stopped but didn't turn around to look at me. I think she was crying again, I couldn't see for sure, but she *was* trembling. I had to tell her one more thing, make her understand the torment I had been living with all my life. I had lost Mel but something inside me would not let me hide from Jess. I walked over and stood behind her. "When Mel and I were six years old, she had a premonition that a school trip I was supposed to go on that day would end in a horrible disaster. 'The bus is going to crash,' she had said, crying, frightened out of her mind that morning. Mel was so hysterical that my mother kept me home just to calm her down. That very morning *that* bus did crash, Jess. A bridge had collapsed minutes before it had come along, killing four kids. Dozens of others were badly hurt, but not me. I was home watching cartoons with Mel. My parents made quite a fuss over her, calling her their little prophet. Man, was I jealous. I still am.

Well, I stewed and stewed about it until one night, about a month later, I had my first nightmare about Mel," I said. "She was in her room, lying peacefully in her bed, when suddenly a tremendous wall of fire was all around her, trapping her in her bed. Burning rafters began to collapse as she screamed, 'Michael, Michael, help me! Please, help me!' I woke up in a cold sweat, shaking like you don't want to know, and ran into her room where I found her sleeping like a baby. I stayed there all night, waiting for something to happen, knowing that I could then rescue her and be the big hero. But nothing happened. I decided to keep quiet and wait for the next time. There were more nightmares after that—lots more—but every time I would find Mel unharmed. They would appear every night for a month or two, then disappear for a few weeks only to return with new vigor and fresh episodes like some insane Thursday night police drama."

"Did you tell her about them?" Jess asked.

"Once," I said. "I'd had a vision that one of our neighbors hit her with his car. It seemed so real that I couldn't hold it in. The green station wagon, the squealing tires, Mel's scream. Mr. Wyler's eyes nearly popping out of his head as he barreled into her. It was going to happen, Jess, I just knew it."

"Well, Mel didn't leave the house for weeks after I told her, and my parents...my parents thought it was the worst prank they'd ever seen. My father was ready to skin me alive and my mother didn't speak to me for a month."

Jess turned toward me slightly, a tiny hint of understanding blossoming right in front of my eyes. There was no way I would turn back now.

"Prank?" she then asked. "Why would they think that? Mel's premonition about you had come true so why didn't they believe yours?"

"I had a bit of reputation by then," I said, confessing. "She was perfect in their eyes and, as I said, I was jealous. But it was all harmless. Dead spiders under her pillow, stuff like that. I didn't know at the time I was building an image my parents would have tattooed on their brains for the rest of my life."

"I decided then that I would never mention another vision to Mel or my parents. If anyone asked about Mel's sixth sense, I would simply say that only she had gotten the paranormal abilities. I got the abnormal ones."

"But the nightmares kept coming. At some point, I began stealing my mother's sleeping pills to ward them off, graduating to booze when my father forgot to lock up the liquor cabinet one night. I think I was thirteen, but already I felt like an old man who'd seen too much and didn't want to look anymore. I didn't want the twin telepathy, not like that, but I couldn't get rid of it no matter how much I drank or how far I distanced myself from my sister. I can see that now. If only I had seen it before, I might have been able to do something."

I knew my mistake. I had to live with it now, but all I could think about was how hard I would fall if Jess walked out that door. I had no idea how to prevent it and so I said the only thing left to say—my confession to her and to my sister. With a sputtering voice I said, "I could have saved her, Jess, I could have saved her."

After what seemed like an eternity, she turned completely around. In her eyes, I saw the possibility of forgiveness. "I miss her so god-awful much," she said.

"So do I, Jess. So do I."

CHAPTER 49

What a beautiful day it is! Harold Smith thought to himself as he exited the Mansion House parking lot and headed home to the punctual dinner he knew his dutiful wife, Dorothy, would have waiting on the table. He had watched the day pass with barely containable glee, listening to residents glow about the Reverend's inspiring editorial, confident that an invisible flood of animosity toward the visiting entrepreneurs and their lascivious plans was filling the streets outside at that very moment just as he had hoped. He was a happy camper, as they say, a man in the mood to gloat.

He had just been talking with Harry, the Mansion House receptionist, and had learned, much to his added pleasure, that the young couple had just told her that they might be leaving tomorrow morning but would let her know for sure later that night. "Oh well, I hoped they enjoyed their stay," he had said with a sheepish grin he couldn't and wouldn't hide. Driving home now, he still carried the same smirk.

"The crusade of the clergy triumphs again!" he shouted aloud. He pulled on one of his red suspenders and then released it, letting it snap back against his chest, as was his habit when he got overly excited and there was no one else around. It stung a bit, but in a strange way, it elevated his excitement. He did it several more times before pulling into his driveway.

He sat outside in his car for a spell, rewinding the events of the past few weeks and relishing the outcome that was now taking shape. The anonymous letter to the paper had been a dicey decision by the Mayor's band of unofficial advisors, of which he was one. The private note he had passed to the woman reporter a risky betrayal. All is well that end's well, that was Harold's motto. Today it fit perfectly.

Harold skipped into the house and kissed his wife passionately on the lips for the first time in many years.

The Mansion House
April 1873

Sarah awoke that morning with black spots and bright circles before her eyes. She had been feeling "off" now for several days, brooding over the doubts and fears, which seemed to be coming upon her much more heavily than they had when she was younger. A turbulent air was swelling inside her, just as it was in the Community, stirred by several rising young members returning as convinced agnostics with degrees from Yale and Columbia, one of which was her estranged lover, Henry. Sarah could feel the tug of war was evolving–young versus old, first generation against second generation, the role of God for man in opposition to the role of man for God–and her own breakdown looming. Overwhelmed, she was scarcely eating her meals or sleeping due to the strain, finding it difficult to fulfill her duties as editor of the Circular, the Community newspaper. Willfully prepared to resume her career in writing, she had returned to work just a few months ago after a long convalescence, precipitated by the stillborn delivery of a baby girl–John's baby girl. *I put all my hopes and desires in God's hands*, she had written in her journal. She now found herself wondering, *does he truly exist?* She turned to her husband, Edward, hoping that he could help exorcise the evil thoughts from her head.

"Do you think they're right, Edward," she said as the two entered the empty dining hall, the first arrivals for breakfast.

"Of whom do you speak, Dearest?" Edward replied. He then pulled out a chair for his wife and assisted her before placing himself at the table.

"The group of young men–Positivists, I believe they are calling themselves–who have been spreading their newfound inspirations all about the Association."

Edward tilted his head up thoughtfully. After a moment, he said, "Yes, yes, the college boys swept up by that infernal Boston influence. *The only authentic knowledge is scientific knowledge,*" he added mockingly. With the flick of his wrist, he snapped open his napkin and laid it carefully in his lap. "I don't believe a word of it. And neither should you."

Noticing her staring off into the distance, Edward realized he would need to bolster his advice.

"They are nothing more than intellectuals, my dear, literary folks with feeble hearts. A brain that is subordinate to the heart ultimately becomes stronger than the heartless brains."

Sarah was not soothed by her husband's words, nervously playing with own napkin and silverware. He placed his hand onto hers, quieting her with several tender pats.

"It will pass," he said. "The darkness and hardness you see in them is a narcotic one, dulling the spiritual sense. It cannot last. The continuing light of God will dissolve it."

A single tear trickled down Sarah's cheek, then, another. Hearing Henry described in such a horrific matter ripped at her heart so ferociously she thought she was going to faint. Worst of all, she knew it to be true. Henry *had* changed. Did he still love her? She feared the answer to that question more than anything else.

"Are you alright, Dearest?" Edward asked.

"I'm sorry, Edward," Sarah said, struggling to stifle the sobbing before it consumed her. "Please, see if you can find a boiling pot. I'm in dire need of my morning tea."

Agreeably, Edward rose from the table, laid his napkin to rest, and headed off toward the kitchen. He was as eager for a cup of tea as his wife, and left convinced that a good breakfast would lighten her spirits and that the Oneida Community would endure the *infernal Boston influence.*

Watching him go, Sarah realized for the first time that she did not love her husband. He was a good man who treated her kindly, but not a man who could reduce her to tears the way thoughts of Henry could. *Has my heart strayed into idolatry and the insincerity of false love? Have I fallen so that there is no more opportunity for me to renew unto repentance?*

Feeling stranded on a rock of unfaithfulness, Sarah asked God for help.

CHAPTER 50

There was a line in a movie I remembered where a little boy cautions his older brother, who is dancing in the ocean surf, to "watch out for the Under Toad!" Robin Williams was in it, I think, playing the father of the two boys, who then authoritatively points out that it was the *undertow* that the boy needed to be concerned with, the dangerous water current returning seaward, not a monstrous frog that the younger boy had imagined after misunderstanding his father's earlier warning. That scene popped into my head as Jess and I sat on a bench on the shore of Oneida Lake watching the sunset. I tried to make a joke, saying, "Sherrill certainly has a strong moral Under Toad." She didn't get it at first, had never seen that movie I guessed, so I explained it. She replied simply, "No, we didn't anticipate the Under Toad, did we?"

We had found our way to the eastern tip of Oneida Lake, about ten miles north of Sherrill, purely by accident after Jess suggested that we "get out of Dodge."

"At least for the evening," she had added. "It'll give us a chance to take a step back and re-evaluate the situation."

Anxious to vacate the Mansion House before a bloodthirsty mob arrived, I had readily agreed. Following an hour of aimless driving through the low rolling hills of Central New York, we had found a little village along the shoreline of the lake that offered free access to the beach and several quaint restaurants along the main street. It looked like a summer tourist stop, only it wasn't summer and there were very few tourists. It appeared to be the perfect spot to clear our heads. Sitting there with the soothing sound of the surf ebbing and flowing, I stared out across the twenty-something mile expanse of water feeling like the weight of the world had finally been lifted off my shoulders. Finally, I had told someone about my nightmares–someone who believed me.

"It's a pretty lake," Jess said.

"Yeah, it is," I replied. "Looks and smells fairly clean, too."

That was all the small talk we could muster under the circumstances. So, we sat on the beach for a good while, deep in our own thoughts until the sun abandoned us and left shivering in the chilly night air.

"Let's go get something to eat," I said.

"I'm not very hungry," Jess replied.

"Well, I am. It's a male thing. Even under stress, our instinct drives us toward food so that we stay strong to protect the women folk. You can watch me eat if you don't want anything."

She bled a tiny smile, the first I had seen from her all day. We walked to a small diner close to where we had parked. It had a huge sign in the window that said, "Friday Fish Fry now on Thursday too!"

"What will they think of next," I said as we entered.

We found a faded-yellow-cushion booth in the corner, its white and silver speckled synthetic tabletop reflecting the ceiling lights like a disco ball. We asked for two sodas, telling the waitress we would need to peruse the menu a while before we'd be ready to order. She told us to take our time, and that they were open until ten. I decided I'd wait until Jess found her appetite before calling back the waitress, which I hoped would be well before the place closed.

"Do you believe in Heaven?" Jess asked, out of the blue.

"That's kind of personal, don't you think?" I said in mock alarm. "It's like asking me if I prefer to sleep in pajamas or in the nude."

"I didn't mean to...."

"That's all right," I said. "I guess I opened my Pandora's Box when I told you about my telepathy with Mel so I shouldn't feel so surprised that you're eager to know more."

"I wouldn't say I'm eager."

"I prefer sleeping in the nude. There, I've said it. Now you know."

Jess laughed and I joined her, happy I was able to lighten her mood. We both then returned to the menus.

"I think I'll get a burger," Jess said. "And maybe a side of fries provided you'll eat some of them."

I agreed.

The waitress returned, scribbled our requests on her little notepad, and disappeared again.

"I already know that you like to sleep nude," Jess said.

After thinking about it for a moment, I embarrassingly realized she was right.

"I believe in Heaven," Jess then said, "and I know Mel's there now. I'll bet she's already writing a column for the local paper–Heaven Today."

"Heaven Today?" I laughed. "That is god-awful, Jess."

"Yeah, it is," she chuckled. After a pause, she said, "You don't feel her anymore?"

My head dropped for a second. I looked back up and said, "Not the way I used to. But sometimes...sometimes when I'm not thinking of her at all, I'll suddenly feel like she's standing right next to me. But when I turn to look, she's not there. Does that make any sense?"

Jess didn't say anything as her eyes grew misty.

"There's probably some fancy word for it, lost-twin-atrophy or something like that. I'm like one of those amputees whose mind thinks the arm is still there."

"And the dreams?"

"The latest episodes seem to all revolve around what happened to Mel in Sherrill, in that damn Mansion House. What my mind thinks went on there, anyway. When she's not being choked to death by a red boa-constrictor, she's happily roaming about in some black and white Charlie Chaplin movie. Only there's no Keystone Cops around to save her. Either Mel is speaking to me from the great beyond, steering me toward her killer, or I'm on a slow train to straight-jacket junction."

"If that's where *you're* headed then save a padded room for me," Jess said, "because I'm right behind you."

"Maybe we could get a room together," I smiled. "Save on expenses."

"Yeah, and feed each other with our feet," Jess added, finding a light-hearted laugh to go with it.

Just then, the waitress delivered our meal. We spent the next fifteen minutes putting solid dents into our burgers and wrestling over the side dish of fries. Exasperated by my overzealous attention toward the potato slices, Jess interceded and doled them out in impartial fashion. "One for me and one for you," she repeated over and over until the bowl was empty. *Just like Mel used to do when we were kids.*

Jess had momentarily forgotten about the whole mess we were in, I thought, seeing her enjoying her dinner. Her obsession with my sister's fate, the push to find a killer had taken a short restroom break. I waited until we had finished eating before I pulled her back.

I said, "Speaking of guys named Charlie, what did your cop friend in Yonkers find out about Charlie Walinski?"

"Oh, right. I almost forgot about him," Jess replied. "There wasn't much in the system about the guy. A couple of domestic abuse visits by the Sherrill P.D. some years ago when Charlie and his family first moved to Sherrill. He spent a night in jail one time for smacking his wife but she dropped the charges the next day. After she moved out, his record has been clean, according to the report. Although, my contact thought it was strange that he didn't find anything about the guy prior to the year he moved to Sherrill. Typically, guys with anger management issues like him have an existing track record of vandalism, assault or petty theft; and very often much bigger stuff."

"What was his name again, your contact at the Yonkers P.D.?"

Jess grinned and, ignoring my question, continued, "I suggested he look for an alias. Our friend Charlie may have changed names before he and his wife uprooted in order to hide past offenses and start fresh in Sherrill."

"That was good thinking. How long does something like that take?"

"There's no way to predict something like that. Buddy might find it in an hour or not trip over it for days or even weeks."

"Buddy?" I said, embellishing my surprise. "His name is Buddy? That's a dog's name."

"Let it go," she said, shaking her head in mild disgust. She stared at me a moment, as if studying my skull for defects, then exhaled a sigh that was more a laugh than a cry. "At any rate, Charlie's a dead end; at least for now. Tell me about the dreams you've been having. What do you think Mel is trying to tell you?"

"She's telling me she was murdered," I said, the serious half of my mind assuming command as I recalled the grisly visions of my sister I had over the past two weeks. "Strangled by something colored red, like that sash thing the Reverend was wearing yesterday."

"Ah," Jess said, finally making the connection between our visit to the church and my sudden hostility toward Reverend Newland. "The snake in your dream is just a metaphor, a symbol of the real murder weapon. Is that what happened yesterday? Did his sash come alive?"

I nodded that it had, saying, "And you wonder why I drink?"

Cautiously, Jess said, "you don't believe...."

"No," I said firmly. "I was just trying on the straight-jacket at that point; testing to see if it was a good fit."

"Although, we shouldn't rule him out," she said. "Not yet."

"Or the city librarian, my pal Gomer and his red suspenders; or the mayor, who seems to have a fetish for crimson colored power ties."

"Did the mayor's tie turn into a snake, too? When we had lunch that day?"

"No, thank God. I probably would have leapt across the table and stabbed him with the butter knife if it had. That would have been an ironic headline: *Mayor of Silver City killed with locally manufactured flatware!*"

Jess said, "He doesn't strike me as a man who could kill somebody. What about the librarian?"

"Mel could have taken him down with one hand tied behind her back. He's just a bug hiding behind a Bible. I'd be shocked if he ended up being the one. No, my money is on Homer."

"Has he been in your dreams? I don't recall anything red in his clothing."

I shook my head no. Except for the dance party scene I had dreamt the night before, he had been conspicuously absent from my dreams and hallucinations. I should have drawn a different conclusion but my gut was telling me he was my man. "He's got the perfect profile," I said. "He looks strong enough to choke a horse; he lives at the Mansion 24-7 so he can wander around without anyone thinking anything of it; and he's probably got a skeleton key for every room in the place. He's got the creep factor working double overtime, what with those psycho eyes and that chainsaw glued to his hand."

"I don't know," Jess said, hesitantly. "He didn't scare me that much."

"Come on, you wouldn't scream bloody murder if he cornered you alone down in that dungeon they call a cellar?"

"I didn't say that," she said, grinning.

"We might as well face it, Jess, we've been here four days and have managed to alienate the whole city while establishing only one truly viable suspect but not a single thread of evidence."

"What about your dreams, your premonitions?"

"I don't think they'll hold up in court."

"You believe she was murdered just as much as I do," Jess said.

"Yes, absolutely, but we have no idea what we're doing. Sure, we could stay a few more days but I honestly think that if something doesn't break tomorrow, we should call it quits and book out of here Saturday morning before more shit hits the fan. I've got some money saved up; we can hire a private investigator to take the case. He can look into Homer's background and follow up with Buddy about Charlie Walinski's past. I loved Mel with all my heart, but we're just spinning our wheels here."

Jess didn't agree or disagree, only turned away and peered out the window into the dark overcast night, her head tilting upward, her eyes scanning the blackness for chance a star might peak its way through the clouds. "I'll never quit," was all she said to me.

CHAPTER 51

The blind date was going much better than either of them had hoped.

They had met in a chat room on the internet several months ago, one labeled *Adventurous Booklovers,* and had been in constant contact ever since, sending flirtatious emails and instant messages from work, home, and even sometimes while lying in bed, each with a laptop computer by their sides. Finally, at her suggestion, they agreed to meet in person, setting up a rendezvous in a bar an hour south of where he lived and an hour north of her. "I'll meet you halfway...lol!" he had typed two nights ago. "It's a date!" she had typed back.

They had noticed each other the first time because of the similarity in their online nicknames: his was FictionBoy69 and hers was FictionGirl44. Each moniker seemed to imply certain attributes, which they had playfully discussed in many keyboard discussions, but tonight was where the rubber met the road, as they say. They had never exchanged pictures or their real names, that was part of the thrill, but the gamble appeared to have paid off and, after several hours of coy glances, blue jokes and nervous laughter, she had asked if he would like to go someplace for coffee.

The man readily accepted the invitation with a nod and a wink before excusing himself, telling the attractive, forty-something divorcee that he needed to use the restroom and would return "in two shakes of a lamb's tail." Standing now in front of the men's room mirror, he smiled at his reflection, complimenting himself on his dapper appearance and the evening's fine performance. "If only my friends could see me now," he said aloud. But he was sixty miles from Sherrill where he had been living for quite some time, and no one in this town knew him from Adam. "Perfect," he thought to himself. He reached into his blazer pocket to check its contents for the umpteenth time since leaving home, smiling at the sight of the tiny vile of clear liquid (*Easy Lay*, the man he had bought it from had called the drug. "Guaranteed to put her out, so you can slide in!") and a red silk scarf that had belonged to his wife.

Tonight would be a piece of cake. He could feel it in his bones as well as in the crotch of his pants. The risk was almost non-existent. His date tonight didn't even know his real name or where he lived. No one in this place did, unlike the near disaster of the prior week when he had let his dick do his thinking and had drugged a woman in a bar only a half mile from where he lived. It had been a spur of the moment thing; an adrenaline rush that quickly transformed into panic after the woman died naked and unconscious before he even had a chance to unbuckle his belt. He managed to cover his tracks as he had done before, thankful that this time he hadn't consummated the act. But it had been too close a call for his liking.

"Never shit where you eat, numb nuts!" he said to the man in the mirror grinning back at him.

He ran through tonight's plan in his mind. He would sneak a drop of the drug into her drink and then spend fifteen minutes asking her detailed directions to her house while the chemical slithered into her veins. Then, he would insist on driving her home when she complained about feeling too woozy to drive. She would be helpless by the time they got there, he concluded.

FictionBoy69 then checked the part in his hair one final time, smiled, and returned to the bar, anxious to finish his date.

CHAPTER 52

It was just after midnight, Friday morning officially, but still Thursday night to my body. Jess and I lay on our designated sides of the bed watching tree limb shadows dance along the wall. On our way back to the Mansion House, the clouds had cleared and now there was a full moon illuminating the courtyard outside our slightly opened window. A light breeze blew into our sleepy room. The crisp, fresh air took me back to when Mel and I used to camp out in a pup tent in our backyard during summer recess. We would lie awake half the night talking about nothing, the Yankee baseball game playing in the background on a pint-sized transistor radio I rarely went anywhere without, before waking up at dawn to go fishing at a pond that was only a ten-minute bike ride from our house. Once in a while my friend Jeff would take Mel's place when my mother and Mel had a girls' night out, but his jokes and ghost stories were never as good as hers, not to me anyway. And I never had a nightmare on those nights, not a single harrowing thought about her when Mel was laying next to me under the stars just like Jess was now. I loved those summers. I missed my sister.

"You never answered my question," Jess said.

"Which one?" I replied.

"Do you believe in Heaven?"

"I guess it depends on what your definition of Heaven is," I replied. "I think the one with angels floating on billowy white clouds and all that was conjured up by some guy whacked out on crack. Probably those twelve apostles started it up, Christ's posse. A bunch of Cheech and Chong types I'll bet, writing testaments day and night, stoked so badly on reefer they couldn't put their quills down."

I knew I was ragging unfairly on a topic I didn't know a lot about but Jess was laughing and that was all that mattered. Then I said in a more serious tone, "I think there's something after this, after life on earth I mean."

"I do too," Jess replied softly, "something completely different."

"Different how? Better? Worse?"

"No," Jess said, the word lingering on her tongue as she thought about it. "Just different."

The stick figure puppet show performing on the wall caught my eye as I pondered what she had said. Maybe there was something to that; something the scientists, astronomers and even the Pope had missed in their carefully calculated explanations of the hereafter. Maybe it was just something other than what we had experienced in our first life, not better or worse, not pearly gates or scorching flames and not George Burns smoking a cigar, pretending to be God. Something like now, only different. *I hope Mel has a good brother there.*

I must have fallen asleep with that very thought in my head because the next thing I knew I was waking up to a scratching noise just outside our door. It sounded like a dog trying to unearth a bone from the wooden floor in the hallway, a small dog like a Chihuahua. I got up, went to the door and opened it a crack, half expecting to see Lassie looking back at me with worried eyes that said Timmy was stuck in a well. The hall was empty. I looked back at Jess who appeared sound asleep, but was at that very moment rolling over onto *my* side of the bed.

The digital clock read 3:22 a.m. I sniffed outside our room for the scent of manure, Homer's calling card, but all I got was a nose full of musty, old mansion air.

I cautiously poked my head out further, gazing up and down the dimly lit corridor. There, standing at the far end and looking directly at me was one of the old ghosts, as I called them, the flannel-shirted, grey-haired man with the iPod. As soon as he saw me, he started walking toward me. I felt the muscles in my neck stiffen as my eyes opened wider than I ever thought possible. My feet seemed to be melting into the floorboards as he drew closer and closer. I wanted to call out to Jess but my tongue had fled down my throat and was now hiding somewhere in my small intestine. The only thing left to my senses was the sound of his footsteps ringing in my ears to the exact beat of my thumping heart.

Two rooms down from where I was standing, the man stopped and opened the door. He then nodded to me, turned and walked away, disappearing around a corner without a word. "Mel's room," I whispered to myself, feeling for the first time in my life that *this* premonition about my sister was one I could believe without hesitation. I walked down the hall, found it unlocked and went inside.

The room was almost an exact replica of the one Jess and I were staying in. It was a modestly adorned square with a simple, white-quilted, queen-sized bed with a nightstand, a chest of drawers and a sitting chair wrapped in a flowery pattern that I couldn't distinguish in the faint moonlight cascading in through the draped window. The blind on the window was drawn halfway down like the one I had seen from outside in the courtyard on the day we arrived. This was where Mel had stayed and I smiled briefly, until I remembered that she had died here as well. Murdered!

I don't know how long I stood in the middle of that room completely lost, searching the four corners for some trace of my sister, before I finally went to the chair, exhausted, and sat down. She wasn't here anymore, in body or spirit. I got a chill thinking that she had spent her last moments here–horrible moments. I forced myself not to think about it, shifting instead to what Jess had said about the next life being something different. I thought about Mel as she had been, full of life and love for everyone she met. That's how she was in the next life, I was sure of that now. A different place like Jess suggested perhaps, but not a different Melissa Gibson.

My body began to complain about sleep. Just before I rose to return to my room, I reached down into the cushions of the chair in search of "buried treasure." For once, my seeking hand found gold!

CHAPTER 53

All the years of patiently awaiting the sunrise had prepared me for this night.

Wedged down beneath the worn cushion of the sitting chair in the Mansion House room where my sister Mel had stayed, I had found a computer data disc. Actually, it was one of those new memory sticks that everyone seemed to have now, labeled MG-NYT 2/2. *Melissa Gibson–New York Times; Second of Two Discs.* It looked like a downsized disposable lighter, but it could hold vast volumes of data and could be hooked to your keychain, serving as a convenient way to transport and safeguard information; the latest rage in the techno-nerd circles.

As soon as I had got back to our room, I quietly pulled out my laptop computer, which had been sitting idly in its travel bag under the chair since Monday (I had planned to catch up on some work, but, hey, you know how that goes) and brought it to life. I then popped the stick into the USB port in the back and set about recreating the events of the week before using whatever files I found. That's where Jess found me in the morning, sitting in the chair with my computer in my lap still feverishly mousing away.

"Have you been up all night?" she asked, wiping the sleep from her eyes. Decked out in Eskimo lingerie–the now familiar faded-yellow flannels–I couldn't help notice that there was an unfastened button innocently exposing her belly button, a non-pierced inny.

"A good chunk of it," I replied, trying not to stare at her exposure. "I found something." I handed her the memory stick and said, "I've copied everything in it onto my computer and now I am almost done reviewing it all."

Jess studied the label, "Mel's?"

I nodded, "Yes."

"Where did you find it?"

"In the room a couple doors down. It was Mel's room. One of the ghosts tipped me off."

Jess threw me a perplexed look that told me it was too early for ghost stories.

"Two of Two," Jess pondered. "Do you think that means there is another disc out there somewhere labeled *One of Two*?"

"I think that's a safe bet. It's probably with her laptop, wherever that is, because it wasn't with the belongings my father and I retrieved."

"Maybe she put this one there on purpose," Jess said. "You know, to provide us with clues."

"I don't think so, Nancy Drew," I said, good-humoredly. "She just misplaced it there. I was always finding her stuff in the couch back home–combs, lipstick, cell phones. You name it; I found it. Sometimes I even gave the stuff back to her."

"Whether she put it there or not, have you found anything helpful, like the picture of the murderer?" She asked as she came over to where she could peer over my shoulder at the computer screen.

"No," I chuckled. "Nothing quite that obvious, I'm afraid, but some extensive notes detailing the story she had been compiling *and* the sources thereof. There is also an interesting email I think you should see." I clicked on the shortcut icon and the message magically appeared on the screen like a rabbit from a hat.

I said, "Based on the date, Mel would have gotten this email early last week while she was here. Now, provided she opened it and read it on that day, she would have had plenty of time to investigate its accusation."

"Accusation?"

"That's right. This email, sent by a 'Concerned Resident,' claims that a woman here in Sherrill has been practicing one of the tenets of the Oneida Community's sexual system. More specifically, she has been teaching young men in the local area about the fine art of Male Continence."

"You're kidding!" Jess said, bending down to get a closer look, perhaps hoping there might be some accessory illustrations. "That's the thing Dorothy told us about. The Community's preferred method of birth control, where the man never achieves orgasm."

"Sounds more like their version of 'Night of the Living Dead'," I quipped.

"It makes you nervous just thinking about it, doesn't it," Jess said in a teasing tone.

"Yes! As a matter of fact, it does. But it answers the question about the rebirth of the Oneida Community."

"I don't know if I'd go that far. It may just be one person and one isolated incident for all we know. The tendency to exaggerate was one of the first unwritten rules of human nature I learned when I began working the streets of Yonkers. A dozen looting youths would always turn out to be just three or four; a robbed and frightened business owner's description of a 'hail of gunfire,' usually proved to be a single round from an equally scared crook. So, the moral to my story is—let's not jump to conclusions."

I said, "You have to admit, it does parallel the anonymous letter to Mel's editor claiming a resurgence of the Oneida Community."

Jess replied coolly, "Both letters are probably from the same person." She then looked at the bottom of the message, at the signature. "Any idea who this *concerned resident* might be?"

"Oh, I have a pretty good idea. Read the last line."

Jess squinted at the screen and read aloud the line just above my finger. "There is no place for this kind of lasciviousness in our fine community."

We looked at each other and said in unison, "Harold Smith!"

"Now look at who he names as the perpetrator of the *bawdy behavior*."

"Oh, my God!" was all Jess could say.

CHAPTER 54

My sister Mel's computer memory stick had a folder labeled simply "OC," *Oneida Community*. It contained several dozen documents detailing interviews with local people, page references and quotes from books she must have found in the City Library or in the Mansion House itself, and a variety of ideas she had jotted down for her final piece. Either she hadn't started the article that would ultimately appear in the *Times*, or it was on the other disc that Jess and I had convinced ourselves *did* exist. After we both had read every line of every file in that folder and then compared thoughts, I felt we had a good picture of Mel's investigative reporting travels on the subject of the rebirth of the Oneida Community. Her spin was very positive, just as we expected, but inconclusive as to whether or not a revival was presently, and perhaps covertly, underway. The members of the original OC, as Mel had referred to them in her notes, were compassionate, hard working, family oriented people who practiced what they preached and held themselves fully accountable to their "alternative" beliefs. She seemed especially taken with the equal rights the women of that time enjoyed, chronicling their role in dozens of pages including an interview with the no-orgasms-for-the-man practitioner. It all seemed complete but I still had a gnawing feeling that there was something missing; something important to our cause; something that was on that other disc.

Jess and I finally decided to take a break from our study. After taking a shower (not together), we were now dressed and considering where to go for breakfast. We had a few people we wanted to talk to, names listed as sources in Mel's documents, but the question was where to start. A knock at our door gave us the answer. Jess guardedly opened it.

"I thought you kids might be hungry," Harriet Kinney, Harry to her friends, said cheerfully. She held a tray filled with bagels, donuts, juice and coffee, and didn't wait for an invitation before walking right in and setting the provisions onto the bed. "I hope you like fresh-squeezed orange juice. My grandchildren won't drink it–too much pulp."

There was a momentary and rather uncomfortable pause before Jess said, "That was very thoughtful of you. Mick and I were just saying how hungry we both are."

"Wonderful," Harriet said. "We can have a little picnic right here on the bed."

We all sat down carefully so as not to tip the juice or coffee containers over and helped ourselves to the spread, I, myself, quickly grabbing the only glazed donut in the pile much to Jess's chagrin. Then we all sipped our beverages and chewed our selections happily as if we had done it together a hundred times before. Harriet made me feel like the always-welcome grandson. She was the first to break the silence.

"I have to confess I had an ulterior motive for visiting you both this morning," she said as her cheerful expression turned somber. "The mayor stopped by yesterday and told me who you both really are. As soon as he left, I knew I would have to speak to you."

Had Harriet come to us before that morning, Jess and I both would have been floored by what she was about to tell us. But after reading the notes in Mel's files that listed Harriet as the source of countless clarifications and quotes about the Oneida Community, as well as insights to the moral "Under Toad" of the current Sherrill community and its inhabitants, we were ready and anxious to hear her side of my sister's story.

Harriet started by telling us how sorry she was about Mel's death and how much she had enjoying talking with her. They had met in Mel's room every evening, she explained, just after dinner so that Harriet could explain or elaborate on anything Mel had learned that day. "She was so inquisitive," Harriet said, "and smart as a whip. She knew a cock and bull story when she heard one and there were plenty of those floating around Sherrill, I dare say." She then said that they were getting along "just swimmingly" until one night when Melissa had a number of uninvited visitors. Coincidentally, it was the night she died.

I struggled to remain calm as I asked Harriet who had come to my sister's room that night and why.

"The first one was the Reverend Newland," Harriet said, "which was a shock to me because I don't recall him ever setting foot inside the Mansion House before. Not that I knew of anyway."

"You were there?" Jess asked. "In Mel's room with them?"

"Sort of," she replied. "We had met that night in her room like we had been all week when there was a knock at the door," she said. "Melissa told me to hide in the bathroom because she wanted to keep my identity hidden in case anyone got into a snit about her article after it came out. She was very considerate that way. Of course, I did as she asked."

"What did the Reverend want?" I asked.

"Well, he was very brief and to the point, exactly the opposite of his Sunday sermons, I might add. He wanted to know what her position was on the Oneida Community–did she find them as lurid as he did?"

Jess asked, "What did she say?"

"I'm sorry, Reverend, but that's really none of your business!" Harriet replied, holding back a giggle.

That's my sister.

"I don't imagine he was too thrilled with her answer," Jess

said, smiling at me.

"He wasn't. He left in a huff with his white collar bent all to hell, if you'll pardon my pun."

"And then there were others, you said?" I asked, "More unannounced visitors?"

"Yes. About five minutes after Reverend Newland stormed off, his wife Abigail came calling with her sister Dorothy. Back into the bathroom I went!"

This one was no surprise to me. We had read about Abigail in Mel's notes. She was the one the not-so-anonymous snitch had written to Mel about–the tutor of climax-less sex, the governess of the shake without the shiver, the teacher of the class I never planned on enrolling in.

As it turns out, according to what Harriet overheard, older sister Dorothy had been an "educator" as well. The "study sessions" had taken place over twenty years ago before the two of them had gotten married, just a few months after Abigail had returned to Sherrill after a long absence overseas. Abigail had quickly become fascinated with the Oneida Community's sexual system after reading several books on the subject her sister had acquired over the years, and true to her adventurous nature, uninhibitedly indulged her curiosity with a number of willing "students." Dorothy had followed suit out of a sudden resurgence of jealousy toward her sister's unbridled spirit, she claimed. They assured Mel, Harriet said, that all the young men were consensual adults and that only one of them still lived in the area.

"Why did they come to Mel and spill their guts like that?" I asked, uncertain about their motive.

Harriet didn't immediately respond.

"Their husbands don't know anything about their past, do they?" Jess said, "And they were scared to death that now they might find out."

Harriet nodded, agreeing with Jess's conclusion.

"Who's the guy that still lives in the area?" I asked, thinking there was still a little juice left to squeeze. Harriet said she didn't know because the two women hadn't divulged that to Mel. "They're protecting someone else, I imagine," Harriet added.

And then, he took things a step further to return the favor by killing Mel. I surmised.

It certainly looked like my buddy Harold Smith had stabbed the Reverend in the back thinking his sister-in-law Abigail had acted alone only to now have the yet-unseen knife flying back in his direction. Was he also capable of murder? He didn't know it yet but somebody who looked an awful lot like Melissa Gibson's brother was about to rock his world, as they say. *I hope Gomer enjoys irony.*

"What did Mel tell them?" Jess asked.

"She told them not to worry," Harriet said. "And I know she meant it."

"You must have been in that bathroom quite a while," Jess said.

"Had I known, I would have brought my makeup kit," she laughed. "After the Talleys left, dear me, I still catch myself calling them by their maiden names, I bid Melissa goodnight and hurried out. It was getting late by then and I had my animals back home waiting for me. Buster, my cocker spaniel can hold his bladder, but little Sophia, my Pekinese, can't go more than an hour without spotting the rugs."

"About what time was it when you left?" I asked.

"Around nine or nine-thirty, I think," Harriet said, squishing her face in deep reflection. "Larry King's television show had already started by the time I got home and took the dogs to the potty. I watch Larry every night; he always has someone interesting on. Do you kids watch his program?"

"Once in a while," I said, though I couldn't remember the last time, if ever.

"Did Mel say what she planned to do the rest of the night?" Jess asked.

"Now that you mention it, she did say something about going up to Shelley's place for a nice glass of wine. She said it had been a frantic day and she needed an hour to unwind before she could even begin to think about falling asleep. I told her that I had the same problem sometimes. I suggested a gin gimlet. It only takes one of those and out I go."

"Did she say if she would be meeting anyone?" I asked.

"Well, she did say that the mayor had told her it was a nice place to go for a quiet drink, so I suppose *he* may have invited her?"

CHAPTER 55

"I think we should tell them before somebody else does," Dorothy Smith said to her sister, Abigail Newland. They were sitting in Dorothy's kitchen, a relaxing blend of primitive antiques and homemade knickknacks, finishing up the morning's pot of coffee while arguing, as sisters sometimes do, over their next course of action in regards to the "snooping young couple holed up in the Mansion House," as Abigail had put it. Her little sister was acting more like the fifteen-year-old brat she used to cover for, Dorothy thought, unwilling to accept responsibility for her actions just like she did when she was little. Her big sister didn't think she was going to let Abigail squirm out of it this time, especially since Dorothy herself had so much at stake as well, but in the end, as always, she would.

"As soon as one of them finds out, that one will certainly tell the other," Dorothy said, believing that her Harold and the Reverend James were confidants. "And then any hope we have for forgiveness will be gone. We must tell them ourselves if we are to have any chance at all."

Abigail shook her head defiantly. "We've kept it a secret for twenty years and can keep it for twenty more," she said. "That couple is searching for the truth about that poor woman's death, not for details of our past *lasciviousness*."

Dorothy grimaced. She hated that word, lasciviousness. Harold had been using it constantly in recent weeks and it was beginning to make her physically ill. It sounded so vulgar, she thought, making her poor judgment of twenty years ago sound so much filthier than she cared to remember it. "Must you use that word," she complained.

"Lasciviousness?" Abigail said grinning. She then quickly apologized, enjoying the acerbic moment nonetheless.

Dorothy said, "I know we've come this far without it leaking out but I've grown weary from the burden of it all, haven't you, Abbey? Wouldn't you rather we just get it out in the open and be done with it?"

"No," Abigail replied firmly. "James would never understand and neither would Harold. You're foolish, dear sister, if you think otherwise. We've built a happy life here and we must protect it. That reporter, God rest her soul, is gone and soon so will that young couple."

"And what about Homer?" Dorothy asked. "Do you really believe that man has kept quiet all these years? He may have talked to them."

"Homer and I have an understanding," Abigail said as her eyes trailed away.

"Abigail!" Dorothy exhaled, "You're not still...."

"Oh, heavens no, dear sister," Abigail said with a light giggle. "He was a strappingly handsome lad at nineteen and one of my brightest pupils, but the years have certainly weathered all that away. No, you needn't worry about Homer, he empathizes with us."

Dorothy was still unconvinced that they were doing the right thing, but the protective big sister in her would not allow her to oppose "sweet little Abbey," as their mother used to call her after forgiving another day's mischief. It had always been that way and it probably always would, Dorothy conceded. She decided to ride out the storm just as her younger sister proposed.

Still, Dorothy wondered what Abigail had said to Homer Tubb. In the back of her mind, hidden to the rest of the world, lived a tiny suspicion that her sister might have been involved in the death of Melissa Gibson, the reporter Dorothy knew Abigail had talked with a few days before she died. She hated herself for even thinking it, but it had lingered all week, and hearing her say so vehemently that they needed to protect their happy lives made her stomach jump. She must have known what the reporter was after. Had she suggested something to Homer–something to protect them all? He *would* do anything for her, Dorothy was sure of that. He had been in love with Abigail since the days of their Community "experiments," as Dorothy preferred to call them. He had followed the younger sister around town like a lost puppy until the Reverend Newland came along and carried her up into the church steeple, as Abigail would describe their courtship. Was Homer still in love with Abigail? Willing to protect her at any cost?

Surreptitiously, Dorothy examined her little sister and, for a moment, saw a stranger sitting before her, clutching her coffee mug, her golden–ringed fingers worriedly performing piano scales against the white porcelain. The Abigail she knew, thought she knew, had not returned from Europe all those years ago. In her place, returned an unusual but worldlier woman with mysterious views and secret compartments that Dorothy was still struggling to understand. But a murderer? Her coffee cold and her head throbbing, Dorothy Smith pushed the ghastly thoughts from her mind, disgusted for having them, convinced that it was her jealously that was twisting her reasoning. Sisters protected each other.

CHAPTER 56

Homer Tubb gazed out at the sky from just inside the Mansion House maintenance shed and decided the day had come. He pulled in a long, deep breath, savoring the moist morning air, placidly pleased that spring had arrived. The observant windows of the old mansion stared back at him, but he did not blink. The battle cries of his enemy swirled about the courtyard like feeble leaves caught in a playful breeze, but he did not turn his head away. He stood firm and lifted a worn, leather bound Bible he held in his left hand so that it faced the world outside. Then, without opening it, he recited a passage from within that he had altered ever so slightly:

"Be strong and courageous, because you will lead these people to inherit the land I swore to their forefathers to give them. Be strong and very courageous. Be careful to obey all the law my servant John gave you; do not turn from it to the right or to the left, that you may be successful wherever you go. Do not let this Book of the Law depart from your mouth; meditate on it day and night, so that you may be careful to do everything written in it. Then you will be prosperous and successful. Have I not commanded you? Be strong and courageous. Do not be terrified; do not be discouraged, for the LORD your God will be with you wherever you go."

Now Homer was ready. All he had to do was wait.

CHAPTER 57

I was surprised when Arlen Bensinger, without hesitation, agreed to meet with Jess and me. There were several things he wanted us to know, he had said. "Incidental events surrounding the night in question," he claimed that the Sherrill P.D. already knew about. Now, as I sat across from the man who may have murdered my sister, I fought back my rage and tried to remember the questions Jess and I had prepared a short while ago.

"We appreciate you taking time off from your regular job to come back and meet with us, Arlen," Jess said, playing the Good Cop. (I had gladly accepted the Bad Cop role.) "Your office is very comfortable."

"Thank you," Arlen replied. He was visibly shaking, fidgeting behind his desk and bending a paperclip mercilessly until it finally broke in half, puncturing his finger. He put the wound into his mouth while he retrieved a band-aid from the desk drawer. Watching him tend to it so readily made me think that it must happen often. With his injury bandaged, he seemed to calm a bit as he said, "I was deeply saddened when I heard of your sister's death. Please accept my condolences."

I nodded slightly, searching his eyes for some semblance of sincerity. They were too murky but then that's what you get with career-minded politicians, I remembered my father telling me once. Jess thanked him.

Arlen said, "I talked with her several times during her stay here, mostly about the current economy and history of the city. I'm not sure if I was much help to her, for her article that is, but I did enjoy meeting her. She was a charming woman."

"Yes, she was," Jess said. "Everyone loved Mel."

At that point, I wasn't sure if I was supposed to cut in with the hot lamp and probing questions but I decided to anyway. I said, "We understand you may have seen Mel that night, the night she died. I'd like to hear more about that, the *incidental events* as you refer to them."

Arlen seized another helpless paperclip and shifted in his chair. He then warned us that everything he was about to tell us was confidential, part of an ongoing investigation and that he didn't have to divulge a single word of it. He would, though, he said earnestly, because he had sisters, three of them, in fact, and that if he were in my shoes, he would be demanding the truth just as I was.

I thought to myself, "Were these the words of a savvy politician or an honest man clearing his conscious?" I decided to hear what he had to say and judge him afterward.

The mayor told us that he had gone to Shelley's bar that night for a quick beer. After spotting Melissa sitting at a table, he went over and asked if he could join her. She invited him to sit down, he said, and, after some small talk about the warm weather, Charlie Walinski joined them. Charlie had been sitting with Mel before Arlen had arrived, Arlen explained, but must have gone to the restroom just as he came in giving Arlen the impression Mel was alone. "Charlie's beer was already sitting on the table, I just hadn't noticed it when I first sat down," Arlen said. "I don't care for Charlie," he said in an uncharacteristic, politically reckless tone. "I've lost all patience for his bullshit."

Arlen then explained how he had asked Charlie to finish his beer at the bar because he had some city business to discuss with Melissa. When Charlie refused, they got into a heated argument, with each man accusing the other of personal motives regarding the "attractive reporter." He had then quickly realized that such an ugly scene would discolor his reputation far worse than Charlie's. He got up and left, leaving the two of them sitting there. He then sat in his car outside the bar for a while to cool down before heading home.

"Was that the last time you saw her alive?" Jess asked.

The mayor hesitated for a moment, a long moment in my mind, and then said soberly, "No, it wasn't."

His words registered in my brain slowly, like the delayed head pain that comes from sucking on an ice cube, and I stared back at him, willing myself to stay in my seat as his crimson tie began to squirm its way up his chest. The snake was coming alive right before my very eyes again. I quickly shut them and pleaded to my soul for control. I lost all track of time, feeling only my throbbing head and the death grip of my hands around the arms of the chair. I opened my eyes again to find Jess and Arlen looking uneasily at me. I spoke, although it felt like someone else, like a demon from within, in a deep, threatening growl, "Did you kill my sister?"

"Of course not, I just said that," Arlen rebutted defensively. "Haven't you been listening?"

Arlen then explained how Mel had come out of the bar alone shortly after he had. He was still in the parking lot in his car and she had smiled at him, encouragement he thought, before leaving in her Mustang. He said he had then followed her back to the Mansion House before going up to her room. She was surprised to see him when she opened her door, he said, and it was then that he realized the attraction between them was entirely one sided. He said he was only in her room for a few minutes, long enough to apologize for the misunderstanding and wish her a good night's sleep. She was very gracious about it, Arlen said, telling him she was flattered and that it would remain their little secret.

Later, Jess would say that she thought he appeared genuinely ashamed of his actions and I would respond that, indeed, he should be since he was married with three children, adding sarcastically, "Who does he think he is anyway–Bill Clinton?"

"That's really all there was to it," Arlen said as we concluded our little meeting. "When I left the Mansion House your sister was alive and well. Although, she did say she was feeling a little groggy as I was leaving."

"Did you notice what she had been drinking at the bar?" Jess asked.

"White wine I believe," Arlen replied. "But she had hardly touched it. I know because I was going to offer to buy her one when I first sat down at her table, until I saw she already had a full glass."

"Did she look drunk to you at that point, or even a little tipsy?"

"Not at all," Arlen said. "But now that I think about it there *was* a noticeable difference in her demeanor between the time we were sitting in the bar to the time I was leaving her room."

"How so?" Jess asked.

"Well, she looked tired and a little groggy, just like I said. It must have come on fairly quickly, too, because I hadn't notice it when she first answered her door."

"And you said it appeared that Charlie Walinski had been sitting with Mel before you arrived?" I asked.

"That's the impression I got."

"Did you see him leave the bar?" Jess asked.

"No, he definitely didn't come out with Mel, I would have seen him. What he did after I left, I have no idea."

Jess was thinking now, drawing conclusions, I imagined, but I was still settling my ebbing rage as the room fell silent. After a few minutes, Arlen said he needed to leave for a meeting back in Syracuse but promised to talk with the police chief later about our conversation. He was confident they would want to talk with Charlie, he said. If Charlie was involved, they would "nail him," adding jokingly that not all police departments were a bunch of bumbling idiots as often depicted on television. Jess then grabbed my arm and led me away, leaving behind a trail of pleasantries.

Outside the Sherrill Municipal Building, it was an agreeably sunny day and I asked Jess if she believed what the Mayor had said, to which she replied curiously, "Most of it."

CHAPTER 58

While she drove us back to the Mansion House, Jess told me that she believed the mayor was not involved with Mel's death. "A no-good cheating husband–yes; a cold blooded killer–no," she said as we waited at the lone red light that caught us every time we went anywhere in Sherrill. When I asked how she knew, she handed me the women's intuition line. "I could see it in his eyes," she said. I told her politicians wear different color contacts for emergencies like this to influence gullible people like her. "When someone's got them by the short hairs, they pull out the baby blues from the special kit they're issued at their secret initiation ceremony, slap on a big smile and maneuver their way out. I think they receive a handbook as well when they're sworn in– Bullshitting For Dummies," I argued. Though I presented what I thought was a strong case, I wasn't able to sway her female-instinct-based opinion.

"Did you buy *everything* that guy was selling?" I asked out of frustration.

"No," Jess replied. "He's not telling us everything he knows about Charlie Walinski. My guess is they're looking at him as seriously as we are."

"Are *we* looking at Charlie seriously? Your friend Buddy said his criminal file was pretty thin."

"It is under *that* name, but something tells me our friend Charlie has had a few other identities."

"Women's intuition again?"

"A little of that, but mostly my experience with the criminal element," she said authoritatively. "The one thing every person with a bad history wants is a clean start, that's human nature."

"And you think Charlie fits that mold?"

"Yes, as a matter of fact, I do."

"Well, my gut tells me, my *male logic* says it's Homer Tubb all the way. The guy is straight out of a Stephen King novel; the Jack Nicholson character in that movie 'The Shining'; a-million-miles-off-his-rocker nuts!"

"You shouldn't judge a...."

"Book by its cover," I interrupted. "I know, I know. You stick with your intuition and I'll stick with my gut logic, and we'll see who nabs who."

"Ok," Jess said with a grin.

It was early afternoon when we pulled into the Mansion House parking lot. The sun was full in the sky, shadowed only by a sea of blackbirds circling the thirty-acre-plus property, hovering like vultures over a mortally wounded elephant. Looking up, I could see they had taken over several of the larger trees; nefarious ebony buds dotting the imposing branches; calling to one another in an annoying chorus of off-key squawks and cackles. The birds seemed to have grown in numbers during the week of our stay and as we walked through the courtyard toward the back entry, I wondered what the attraction was along with worrying about their lack of toilet training. Jess seemed distracted by them as well.

"I hope they don't have a taste for human flesh," I quipped.

"Don't even joke about it," she replied, "that old Hitchcock movie about the whacked-out birds scared the living daylights out of me when I was little. Why my mother let me watch it, I'll never know."

"I'll bet she told you not to and yet you went ahead and watched it anyway."

Jess just smiled, telling me I was right.

The sudden, unmistakable roar of a chainsaw interrupted the moment. I quickly turned to my left, toward the source of the sound, and there, coming around the corner, was Homer himself, the grounds-keeping psycho and my number one suspect. His eyes were lit with fury; his hands white-knuckled around the rumbling, prey-eating machine; his waist belt bejeweled with menacing steel blades of various shapes and sizes. He was entering the courtyard the same way we had, through the only existing gap between unattached buildings of the four-sided estate, and effectually blocking our escape.

Before I could blink, Jess had unexpectedly grabbed my arm at the elbow and was pulling me away, urging me to follow her. "Come on!" she shouted over the din of the ripping motor and the startled crows. Still dazed by the sight of Homer, I ran clumsily in her wake the remaining twenty yards of the courtyard to the back door to the old mansion. Locked!

"It's never been locked before," Jess said in a panic that only heightened my own. She shook the door wildly but it didn't budge.

"*He* probably locked it," I said, looking back at our pursuer, who was already half way across the courtyard, walking briskly straight toward us. "I'm not one to say I told you so, but I told you he was a killer!"

"Let's try another door," Jess said. We fled in the most logical direction available to us–the opposite direction of Homer.

We ran, frenzied and gasping for air, to each inviting door we could find in the quad. Every one them, locked. With the obsessed Homer hot on our heels, we had no time to ring doorbells.

"This is just like that movie," I yelled as we scampered from door to door, "This guy really thinks he's Nicholson."

Finally, with our options depleted, we stood on the porch of what I assumed to be one of the apartments Harriet had mentioned and prepared to face our adversary. *A pleasant enough place to die*, I thought, spying two weathered wicker-back rockers sitting serenely to one side. I pushed Jess behind me, protecting her, and began a stare-down that I hoped would scare Homer away. It didn't. He kept coming and coming, bursting growls and puffs of smoke from his weapon as he advanced. He came to the bottom of the three steps that led to the porch where we stood bug-eyed and helpless, and stopped, his greasy finger still twitching against the chainsaw trigger, revving the motor as if to some hidden melody. Rat-a-tat-tat-tat-tat… Rat-a-tat-tat-tat-tat.

Above us, the sky was a black blanket. The crows were fleeing. *Wait, come back. Take us with you!*

Just then, the door behind us opened and out popped old George, the Mansion House "comedian" we had met at dinner our first night in town. He wasn't exactly the cavalry commander I was hoping for, looking more like a Geisha house customer in his oriental robe and sandals, but I wasn't about to complain.

"What is all the dadburn ruckus out here!" George snapped before stepping out onto the porch. He quickly assessed our frightened faces, and then aimed a stern scowl at the man at the bottom of his steps. "Homer!" he yelled like a father who had just caught his son smoking cigarettes in the bathroom. "Are you mucking with the guests again?"

Homer smiled sheepishly, turned, and walked away without a word.

George then noticed the bolting birds overhead, a huge black wave rolling out to sea, their fading caws protesting the hostile encounter. "Homer sure does hate crows," he said. "Works himself into a real nasty frenzy every spring knowing they'll be back looking to roost in our trees. It's a religious thing with Homer and those birds are the devil."

"Are you telling me he was only trying to scare away the crows?" I asked as my heart crawled back into my chest.

"Yup," George replied. "That chainsaw seems to work best. Those blackbirds can't stand the noise and it sure beats the hell out of those firecrackers he tried one year." He started to chuckle as he said, "I remember one spring we were having a birthday party right out here in the courtyard, I can't remember who it was for, my memory isn't what it used to be, when Homer fired that thing up and started turning laps around our tables, gunning the engine like a race car. We nearly lost three of the retirees to heart attacks but it sure put a fright into those crows. They stayed away all summer after that."

"I guess you had to be there," I said, failing to see the humor in it.

"Yeah, Homer's got a weird sense of humor," George said as he slapped me on the back. "He keeps us on our toes around here. And you folks, too, by the sound of it."

"He looks deranged to me," Jess said.

George laughed again and said admiringly, "Doesn't he!" He explained that his lunch was on the stove, and suggested we give his rocking chairs a try. He then bid us a good afternoon.

I turned to Jess and asked, "Are we in the Twilight Zone?"

CHAPTER 59

I surrendered to George's suggestion, collapsing into one of the rockers on his porch. I stared blankly out into the Mansion House courtyard, feeling the certainty of Homer's guilt evaporate as if sucked away in the updraft created by the vanishing winged nuisance. It would have made a nice ending to our week as amateur private eyes, I thought to myself, to catch the psycho-killer and avenge my sister's death *and* in the process, save the Silver City from further loss of human life. A really cool newspaper headline that I'm sure even Harold Smith would have appreciated. But it was not to be, it seemed, and as I began to mentally prepare for the melancholy trip home, Jess took a seat next to me. I could tell she sensed my feeling of failure.

"Well, look at the bright side," she said with a weak smile. "If Homer had been our man we both might be two piles of ground chuck right now. So, it's a good thing he's just a weirdo with a taste for blackbird blood and sick pranks."

"So it would appear," I said, before exhaling my frustration. "So it would appear."

We sat on the porch for quite a while, quiet in our own thoughts, rocking tunefully, whittling away at the tension that had accumulated like road salt residue on a car after a long Northeast winter, its corrosive desires threatening to render us worthless rust. I told myself I might never find the truth about my sister's death; Mel was dead and that wouldn't change no matter what happened from this day forward. I argued, not completely convincingly, that in time I would come to terms with my actions, my lack of action as it were. After all, Jess had forgiven me, hadn't she? *But could I forgive myself?*

All around me, life went on, seemingly oblivious to my anguish. I could hear George inside his apartment talking enthusiastically to someone on the phone, his grown child perhaps or a sibling. Homer was off tormenting another flock, the distant rat-a-tat-tat-tat of his chainsaw spilling over the mansion walls and falling at our feet like tiny ocean waves. An elderly couple was strolling through the quad, heading for the awakening gardens, the birth of spring. Jess was still living and breathing as well, rocking steadily next to me, thinking of Mel I had no doubt, but also about returning to Yonkers, to her job, family and friends. I would have to do the same, although that reality seemed like a faraway fantasy as distant as the faint afternoon moon looked now. I had left my sister behind before but I honestly didn't think I could do it again. Something had changed, something inside me, and I knew that one way or another I would keep searching for the answers to Mel's death, which in some odd way held the answers to my own life as well. I am not a religious man but being in this place, this ancient Christian Utopian commune at this moment in time, majestic buildings of brick and human devotion, I began to sense a broader purpose to my sister's death. I began to think that perhaps Mel had died to save me, to force me to confide in someone about the nightmares and my drinking. Had Mel known all along that it would take her death to open my eyes? Had she had *that* premonition? I could already hear the skepticism in Jess' voice.

Then, there she was, in the window again, Melissa Gibson, my twin sister looking down upon the courtyard. But she wasn't smiling and she wasn't looking at me. She was gazing off into one of the far corners, frightened, it seemed, and cowering behind the curtain. A sudden rush of adrenaline surged into my veins. I alertly followed the line of her gaze and found the source of her worry, a man unlocking a thin door partially hidden by a tall evergreen shrub. Just as my eyes struggled to register the indistinct figure, my mind electrified with the image of Homer Tubb, the Texas Chainsaw Massacrer. In the next split-second I realized it wasn't him. It was Charlie Walinski and he was just then sneaking into the Mansion House.

"Come on," I said to an unknowing Jess. "The fat lady hasn't sung yet!"

"Where are we going?" Jess asked.

"To catch a killer," I replied.

Charlie had a good head start on us but that didn't matter because I knew where he was going. I ran around to the front of the Mansion House with Jess in tow. We entered through the visitor's entrance and hurriedly ran past Harriet and a small gaggle of tourists preparing for the ten-cent tour. "Call the police," I shouted as we climbed the sturdy oak stairs, "and send them up to our floor." Later, Harriet would tell us one of the visitors asked excitedly if we were part of the tour. Impulsively, she had told them we were.

Judging by the distance Charlie needed to travel through the dark basement compared to our own aboveground route, I was confident we had arrived at Mel's former room first. As I expected, the door was unlocked. We went inside, locked the deadbolt securely behind us and slipped into the bathroom where we could observe the main room, adequately hidden by a jut in the wall partition.

"Ok," Jess whispered, "What are we doing?"

"Waiting for someone," I whispered back.

"Who...."

"Shush," I snapped, just as I heard the telltale sound of a key entering a lock. I looked at Jess and held my index finger to my lips. I turned my eyes to the bedroom.

With my heart pumping wildly and Jess's anxious breath skidding along my neck, I heard the deadbolt pop open, then the rusty creak of the door hinges once, then twice–the door opening and closing. Footsteps drew toward us as I hunkered down deeper against the bathroom wall. I could actually hear Jess's eyes widen and her pulse pounding against my back as I waited for the figure to appear, the only other person besides me needing to step inside Mel's room—my sister's murderer returning in search of loose ends. I knew why he was there. As his eager hands slid down into the cushion of the sitting chair I had sat in the night before, I stepped out of my nightmare and into his.

With a cold stare, I asked, "Are you looking for this?" I held up my sister's computer memory stick, the one labeled 2/2 (the second of two discs). His reaction told me what I already knew.

"There's a lot of juicy shit in here," I said as I walked slowly toward him. "A second helping of what's on the other disc, the one we know you've already got."

Charlie didn't say a word, his eyes darting between Jess and me.

"Juicy enough to blackmail someone, I would bet," I continued. "The mayor? The Talley sisters? The Reverend Newland? People with that kind of pull in this town could help you get a job; a good job; a job that your wife and kids would come back for."

One more step and I would be nose to nose with my sister's killer.

"A once-in-a-lifetime opportunity that you stumbled upon *after* you killed my sister."

As my march ended, my eyes locked and I could feel my muscles engorging with blood, pulsating–a rising cry to battle.

"Am I getting warm, Charlie?"

CHAPTER 60

Jess called it a rage blackout but right now, I was calling it a god-awful headache. She wouldn't elaborate anymore, saying only that I had been "inspiring" during my scuffle with Charlie Walinski, whom she said was now sitting in the back of a police cruiser driven by an extremely excited Officer Callahan.

"Well, I'm glad I was finally able to make her day," I said, rubbing the welt under my eye that seemed to have doubled in the short span since my return to normal consciousness. I also had a loose lower front tooth and a matching pair of bloody, sandpapered knuckles. Other than that, I felt pretty good, satisfied.

"The Sherrill P.D. had been interested in Charlie from the beginning," Jess said. "In fact, they had just put out a bulletin for his arrest in connection with a woman who claims he raped her just last night."

"So I guess I did them a favor."

"You sure did!" Arlen Bensinger said as he trotted into the Mansion House lobby where Jess and I were sitting on a bench. He stood before us, admiring my battle scars. "Damn, that must have been quite a fray," he said.

"Enough to warrant a little combat pay?" I asked, attempting a painful smile.

The mayor laughed, "I don't know about that."

"Is there enough evidence to prove Charlie killed Melissa?" Jess asked.

Arlen hesitated for a moment before saying, "Normally, I wouldn't tell you anything about our investigation but under the circumstances I think you deserve more than the standard *no comment*. Let's take a walk."

As we wandered around the neatly manicured grounds, cultivated generations ago by the original Oneida Community, Arlen explained how they believed that Charlie was a sexual predator who had used a number of aliases that they had finally identified just that morning. They had found on his possession the drug Gamma Hydroxy Butyrate, a date-rape drug commonly referred to as "Liquid Ecstasy" or "Easy Lay." Arlen believed that Charlie had secretly tainted Mel's wine with the drug the night she died. "My guess is he somehow dropped it in her drink after our argument, thinking Mel would hang out a little while longer. He could then offer to drive her home when she began to feel drowsy," Arlen said. "But she left before the drug kicked in, so he must have gone to the Mansion House later, and, after seeing me leave, went up to her room."

"Mel had told you that night that she suddenly wasn't feeling well," Jess said. "So the timing in your theory sounds right, but I don't think she would have let Charlie into her room. She was always good at spotting creeps."

Arlen said, "Charlie had a number of keys to the Mansion House in his pocket according to Officer Callahan. The outside entry variety, mainly, but a few that looked like guest room keys, one of which you already know opens the door to the room Mel stayed in. This is an old place and the locks have not been changed very often, I'm sad to say. How he got them is something we plan to find out."

"Did he have anything else on him, like a red necktie or a red scarf?" I asked.

"Not that the officer mentioned," Arlen replied. "I could call over to the station and find out."

Jess put her arm over my shoulder as I said, "Never mind, I

don't really want to know."

"Whatever went on in that room that night, we'll dig it out of him," Arlen said. "You've got my word on that."

I just nodded. There wasn't anything more I could think to say. Mel was still dead and that wouldn't change no matter what Charlie said. A voice inside was telling me I had done all I could do. I think it was my sister's.

The three of us eventually found our way back to the main entrance but not until after Arlen had confided to us that he had told his wife about his "pitiful" behavior. He said he hoped she would forgive him one day. "We've got some things to work out," he said.

As he left, he was his mayoral self again, reminding us that Sherrill was a great little city with wonderful people that shouldn't be judged by the actions of one man. He even invited us to come back under more pleasant circumstances and he would personally show us all the wonderful sights and sounds found in Central New York, no more than an hour away. I didn't say it at the time, but I didn't think I would ever take him up on it.

The Mansion House
June 1879

"It would appear that I have come full circle," John said to his loyal friend Marquis.

Solemnly, Marquis nodded. It had been over thirty years since he had felt the firm grip of John's handshake for the first time as the two greeted each other in the quiet valley of Upstate New York, a hopeful occasion filled with promise that he remembered warmly. *A new beginning*, he recalled thinking when John and his small group of followers had arrived from Vermont, with a smile so broad and lasting that his wife remarked he must have snuck off and gotten it tattooed upon his face. This moment, he knew, would not stand the test of time so favorably.

The two men were pacing nervously about in the otherwise empty upper sitting room. Exhumed newspapers littered the table and floor, each filled with righteous fury and impassioned calls for action, savage dogs of intolerance nipping at their heels. Dozens of columns written by their "neighbors" were being read all across the nation, branding John as one of the country's leading Communists. It was being unanimously reported that John was to be arrested; legal proceedings to be commenced; a trial to be pushed by gentlemen who were prepared to go to the very foundation of it; testimony taken that would stamp the Oneida Community as far worse in their practices than the polygamists of Utah.

"I hear tell, John," Marquis said, "that a Mormon has been recently imprisoned upon being found guilty of polygamy. Also, that several other Mormon leaders are awaiting trial on similar charges. The storm is blowing hard, John. It's headed our way."

"Yes, I know," John replied. "I've heard it outside the windows and I've felt it in our halls. From the winds of change, there is no shelter."

"Inside these very walls?" Marquis asked disbelievingly.

"I refer to the political lines being drawn, Marquis," John said, Marquis nodding in understanding, "for control of the Community. The Townerites, as they are referring to themselves, do not care for my autocratic style of government. They want a freer system of Complex Marriage and demand more voice in the management of our businesses. They've found considerable backing from relatives and friends, I must say, an increasing gale that a mere raised collar cannot shield."

"It surprises me that James has fallen upon such a path," Marquis said.

"Every man must be persuaded in his own mind, my friend–I in mine and you in yours. James is only following his and I have no quarrel with it."

"And your thoughts," Marquis said, "regarding the third weed that has found its way into our garden. Positivists I believe they call themselves."

"The college boys," John said with a knowing grin. "We send them off to school and this is how they return our liberality? They return and question the Old Testament, the very foundation of our existence."

Marquis said, "You reconcile better than I, John. They have so many of the young women bound up in slavery to their opinion they dare not say their souls are their own!"

"Do not mistake my comprehension for reconciliation. That I understand them does not mean I accept them. We are a peculiar institution and a peculiar people. Having seen the outside world through impressionable eyes, these young men seek only balance.

Their voices sing, alas, just a different song. I cannot begrudge them that."

The room fell quiet, both men sorting through their thoughts as their tired eyes wandered tenuously over the scattered newsprint like two old bears navigating a thick patch of thorn bushes.

"It is not from within that I fear the Association will fall," John then said. "Different social arrangements can respect and tolerate each other, all working together to make a happy home. It is the outcry that surrounds us that we must now chastely appease if we are to keep this great machine–the business organization which shelters and feeds us–going with unfailing momentum."

"The clergy?" Marquis asked, to which John confirmed.

"At the time of their *secret* meeting several months ago I was unconcerned. New applications to join poured in after word of their small-minded affair spread. In fact, I received a confidential and quite sincere letter from a student of the hosting Syracuse University–Charles, I believe his name was–stating that the private meeting held on campus in opposition to the Oneida Community had awakened an unusual interest amongst the student body, especially since the doors were closed against them. He requested that I reply with a short communication representing my views on the subject."

"And did you?"

"I did, in a jocular letter that I'm sure you would have appreciated."

Marquis smiled briefly, his worrisome thoughts of the clergy crusade only briefly interrupted.

"But several coals from the fire that burned that night have lingered, consuming many of the weaker samplings in the forest around us since then."

"We have faced it before, John."

"We were younger then, Marquis. The times were different. The wind of change is fueling the fire now, one we cannot repulse. I'm afraid retreat is the only answer."

Marquis' head dropped, his empty eyes staring at his shoes. He could muster no argument.

"As it was in Putney," John said, "so is it here. I am the true target and so I will leave and draw off their fire."

Marquis feared in his heart that this time it would not be enough to extinguish the blaze. He raised his head once more, looked John in the eye and asked him the question anyway. When John looked away, gazing out the window to the courtyard below, Marquis had his answer.

"My hope," John said with a heavy heart, "is that the Community holds together. That the best form of social life will finally emerge out of all these debates and turmoil, and carry with it a moral and spiritual power that will really be, and be known to be, the judgment of God. For if it should break up, my supreme anxiety is that many of those who have always lived here would suffer the miseries and anxieties of common life in a world that impresses me more and more with an awful sense of woe.

So to endure, I believe, we must strip from our constitution that which the outside world defines as immoral. Conform to worldly custom for the sake of avoiding offense. Define our Communism in terms of property ownership and business interest alone. We must stand on the same practical platform as that of ordinary society and give up the practice of Complex Marriage.

I am confident that these modifications will compel the clergy not only to let us alone but to encourage us, as they have lately promised to do. Such a platform would provide new liberty and harmony within the existing Community. New communities could be started anywhere without fear of persecution. With the assurance that John Humphrey Noyes, the original and principal offender against sexual decorum, has left the Community and retired to private life, this new platform could be fearlessly put before the world in our paper, acceptable to all."

"If you write it, I will personally put it before the counsel," Marquis said before saying goodbye to his friend.

CHAPTER 61

"Let's walk through the courtyard one last time before we go," I said to Jess as I closed the trunk to her car. It was early Saturday morning and only the robins and the sparrows had come to see us off. (No crows, they were long gone.) We had a long drive ahead of us, about three hours to my place and another two or three for Jess, depending on the New York City weekend traffic. I can't say I was anxious to go but then I can't really say I wasn't either. Jess was ready, I could see that, but I think she understood what I needed to do.

"I'll wait here for you," she said. I nodded and left her standing there.

The Mansion House made no apology. It stood tall as it had for well over a century, secretive and silent, its placid windows reflecting the golden sunlight of a fresh new day just as it had in the days of the Civil War. Time marches on, it was saying, and I accepted that. This place was not an enemy of its neighbors, Christian or otherwise; nor were the beliefs that it was built upon or the people who mortared the bricks together. It was a testament to what a daring group of people was at one moment in time and what brave people can be if they are true to their hearts. That's what my sister would have seen and that is the story she would have told if she had lived to tell it.

Looking up at one window in particular, I made my peace and left.

"Was she there?" Jess asked as I returned to the parking lot.

"She's smiling now," was all I could say.

As I slid into the passenger side ahead of Jess, I noticed a book sitting in the driver seat. "Did you steal another book?" I asked as I pick it up so she could settle in.

"You took the other one," she said. "Let's keep the record straight on that."

She was right and I couldn't help but laugh remembering her woeful face as Officer Callahan escorted us to the station. It seemed like a dream now, stupid and funny compared to the dreams I used to have.

"It's a book about the Oneida Community," I said as I studied the cover.

Jess started her car, that rustling-leaves sound again. "That would seem appropriate," she said. "I'll bet Harriet left it for us."

"But wasn't your car locked all night?"

"Yeah,"

We looked at each other and asked, warily, "The ghosts?"

I opened it up, its pages parting to a specific picture as if the book had a mind of its own. It was a group shot, several dozen people gathered around a woman seated at a piano.

Jess leaned over and peered into my lap. "The woman at the piano looks like our ghost friend."

"Your right, she does," I replied. "A younger version, anyway. Maybe one of the guys in the picture is the iPod man?"

"Maybe...." Jess said as she scanned the picture. "There! The young man holding the violin." She pressed her finger into the page, highlighting her target.

"You think so?" I asked, uncertain about the resemblance. I examined more of the grainy, black and white faces staring back at us. "I think this guy over here, the stern-looking one in the stiff-collared suit."

Jess gave my choice a quick glance. "No, I don't see that. It's definitely the handsome one with the violin."

"Handsome? You think that guy is handsome."

"Yes, I think he is," Jess said. She then scrolled her finger across the names listed underneath the picture. "His name was Henry and I like his passionate eyes."

I shook my head. Lining up my guy with the names below, I said, "My money is on Edward."

"I don't mind taking your money," Jess chuckled.

I gazed at the picture, recalling how the man–the ghost–had led me to Mel's room and the clue that ultimately solved my sister's murder. I owed him one–a big one. I sighed, thinking that maybe Mel would thank him for me. "Well, we've got no way of knowing," I finally said.

"We could go back inside and ask them?"

We looked at each other again and laughed. "No."

After shifting the car into gear, Jess began backing out of her parking space. "What was the woman's name?" she asked.

"Ah, Sarah," I replied. "According to the picture, her name was Sarah."

"That's a pretty name," Jess said.

Pulling onto the street, we waved goodbye. Goodbye to the ghosts, to the Oneida Community, to the only bad memory I ever had of my sister.

We drove east, back to our lives, marveling the whole way at how much spring had sprung during the week. It made the world outside the windows of Jess' little car look like a world different from the one we had scurried past almost a week ago. Maybe this was heaven, the different place that Jess imagined, and we just didn't know it.

EPILOGUE

I had made two promises to Jess during our trip home. One month later, I was fulfilling the second one (the first one was that I would *not* send an anonymous letter to Harold Smith, forever Gomer to me, detailing the *lascivious* activities of his wife Dorothy. I had fulfilled it–so far). I was in Yonkers, standing by the side of the road in front of Jess's apartment as we eagerly awaited the delivery of the *New York Times* newspaper. The sun wasn't even up yet, but there we were in our robes and pajamas (Jess was wearing the new *red* thermals I had bought her as a kind of thank-you present), looking and acting like a couple of six year olds, anxious as all hell to see the article on page five of the regional section. I had not had a drink since our time in Sherrill, a promise I had made to myself and to my sister just before I said goodbye to her in the courtyard. I was very happy to be with my new best friend.

Jess and I already knew what the piece said; we had stitched it together ourselves using the draft Mel had started, the notes she had accumulated and the memories we held of her in our hearts. We had sent it to her editor with the only stipulation that he print it as is. He agreed before even reading it. It was short, simple, and every word, Mel's:

The Good Silver

By Melissa Gibson

When I was little girl I would always help my mother set the dinner table. It was a small task really, since there were only the four of us, my father and mother, my twin brother and me, but one I took great pride in nonetheless. "A place for everything and everything in its place," I recall her saying as she taught me about the special rules to observe when laying out each place setting; a mysterious set of laws, I imagined, that no hostess dare break for risk of social embarrassment. The flatware should always be laid out in order of use, my mother explained, from the outside in, toward the plate. Spoons and knives go to the right with their cutting edges toward the plate, with forks arranged to the left. "What could be more charming than a perfectly set table," she had said on more than one occasion. I always enthusiastically agreed.

Then, one Christmas, much to the envy of my brother Michael and me, my father gave my mother one of her presents a few days early. I remember as if it were only yesterday, my father setting a beautiful, dark mahogany box with brass handles and a bright green bow on top into my mother's lap and the look of astonished joy on her face as her trembling hand reached out to open it up. I was standing right by her side as she slowly tipped the lid, revealing a wondrous treasure of gleaming silver. "It's exquisite!" I had said with such aplomb that it triggered a chorus of laughter from both my parents (I was only seven at the time and was merely mimicking a phrase I had heard on television).

I had asked my mother that evening if we could use the new silverware for dinner, but to my disappointment, she said we couldn't, explaining that it was *the good silver*, and would only be used on special occasions. She then quickly reminded me about the Christmas Eve party we were having the next day and that she would need my help setting the table with "Daddy's wonderful gift." Of all the Christmas's I had as a child, that is the one I remember most often, when the bond between my mother and I blossomed from something as simple as setting a dinner party table. Through all the years since, my mother and I have never talked as openly, or laughed as heartily, as when we are polishing the good silver in preparation of a holiday celebration. I know it may sound odd, New York City, and tarnish (no pun intended) my gritty image, but its true.

Now, my loyal readers know that I would never bore you all with such an enchanting personal tale if it didn't relate to the cerebral nourishment I have for you today; a veritable feast of social experimentation and sexual revolution that not only honored community and commitment, but also launched a small slice of the nation's populace down the road to prosperity. This is a story about the Oneida Community, a small band of people, courageous and daring whom, over a century ago, went searching for the kingdom of heaven on earth, and found brotherhood, equality and love. With their feet firmly anchored to Christ and the Bible, their hearts to each other and their neighbors, they marched forward through poverty and intolerance, oppression and prejudice, and built not only a home for themselves and every generation that followed, but also a spirit of hard work and devotion that lives on today as boldly as it ever had. It was their hands that forged the very first set of "the good silver" that my mother and I, and millions of other admirers worldwide turn to for hostess immortality (and yes, that includes you, NYC!).

Alas, I must make a long story short. The meager allotment of space my editor has provided me for this piece (please give him a call and let your voice be heard!) does not afford a deeper exploration of the Community, as they were often referred to. Only a mere snapshot of what I discovered when I traveled to Sherrill, New York and spent a week at the Mansion House, a large stately mansion and the original home of the Oneida Community. You all know how much I love to explore and this, I dare say, was a once-in-a-lifetime experience.

The Oneida Community essentially formed in the 1850s as a communal living experiment. Built on interpretations from the Bible, it was as much a product of the turbulent decades before the Civil War, as a revolt against the suffocating religious dictatorships of the era. With its alternative lifestyle system of "complex marriage" (a fancy word for immoral "free love", challengers would argue) and equality amongst the sexes, the Community was one of the most fascinating and successful orders of Communism, as well as being the most controversial. Female members owned their fair share of the group's property some seventy years *before* American women would receive the right to vote. You heard me right, ladies, seventy years before!

At its zenith, the Community had several hundred members comprised equally of men, women and children, all living under one roof in the Mansion House, which they built themselves in the 1860s. (It still stands today as an historical landmark.) They managed an impressive thirty-year run, fending off an enraged clergy regularly over their "licentious" sexual practices, ironically succumbing in the end to the gradual loss of religious faith by not only the second generation of Community members, but also the nation itself. The world was changing and so then did the Community, eventually returning to the accepted form of marriage while creating one of the earliest joint stock companies in the land.

I had traveled to Sherrill in the spring of this year to see if the Oneida Community still existed, to discover if perhaps these difficult societal and economic times had spawned a rebirth in their beliefs and a rebuilding of their structure. Did I find it? I guess you could say yes, because what I found was a spirited community full of happy children, loving parents and caring neighbors all equally sharing the enchanting place they call "The Silver City" just, I believe, as the founder of the original Community would have wanted it.

HISTORICAL NOTE

The Oneida Community disbanded in 1881 and formed the joint-stock corporation, Oneida Community Ltd. Eventually changing its name to Oneida Ltd., the company achieved world wide recognition for the silverware it produced in Sherrill, New York.

A non-profit organization chartered in 1987 by the New York State Board of Regents oversees this magnificent National Historic Landmark. Continually inhabited since 1862, the Mansion House features a museum, 35 residential apartments, nine guestrooms, dining and meeting facilities. Century old trees define the grounds where meandering paths lead to peaceful gardens that change with the seasons.

To learn more about the Oneida Community and the Mansion House, visit www.oneidacommunity.org.